I0451780

Love You Like a Catfish

Faux in Love, Volume 1

J. Leigh James

Published by J. Leigh James, 2020.

LOVE YOU LIKE A CATFISH

First edition. September 25, 2020.

ISBN: 978-1735860923

Written by J. Leigh James.

Chapter One

Fiona

My parents are risk-takers. I grew up hearing the phrase *no pain, no gain* my entire life. Which made me their biggest disappointment. I hate risk. I like knowing what's going to happen, when it's going to happen.

So, when my parents suddenly decided to move out of state for a business opportunity, they decided to leave me. They left me and took my little brother. Because I was in high school and needed to focus on my education, so they claimed.

I wanted to believe them, but I didn't.

Here I was, watching my parents fork over money to Uncle George and Aunt Lisa to cover my living expenses. Great. My father was paying his younger brother to keep me for a year. I felt like a pet being shipped off to a boarding kennel. While they all sat in my uncle and aunt's over-designed, way-too-expensively decorated living room acting like a financial transaction hadn't taken place.

"We're going to miss you, Fifi," my dad kissed my temple. Fifi, short for Fiona, yet another thing that made me feel like an inconvenient pet.

"Fi," I reminded him under my breath. Though what was the point? He wouldn't see me again until Thanksgiving — four months from now.

"Behave yourself," my mother said and kissed the other side of my face. "We'll fly you out to us on school breaks, but don't overstay your welcome. They're doing us a big favor."

I wanted to point out that you didn't pay off favors, but I kept my mouth shut. The risk of making my parents angry, or even worse — disappointed in me — was too great.

"Why are we leaving Fiona?" Franklin, my five-year-old brother, began crying, tears sliding under the rims of his nerdy little glasses to trace down his cheek. "Don't you love her anymore?"

"Of course, we do," Mom wiped the moisture from his face while I mouthed the word *no*. "She's going to school. School is important."

"I'll go to school with her," he said. I loved my little brother. He was the best part of my life, and I'd do anything to make him happy, even pretend that everything was going to be alright.

"Franky Tanky," I hugged him. "It's OK. We'll talk on the phone every week. You'll tell me all about your adventures."

He sniffled and wiped the tears from his eyes. "Adventures?"

He was a risk-taker, like our parents, and having an adventure was his dream come true. "Yes, you're going to have so many adventures. It will be boring here."

"No adventures?" His bottom lip trembled as if the thought of no adventures was a death sentence.

"Not even one." I pulled him into a bear hug.

He sniffled and nodded again. "I'll miss you, Fiona. I love you."

"I love you, too." I ruffled his sandy blond hair, a few shades darker than my own.

"Everything will be fine," my aunt said to no one in particular. "Now skedaddle. The sooner you get on the road, then sooner you'll be at your new home."

Mom and Dad had found a place to live while they started their new business and needed to sign the lease in a couple days. Which is why I was being dumped a month before school started with only a day's notice.

We crowded onto my uncle's small front porch, hugs all around, and then my family piled into our SUV and rode off into the sunset.

I stood on the steps watching them become a speck on the horizon. When I stepped into the house, Aunt Lisa motioned to my suitcases.

"Follow me," she said, "and I show you to your boring room."

My shoulders sunk in defeat. I hadn't been here ten minutes yet, and I'd already insulted them. "I was just trying to stop Frank's crying."

"Sure," she said. She didn't believe me. "Your cousin will be home soon, and we'll break the news to her." Her tone said this would not be a pleasant surprise.

Lisa motioned to a small room with a crisp white bed and a small desk in the corner. "She doesn't know I'm here?" I'd only known for a day, but I never imagined I'd show up and Cindy not know.

Cindy was my only cousin, and even though she was my age, we'd never gotten along. We didn't hate each other, or anything like that. It's just we had nothing in common and had never developed any kind of camaraderie.

She was the center of her parents' universe, and she knew it. For as long as I could remember, she did whatever she wanted and got everything she asked for. If she didn't like me staying here, then who knew how long it would last.

Lisa's lips stretched into a tight, humorless smile. "Your uncle is forgetful sometimes. None of us knew you were coming until this morning. This boring little room will have to make do."

I'd struck a nerve. I wanted to tell her the small guest room she'd shown me was quaint and cute, but that would be a lie. It *was* boring. A small white, wood-framed bed, positioned in the middle of a room with beige carpet, white walls, white curtains covered a small window, and a tiny white wood-framed desk sat in the corner.

"I really appreciate you letting me stay here. I'll take good care of this room," I told her. And that was the whole truth.

"I'll leave you to it," she said and closed the door behind her as she left.

The room was so white, I was afraid to breathe, just in case my mere presence left a mark somewhere. I walked to the window and looked out. Below me was the driveway and the street. There were two houses across from us, but since this was a new subdivision, we were the only homes currently occupying this street. Outside the large white house directly across from me was a couple young boys playing basketball in their driveway. They were my neighbors now. This was my room. This was my life for the next nine months.

This was depressing.

Nathan

I perform under pressure. That's why I was our best running back on the football team, why I had better-than-average grades, why my dad pinned all his hopes on me taking over the family business. I kept my cool and made rational, well-thought-out decisions.

But there's a difference between pressure and manipulation. Manipulation, I didn't deal with well. I was a reasonable person, and if someone wanted something from me, I'd consider it. Unfortunately, my current girlfriend, Cyn Houghton, didn't understand that.

In a small town like Wildwood, the dating pool is shallow. Being a Hollingsworth with the most influential parents in town made that an even smaller pond of possibilities. Not that I wouldn't date someone outside my social circle, just that it was hard to tell who wanted the real me versus who wanted a piece of my popularity. I tended to date girls who were just as popular as I was, hoping they were dating me for me.

Which is why when a relationship went bad, I usually stuck it out longer than I should. I'd realized almost immediately that

Cyn Houghton and I weren't compatible. But I gave it a chance. When school ended a month ago, I gave her the whole let's-not-tie-each-other-down-for-the-summer speech. I'd used it last year on Juliet Davidson, and it had worked like a charm.

But Cyn was different.

One of the reasons I'd been drawn to her was her tenacity. That personality trait suddenly wasn't so attractive when she refused to break up with me. I'd tried all the euphemisms that had worked in the past: it's not you, it's me; I think we should see other people; I don't want to tie you down. It didn't matter. She found a way to twist my words, and I was still firmly stuck.

I could have outright dumped her, but I had wanted to be kind, to let her down easy. But apparently Cyn Houghton didn't do subtle.

Manipulation, however, she did very well. I'd invited her to go to our local arboretum with me. They had a seminar I wanted to attend, one that might work nicely with a special project I'd started. A special project that only four people in Wildwood knew about. Every time I'd considered telling Cyn about it, something held me back. I wasn't ashamed of it. I just didn't want anyone taking over or taking credit. Deep down, I knew Cyn would.

I'd told her I wanted to go to the seminar and afterward, we could explore the grounds. She'd interpreted the date differently, making it sound like I'd planned this romantic date for us, like I'd planned a special surprise for her. The more I'd tried to downplay it, the more insistent she'd become, hinting that she expected whatever I had planned to do would take her breath away.

Incredible that's she'd expect that since she had to know I'd been trying to break up with her for the last two weeks. The girl wasn't dumb. In fact, she was in the top 10% of our class. She just wouldn't let me go without a fight, and I'd been trying so hard to be a nice guy, that I'd let her manipulation work. It had to stop. I was done.

We were sitting at Tucker's Burger Bar, a local diner, when she'd gotten a call to come home.

"I've got to go," she said between clenched teeth as she threw her phone into her purse, took a last slurp of her soda and slid out of the booth we'd been sharing.

"Is everything OK?" She looked furious.

"Stupid family drama," she said and in an instant smoothed her features and pasted on a smile. "Don't worry. It won't ruin our special day tomorrow."

"It's just a seminar," I reminded her.

"Right," she winked at me and flung her jet black hair over her shoulder. Then her face morphed back into the irritation she was truly feeling and rushed out of the diner.

Seconds later, Genivive Scott scooted into Cyn's vacant seat. "What happened to Cyn? She didn't look happy."

I shrugged, realized Cyn had stuck me with the bill for her soda and cheese sticks. It wasn't the money. I could afford the five dollars. It was the assumption. She always expected me to pay. Most people did. It hadn't bothered me in the past, but now that I was earning my own money, it frustrated me that my girlfriend and friends weren't more considerate.

"You know," Geni picked up a remaining cheese stick and pulled it apart, letting the melted cheese ooze from the breaded shell. "I hope I'm not overstepping, but I'm surprised you're still together."

I watched her take a delicate bite of the snack. Geni was Cyn's best friend. They were a lot alike, only Geni was less — intense. If she brought up my relationship with Cyn, she was either worried about Cyn or snooping for her friend. Either way, I wasn't talking about my relationship with my girlfriend's best friend. I remained quiet while she slowly finished the snack. It was almost like a staring contest. We were waiting to see who blinked first, who would break the silence. It was a contest I knew I'd win.

Geni smiled at me. "Not to offend you or anything, but you have a habit of ending relationships over summer break. Does that mean that Cyn is your true love?" Her tone held the slightest hint of derision, like she thought I'd be a fool to fall in love with her best friend.

"Don't you think that's between Cyn and me?"

She blinked a couple times, then softened her features. I could spot manipulation a mile away. Geni was a lot like Cyn in that way. Only she wasn't as good. "You didn't look very happy a few minutes ago, and I know Cyn isn't happy. I hate seeing you both miserable. Especially when we could fix it so easily."

I sat back in my seat and draped one arm over the back of the booth. "I seem miserable to you?"

I was miserable dating Cyn, but I hadn't expected anyone except my best friend Ben to realize it.

"You both are," she said and lightly placed her hand on top of the one I had resting on the table. "I've told Cyn a hundred times that she won't break your heart if she breaks up with you, but she's so worried she will. And I know you're just hanging on so you won't hurt her."

Genivive's words stunned me. Not that I believed them, but that she'd have the nerve to speak them out loud. She was telling me to dump her best friend. That doing so would actually make Cyn happy. It was an obvious lie, and I wanted to call her out, but that's not the way manipulative girls operated. She'd only double-down on her story.

"Why are you telling me this?"

"I'm tired of seeing people I care about hurt each other," she pouted. "Especially when there's no need."

"So, you think I should dump her?"

"It's not really dumping," Geni batted her lashes at me, "It's letting her go. Not holding her back." As if she felt I wasn't getting the message, she added, "She needs to follow her heart."

I almost laughed at that statement. Geni had gone too far. Definitely not as skilled as Cyn in emotional manipulation.

Somehow I kept a straight face. "So, I need to let her pursue someone else."

She lowered her eyelids and peered at me between her lashes. "You could, also."

It was cowardly. I recognized it the second I thought about her not-so-subtle offer. Geni was stabbing her best friend in the back. Not exactly the quality I wanted in a girlfriend. But she'd be a lot easier to dump when I was ready. And Cyn couldn't twist my words or manipulate my intentions if I was already dating someone else.

I saw a desperate chance for an escape, and I took it. "I can't believe Cyn would be happy if I broke up with her and started dating you. Isn't that breaking some kind of girl code?"

Geni smiled. "Are you kidding? She'll be thrilled. She's been so worried about breaking your heart. If we started dating, then she could pursue her true love guilt free."

She lied. I had no doubt. But Geni had given me plausible deniability.

I felt like a complete jerk the second I agreed to Geni's plan. I should have dumped Cyn straight out. Told her I wasn't interested in her any more and that it was over.

Instead, I broke up with her via text like the total moron I had become.

It's OK that you love someone else. I only want to see you happy. I wish the best for you and your guy, and I hope you feel the same for me and Geni.

I showed the message to the girl sitting in front of me, and she nodded her approval. Genivive watched with pure glee, like a child opening a present they already knew they'd love, as I hit the send button.

A sense of relief washed over me. My relationship with Cyn was over. She would be furious, but there wasn't much she could do if I already had someone else. I wasn't proud of myself, not even a little. I'd gotten myself into this mess, and I'd chosen a messy path to get myself out.

Geni pulled out her phone. "Should we make it official?"

I glanced at her screen to see she'd already pulled up her social media account.

"Not yet," I said, "not until we know for sure Cyn got my text. I want her to hear it from me, not see it online first."

Genivive smirked. "I guarantee you she's already seen it. Cyn is glued to her phone. Something catastrophic would have to take place to prevent her from reading your text immediately."

That was true. But I held my ground. "It's the right thing to do, Geni. Even if this was what she wanted," I let my tone hint to her that I didn't completely believe it, "It's disrespectful to let her hear it from social media first."

She sighed. "You're right. I just got carried away. I'm so excited that we're finally together."

I nodded, because not having a reaction seemed mean. "I have an extra ticket to the arboretum tomorrow," I said, "there's a seminar I want to hear."

Geni's lips spread into a wide grin. "I'd love to go."

I had intended to ask her, but it would have been nice if she hadn't assumed I was. I brushed the frustration away. "Great," I said and stood from the booth. "I'll pick you up tomorrow."

I grabbed the handwritten check and went to the front counter to pay. I was in the same situation as before, stuck with an unwanted girlfriend. Only with a different girl.

I'd date Genivive for a little while, perhaps the whole summer, if she was drama-free, and then I'd break up with her before my senior year started.

Being single my senior year held a certain appeal.

Being single right now did, too.

But until Cyn accepted that we weren't together anymore, I was stuck with a girlfriend.

Chapter Two

Fiona

Every second I lived here was one second closer to going home. I'd decided that would be my mantra during my stay here. I'd chanted it in my head almost the entire hour-long drive here and thought it would get me through the awkwardness and frustration of being foisted onto my relatives. It wasn't as powerful a motivator as I'd hoped.

The room didn't have a chest of drawers, so I opened the closet to see if there were shelves inside. Unfortunately, it was a small closet with a single pole to hang my clothes. The one bright spot was literally that. A spot of pink in the corner of the closet. Either someone had left a hidden stain or the painter had missed the spot and never come back. I liked it. It was a tiny bit of chaos in all the stark-white order. Even though pink wasn't my favorite color, I felt a connection to the quarter-sized splash of color. Like me, it didn't belong here.

There were no hangers in the closet. So, instead of pulling my clothes from my suitcases, I shoved them into the closet and shut the door. I didn't want to bother Aunt Lisa for hangers. My plan was to stay out of their way as much as possible. I'd be the model student and house guest. I'd be so unobtrusive they'd forget I was here.

I zipped open my backpack and pulled out my laptop, ereader and my phone and chargers. I slid the desk closer to one of the few wall outlets in the room and plugged in my equipment.

My parents left me with nine hundred dollars, and I was to budget the money to a hundred a month for any miscellaneous expenses I had. I figured I could spare a couple of dollars for cheap hangers.

I sat at the desk and slowly spun in a circle, taking in the white, white, white of it all. I wondered what had made them pick this color. Even the hallway was more of a warm beige.

My door flung open seconds after a swift knock and Uncle George stepped into the room. I'd always liked him. He was big and loud and energetic, the type of guy everyone liked, and even though his enthusiasm bordered on delusional, he always made me smile.

"Ah," he said, and his big voice echoed around the small room, "you're all settled. Excellent. Isn't this a great room?"

I smiled at him and didn't answer. In times like these, sometimes I struggled with what to say. My parents were super strict about lying, and since I wasn't good at it, I never did it.

"Cynthia should be home soon," he said, "and then we'll go out to eat. I can't wait to show you our little town."

I widened my smile, because, really, what could I say?

"Is there anything you need?" he asked. "We can pick stuff up while we're out."

"No," I swiftly shook my head. "I don't need anything. I appreciate you letting me stay here."

"Pfft," he grinned at me, "Of course, you're staying with us. You're family."

"Hi Daddy," a tall, thin girl with jet black hair walked into the room and wrapped her arms around George's waist.

"Kitten," he said and kissed the top of her head, "Look what a great surprise I have for you."

Cindy did a fake squeal and rushed over to embrace me in a tight hug. "What a great surprise, Daddy! I can't believe you didn't tell us Fifi was coming." The girl backed away and narrowed her amber eyes at me. She remembered I didn't like the nickname, and my bet was she wasn't thrilled at all about my being here.

"It's great to see you, Cindy. You look amazing. The black hair really looks good on you." Her hair had been the same sandy blond as Frankie's, and she'd always been pretty. The dark hair shouldn't have worked with her coloring, but it did. Her pale skin practically glowed.

She tilted her head slightly, like she was judging if I was being sarcastic or not. "Actually," she said sweetly, and I knew it was a show for her father, "I go by Cyn, now. Or Cynthia. So much more refined than Cindy, don't you think?"

"Sure, Cyn," I said. "I'll work hard to remember that. What a coincidence, because I go by Fiona." I smiled at her and tried to let my annoyance roll off me. If our situations had been reversed, I'd probably have the same reaction.

Her smile relaxed into a genuine one. Too late, I realized that my words might have been interpreted as a threat. And somehow that made her more comfortable. "Good to know," she said.

"I was thinking about taking my girls out to The Wharf. How does that sound?"

"Perfect," Cyn said, and I nodded. After all, what could I say? I had no idea what the place was or if I'd like it. But I wouldn't cause a disturbance. I was going to fly under the radar and be as unobtrusive as possible.

George grinned at us. "Better go tell the Misses," he said and left the room.

"Better grab a jacket," my cousin told me. "They really love their air conditioning in that place."

I nodded and opened the closet door. Pulling open my largest suitcase, I found a light-weight bomber jacket and threw it on. When I turned around, my cousin was peering over my shoulder. She had a smirk on her face and then glanced at the closet in surprise. She marched to the door and yelled, "Mom."

Within minutes, Aunt Lisa appeared. "What? What's wrong?"

"Fiona needs hangers," she pointed to the closet.

"Well, it's not my fault," Lisa placed her hands on her hips. "Your father surprised me, too."

"I'll give her some of mine," she said, and I smiled.

Maybe my relationship with my cousin would be better than I'd thought. Maybe she had matured, and we'd find a way to get along.

"You can replace them with those velvet hangers I've been wanting for forever."

And maybe not.

Lisa smiled at her daughter. "How did I get so lucky to have you?"

"I don't know," Cyn smiled back.

Lisa left the room, and my cousin's smile dropped from her face. She shut my bedroom door and then marched over to me. "We need to set some ground rules."

"OK," I said and tried not to show fear. Cindy had always been a bit of a bully, though it was usually mild stuff she lorded over me. Things like having ice cream for dessert instead of pie or playing hopscotch instead of board games. It was always easier to just go along with her than challenge her over things I really didn't care about.

"This is my house," she started, and I cut her off.

"Listen, I don't want to be here any more than you want me here. My parents had this crazy idea that I wouldn't get a good education where they were going, so I'm stuck here. All I want to do is get through this with no drama and convince my parents to let me join them."

Cyn grinned at me. "That sounds perfect. Let me tell you how to avoid any drama with me. Don't embarrass me, don't call me Cindy in front of my friends, and keep your hands off Nathan Hollingsworth."

"Not a problem," I said. "I don't plan to hang around you and your friends. I'm flying under the radar, just another student in the yearbook that no one remembers."

She rolled her eyes. "Yeah, that's not going to happen. You're too cute," she wrinkled her nose in displeasure. "I don't suppose you'd ugly up for me, would you?"

"I have no idea what you're talking about."

"Wouldn't work anyway," she said, leaning close to my face. "You look like that without any make-up on. Nope," she twisted her lips in thought, "Our best bet is to get you a boyfriend immediately so that you're off limits."

I stared at my cousin like she'd just turned purple. She might as well have. What she said was just as crazy to me as if she'd tie-dyed her skin.

"What?" she asked when she noticed my expression.

"I don't date."

Now she looked at me like I had abnormal flesh. "What do you mean? You're sixteen. Of course, you date."

"My parents don't let me date." I raised one shoulder like my answer was obvious.

Cyn pursed her lips. "Your parents aren't here."

"Don't set me up," I said to her. "I'm not going."

She frowned. "We have to do something. A pretty new girl in school? That's like catnip to cats. Teenage boys can't resist them." She tapped the bedpost as she thought. "Any guy friends back home? We could say he's your long-distance boyfriend."

"I went to an all-girls private school."

Cyn cursed. "We have to come up with something. I'm hanging out with Nate tomorrow. We have to have our stories straight."

"I don't see why," I said. "I'm not meeting him tomorrow. I don't have to meet him at all. I told you; I'm flying under the radar."

Cyn rolled her eyes at me like I was stupid. "We'll talk about this later."

I didn't see what else we had to discuss, so I silently followed her down the stairs to the living room where her parents waited. We bundled into a luxury sedan and after a short drive, pulled into the parking lot of a kitschy seafood restaurant.

We ordered our food, and as we waited, Lisa asked, "Cynthia, dear, where is Nathan taking you tomorrow?"

She slyly smiled at her mother. "He didn't say. It's a surprise."

"Aw," Lisa grinned at her husband, "young love."

"You've got yourself a good one, Kitten," George said. "He's a lucky boy."

Cyn beamed at her parents. It looked like my cousin was really in love, but I wondered what kind of relationship she had with this Nathan-guy if I was a threat. I knew my cousin was popular; she rubbed it in every holiday when we both visited our grandparents. I really missed them. If they were still alive, I was sure I'd have been living with them. I would've jumped at the chance. Instead, I was here as an unwanted guest in my relatives' house.

The food arrived, and as we dove in, the family spoke about other topics. They didn't bother to explain their inside jokes or identify the people they talked about. I didn't ask, either. If I wanted to be non existent in their lives, this was how to do it. I suddenly felt very lonely. It was going to be a long, long nine months.

"Mommy, Daddy," Cyn used a baby voice that I was quickly learning meant she wanted something from her parents. "Are there special rules for Fiona while she stays here?"

I paused with my fork midway to my mouth. As much as I hated being invisible, having my relatives' eyes boring into mine was infinitely worse.

Aunt Lisa glared at me and said, "She won't get any special treatment just because she's our guest."

Wow. This woman really didn't like me. "I'm not asking for special treatment, Aunt Lisa. I don't want to be a bother."

"Too late," the woman said under her breath, and we all pretended we didn't hear her.

Cyn must have realized her tactical error. If Lisa thought I wanted special treatment, she might go harder on me that usual, and that wouldn't work for her daughter's plan. "Oh, no, Mommy, I just meant that she can be a normal girl. Like me."

"What do you mean, Sweetheart?" George asked.

"You know how much I love Uncle Harry and Aunt Jillian, and I would never say anything bad about them."

I braced myself for whatever she said next, because obviously, she was about to slam my parents.

"They don't let Fi date."

Surprise poured over their faces, and I rushed in to say, "I don't want to do anything they'd disapprove of."

George looked confused while his wife's anger increased. "Well, that's not a problem," George said. "I'm sure they just want to ensure their daughter hangs out with the right people. When you're ready to date, I'll check the boy out. It will be fine."

My cousin beamed at her father. "Thanks, Daddy. In fact, I was thinking it'd be great if Nathan and I took Fiona on a double-date. Mommy, who do you think would be a good match for Fi?"

Lisa sized me up. "I'd say Finn Devlan, but couple alliteration is out of fashion these days."

I tried to hold in my surprise. Did my aunt really try to choose a boyfriend based on his name?

"So, true," Cyn said. "Finn and Fiona sounds like an old sitcom."

Lisa laughed. "How about Nicolaus?"

"Nathan's little brother?" my cousin asked in horror.

"You're right," Lisa said. "That would be awkward."

"What about Ash?" George joined the game. "He's a good kid and an excellent lawn mower."

"Ugh, Daddy, really? Dating the lawn boy is so 80s romcom."

George smiled at me and shrugged. "I gave it a shot. I'll leave the matchmaking to the experts."

Matchmaking was finding someone compatible. This was more designer set-up. They didn't want to know what kind of boy I liked, what hobbies or interests I had to find someone similar. No, all they wanted was a guy they thought worthy of me, or maybe I was worthy of them.

"You really don't have to go to the trouble," I said. "I'm OK not having a boyfriend."

My female relatives ignored me. George, however, reached across the table and patted my hand. "Let them have their fun. A few innocent dates with some of our local fellows will help you feel welcomed to the neighborhood."

I didn't know about that. Besides, I didn't need to feel welcomed. But, if forcing me on a date made my aunt happy, I'd do it. Anything to break the tension between us.

The rest of the meal, my aunt and cousin named and eliminated potential dates for me. I stopped listening after a few minutes and concentrated on my shrimp scampi. After we made it back to the house, I thanked my aunt and uncle for the meal and then retired to my stark room. I closed the bedroom door and immediately pulled out my phone. I typed a text to my mother.

Am I supposed to follow our house rules or Uncle George's? He gave me rules about dating.

My parents weren't horrible or anything. It's not like they didn't trust me. It's just they'd always wanted me to focus on my education instead of boys. They didn't want me dating because school was a struggle for me, and they were afraid a boy would hurt my grades.

My parents thought I had a disability, though my school could never find anything wrong with me. I just figured they didn't know how to teach in a way that made sense to me. I felt like everything I'd learned in my life I'd had to teach myself.

I hit send and a few seconds later, my mother replied. *Grades come first.*

Of course, I sent back to her.

"No!" I heard Cyn screech from her bedroom next door.

I don't like it, but we trust George. Just follow the rules he set in place, Mom texted back.

"No, no, no, no, no, no, no, no, no!" my cousin's voice grew louder, the last word ending on a sob.

OK, I quickly texted back, *I have to run. Love you.*

I tossed my phone on my bed and rushed to my cousin's room. I knocked on the door as I opened it since I wasn't sure she'd hear me knocking over her hysterical sobbing. Cyn was curled into a ball on the floor, clutching her phone to her chest. I had no clue what to do, so I knelt by her side and placed my hand on her arm. "Are you OK? Can I do something?"

Cynthia twisted her body until her soaking wet face was planted on my shoulder. "My life is over," she moaned into my shirt.

"Your life isn't over," I tentatively patted her back. "Whatever it is, I'm sure it will be fine."

"No, it won't," she said and cried harder.

Aunt Lisa sat next to me and gathered her daughter in her arms. "My poor baby," she cooed, "what happened?"

"Nathan," Cyn gasped, "dumped me."

"That can't be true," Lisa said.

Cyn held her phone out with one arm. "Read for yourself."

Lisa scanned the text message, her eyes filling first with horror and then with tears. "I'm so sorry."

My cousin burst into a fresh round of wailing.

"Is there anything I can do?" I asked my aunt.

She blinked as if she'd forgotten I was there. Curtly nodding, she said, "Go get a large glass of water. We're going to need it."

I raced out of the room and down the stairs to the kitchen. Finding the largest glass I could, I filled it with water and rushed back. A loud hiccup greeted me at the door. It was raw and raspy and sounded intensely painful. From the look on my cousin's face, it hurt as bad as it sounded.

I held out the glass of water, and Cyn took it, gulping the liquid as quickly as she could.

"Thanks," Lisa said. "I think she wants some privacy."

I nodded and backed out of the room. Before I turned to go, I said, "I'm sorry, Cyn. I hope he gets what he deserves."

I'm not sure what made me say that, but it brought a small smile to my aunt's face.

Back in my room, I crawled into bed with my ereader and tried to lose myself in one of my favorite stories. As hard as I tried, I couldn't ignore the occasional sobbing filtering in from the room next door.

And they wanted me to date? I was thinking my parents had the right idea.

Focus on grades, not boys.

Nathan

I'd gone home immediately after and thrown myself on my bed, torn between relief that my relationship with Cyn was over and self-loathing that I'd been such a coward. From now on, I vowed to myself, I'd be straightforward. Even if the breakup was painful. No more platitudes or trying to get out of a relationship the easy way.

My bedroom door flew open with a force that had it banging against the wall, and my younger brother Nicolaus stormed in. We closely resembled each other. Same build, same dark brown hair, same blue eyes, similar features. Same expression when we were pissed off, which he obviously was.

"Why Genivive?" he said as he loomed over me.

I frowned. She was supposed to wait until tomorrow before telling people. She'd agreed. "How did you find out?"

"She told me. Why? Why her?" My brother scowled, and I slowly shook my head. Maybe dating Genivive wasn't such a good idea.

"It just happened." Despite our looks, Nic and I weren't close. We had almost no interests in common and where I was laid back and didn't get worked up over stuff. He willingly, passionately jumped into any drama around him. "Why did she tell you?"

"Well, Romeo, you asked her to be your girlfriend the day after I asked her out." He waved his cell phone in my face. "She just called to cancel because she isn't single anymore."

"I didn't know."

"You didn't care," Nic yelled at me. "You take whatever you want, and you don't care about anyone except yourself."

He was wrong, but I didn't argue. There was no point. He wouldn't believe me, anyway. He'd have his temper tantrum and then move on to the next drama. That's the way it always worked with Nic.

"Ugh. You suck as a brother, man. Completely suck!" My little brother spun on his heel and tramped into the hallway.

"Close my door," I yelled after him. I heard him stomp back to my room, slam my door, and stomp back down the hall. Probably to tell my mother what I'd done. She'd stroke his wounded ego, give him a wad of cash and hope we'd bury the hatchet without her interference. Gotta love passive-aggressive mothers.

I wondered what she'd give me if I went to her crying like a baby because I'd dumped my annoying girlfriend and was feeling guilty. Knowing my mother, she'd probably hand over cash and send me on my way. She didn't do emotions very well.

But I didn't want or need cash from her. I didn't blow through my allowance the way my brother did, and my side business was earning a small profit. That money, though, was reinvested into my business. The only support I needed from my mother was her business-savvy advice. She wasn't the millionaire my dad was, but her personal consulting business did well.

My phone dinged with a text from my girlfriend. The one who'd conveniently forgotten to tell me that she had to dump my brother in order to go out with me. She wanted to wish me a good night and tell me how excited she was about our date tomorrow.

I wondered how long was long enough before I dumped her, too. Playing brothers against each other wasn't cool. The problem was, I couldn't dump her too soon because Cyn would use that as an excuse to get me back. I hated how weak that sounded. Like I couldn't protect myself from my ex. But I didn't know how else to navigate this without causing more drama.

I debated if I should confront Geni about Nic. My resolve to be straightforward said I should, but if I did, then the right thing to do would be to dump her. And I couldn't do that yet. I groaned and rubbed my hands over my face. The whole situation was ridiculous. Totally ridiculous.

Not knowing what to do, I decided I'd sleep on it. Maybe in the morning I'd have some clarity and a better solution.

I waited a few minutes and then told my new girlfriend that I was looking forward to tomorrow. It wasn't exactly the truth, but it was the right thing to say to a brand new girlfriend.

She sent a bunch of texts back about how much she liked me and was excited to be with me.

I read them and then tossed my phone away, letting it bounce on my bed a couple of times.

I'd feel less guilty when I dumped her. Any girl who stole her best friend's boyfriend and dumped one brother to date another didn't deserve a lot of pity.

Being single looked better and better by the minute.

Chapter Three

F iona
    The next morning Cyn was surprisingly calm. I'd expected her to be wallowing in her misery after the night of crying she'd had.

Apparently, wallowing wasn't her style.

"Nathan's going to pay," she randomly announced at the breakfast table.

George smiled at his daughter. "Good for you, Kitten. Work through the grief process. Is anger step two or three?" he said, smiling at the room. "I always forget."

Lisa ignored him and patted her daughter's hand. "Give him some time. I'm sure he'll come running back to you."

She ignored her mother and said, "He forgets who he's dealing with. What I can do to him."

It didn't sound like an idle threat to me, but her parents nodded and continued eating their food.

"I need a killer outfit," Cyn said.

Lisa smiled. "Retail therapy always makes me feel better."

Cyn stared at me, and I could practically see the wheels spinning in her brain. "Fiona does, too. We're going to have the most fabulous night tonight, and Nathan will be consumed with jealousy."

"I'm sure he will," George said and opened his wallet. Lisa frowned at him until he added, "I think all three of you beautiful women should buy something pretty." He handed Lisa a credit card, and from her giddy expression, I gathered he'd just unlocked a vault of money.

"Daddy, you're the best!"

Lisa agreed, "You really are."

"Thank you, Uncle George."

He grinned at us, and for the first time that morning, Cynthia smiled. "Just what the revenge doctor ordered."

I'd never heard of a revenge doctor, and I never wanted an appointment with him.

The tension at the breakfast table lightened, and soon after we were headed to an upscale mall some distance away from small town Wildwood. We spent hours going from store to store, and Cyn and Lisa held several bags from each. I didn't feel comfortable spending Uncle George's money, and I'd planned to only get a nice top or maybe some new jeans.

My cousin had other ideas and insisted I try on several outfits, none of which were my style and were way too sexy for me to wear in public. When I refused to let her buy them, Cyn made me pose in the pictures. She said I'd later regret not getting them, and the pictures would help me remember what I had on. I highly doubted her logic, but I went along with it. Shopping made my aunt and cousin happy, and if they were happy, my stay would be more peaceful.

I did finally give in to three outfits. They were a little outside my comfort zone, a short sundress with strappy heels, a sequined top that showed a little cleavage paired with ripped jeans, and a bikini with a matching wrap. The sundress was the only thing my parents would approve of, but I wasn't typically a dress kind of girl, so I couldn't imagine actually wearing any of these. I decided I'd keep the tags on everything and after a couple of months, I'd make Cyn return them.

Before we came home, my family insisted we stop by the make-up counter. Here again, I was given the full treatment. My mother barely wore make-up, and the only thing she'd ever approved of me wearing was natural-colored eye shadows and lip glosses. There were girls at my school who glammed up the make-up, but I guess since there weren't boys to impress, most of us didn't bother.

Looking in the mirror at the make-up counter in a very high-end department store, I didn't recognize the girl staring back. The deep plum liner around my eyes made them morph from an average green hue to the bright green of a new leaf. The contour hollowed out my cheeks to make my cheekbones look incredibly high and chiseled. I stared at myself, not believing the transformation a little color could give me.

My aunt was just as surprised, and I got the distinct feeling she didn't approve. Cynthia, however, seemed delighted. "This is just perfect," she said to the saleslady, "we'll take all of it."

"Darling," Lisa said, "are you sure?"

There was an underlying question I didn't understand. Cyn's lips twisted into a scary, smug smile. "I know what I'm doing."

My attention darted between the two. Nothing about them gave me any clues to the hidden discussion they were having. I debated asking them and decided now wasn't the time. Maybe later, when I didn't have my aunt as an audience.

I closed my eyes as the saleslady squirted something called finishing spray on my face and guaranteed us that the look would last all night.

"Just what we need," Cyn said.

As we drove back to the house, my nose began to itch, and I started to scratch it.

"Don't touch your face," Cyn nearly screeched. "You'll mess it up."

Lisa glanced over to her daughter. "Does that mean you're going out tonight?"

"Yes," she said. "Fiona and I are going to hang out with the Danvers."

Lisa frowned and kept her eyes on the road. "I thought Nathan hated the Danvers."

She shrugged. "He does. But he broke up with me. So, he has no say in what I do, and I haven't seen Charlie and Oscar in ages." She glanced at me. "They're hot, and Oscar is in college. You're going to love them."

I felt like my eyes were going to pop out of my head. Hanging out with a college guy? I was barely sixteen. My parents definitely wouldn't approve.

Cynthia laughed hysterically at my reaction. "Don't freak out," she said. "They're like big brothers to me. Flirty, hot big brothers. We'll hang out, have some fun, and you'll have pics on your social accounts that will make your friends die from jealousy."

"I don't have any social accounts," I told her, and it was her turn to be shocked.

"Why not?" she said.

I shrugged. It wasn't that my parents forbade it. They were both active on social media. I just had a risk-free, boring life and didn't see the need to advertise that to the whole world.

"Well, we're going to fix that."

I didn't see it as something that needed to be fixed, but I didn't argue with her. What did it matter if I created a social media account? It's not like I'd have a bunch of followers or anything. "OK," I said.

"Today."

She meant it. The moment we got to her house, she ordered me to bring my laptop to her bedroom. The first time I'd stepped into her room, I'd only focused on her. Now, looking around, I realized her room was an explosion of color, with her walls being the same bubblegum pink as the splotch in my closet. I made a mental note to ask her about it later.

She pulled an extra chair to her seaglass-green desk and placed my laptop next to hers. "OK," she said, "Let's start here."

She pulled up a social media site and insisted I do the same. "I'll make a fake account while you make a real one."

"You can make a fake account? Isn't that against the rules?"

She shook her head in disgust. "What century have you been living in? You don't date. You don't wear make-up. You don't have a social presence." When I didn't answer her, she huffed. "Whatever. Just do what I do."

She created a profile for a 20-year-old female and added an email account.

I followed her steps using my own personal information and an email Cyn created for me on the spot from a free email provider.

Next, she added a fake name Audra Houghton to the profile and uploaded one of the pictures of me from the dressing room. She'd captured my side profile and filtered the picture so it looked more moody than a simple dressing room picture. The effect was stunning.

"You're really good at photography," I said.

She shrugged it off. "I've taken a lot of selfies."

That wasn't it, though. The picture really was amazing.

"Now," she said, "Upload one of the pictures from today. I've sent them to your new email account."

I chose a pre-make-up one and cropped it to only show my face. I added my name and the picture, and then we both published the pages.

"Alright," I smiled at her. "I'm on social media."

"Barely," she said. "You need some posts and some followers."

"I don't know a lot of people."

"You don't have to. All you need are some hot pictures and a few cute boys. The rest will take care of itself."

I laughed. "I don't think so."

"Watch and learn," she raised one eyebrow at me. Then she uploaded more of the pictures she'd taken today. Some angles emphasized the low-cut shirts she'd had me try on, as well as a fully glammed picture of my face. After that, she said, "We'll start with the Danvers."

She sent a connection invitation to the college guys, and within seconds, they had accepted the invitation. Cyn laughed, "Boys are so predictable."

Within the next hour, Cyn had connected the Audra profile to several people, and to my surprise, Audra began receiving requests from strangers.

I found a few friends from my old school and sent requests from my real profile, but I didn't dare reach out to strangers. Cyn thought my low number of followers was pathetic, so she connected her account and our fake one to mine.

"Now start posting pictures and updates." Cyn uploaded another picture to the Audra account. This one was a picture of her feet next to a pool. She wrote *having the best day with @CynHoughton and @FionaHoughton.*

It wasn't long before one of the guys who'd connected to Audra made a comment about seeing her in a bikini instead of just her feet. Cyn rolled her eyes and made a gagging noise; then she replied back to him *I like to keep you guessing, Gorgeous.*

"Why didn't you put him in his place? Now he'll think Audra likes his crude comments."

My cousin frowned. "He's the mayor's son, and he's an entitled brat. If he thinks we're insulting him, he'll attack us, and we'll lose followers."

"Who cares? This is a fake account. We can delete all this, can't we?" I suddenly felt very uncomfortable about her using my face for this little demonstration.

"We can deactivate the account," she said, "But if they download one of your pictures, there's nothing we can do about it. So don't post anything salacious."

"Like my boobs spilling out of a dress?" I pointed to one of the dressing room pictures she'd posted on Audra's page.

"Please. That's nothing. You should see some bathing suits posted on here." She glanced at me. I bit my bottom lip, and she read my expression correctly. "Stop worrying. We'll deactivate this account. Eventually. Right now, it's too funny seeing these guys try to wiggle their way into a relationship with you. Look at this one."

She pointed to a guy's message that said, *Didn't we meet at Brewster's party last week?*

Cyn cracked up. "Watch this," she said.

I thought you looked familiar.

"Who is Brewster?" I asked.

"I have no idea," she laughed.

Are you going to Paddy's tomorrow? the guy replied.

"Paddy's?" I asked.

Cyn grinned at me. "No clue."

I'm not sure. Any reason why I should?

The guy answered immediately. *I'll be there.*

Cyn burst out laughing. "This guy is going to show up and spend his entire night looking for a girl that doesn't exist."

"That's mean," I said. "Let him down easy."

"Fine," she huffed. *That's a compelling reason to go. I'll try to make it. My mom's coming into town, and if I can get rid of her, I'll be there. But you know how it is when mothers visit their babies in college.*

"Happy?" Cyn asked sarcastically.

"He's still going to look around for Audra all night."

"I had to have some fun," she grumbled. "Speaking of fun. We need to get dressed for our night out. Wear the sparkly top and jeans."

"Um," I didn't know how to tell her I planned to wear my regular clothes.

She pointed her index finger at me. "Don't even try to weasel out of this date. It's happening."

"OK," I said, "but I don't want to wear that outfit. It's not really me."

"That's the point," she said. "You're not going to waste my dad's money. Wear the clothes."

"We can return them," I said.

"No. Wear the clothes. Daddy will want to see what we bought."

There was hope, after all. My father would never let me out of the house in a shirt that showed cleavage. I'd get dressed, show Uncle George, and he'd demand that I change. Problem solved.

Only, he didn't. He beamed at us with pure pride and told "his girls" to have a good night. I should have known my plan wouldn't work when my cousin trotted out of her room with an even more revealing outfit than mine.

The Danvers brothers picked us up in a modest sedan, and on first impressions, they were not only gorgeous but also really nice. Oscar, the older brother, had golden brown hair that curled around his face, a wide welcoming smile, and larger biceps than I'd ever seen on a guy. I got a really close up view of them as he held open the front passenger door for me.

"No sports car?" Cyn said as Charlie opened the back door for her.

"Back seat's too small," Oscar said and climbed behind the wheel. "I'd never force you to sit in Charlie's lap."

They laughed at Oscar's joke, and I loved the warm sound of it. Maybe this wouldn't be so bad. It wouldn't be a romantic thing. Oscar was 21, definitely too old for me, and the way 18-year-old Charlie stared at my cousin, it was obvious his interest wouldn't settle on me anytime soon. I relaxed into the seat, feeling optimistic about the evening.

"Where are we going?" Cyn asked.

"It's a surprise," Charlie said and rubbed his hands together in anticipation.

"So, Fiona," Oscar said, "Welcome to Wildwood."

We made small talk for a few minutes while Oscar drove. Nothing memorable or uncomfortable. Just the basics like where I was from, how long I was visiting. That type of thing. Not one word beyond polite, ordinary small talk. Until....

"So," Oscar said during a lull in the conversation. "Who is Audra?"

"What makes you think we know any Audra?" Cyn said.

He laughed. "Besides the fact that she tagged you in a picture, you have the same last name."

I wrung my fingers in my hand and hoped the boys didn't get made when they found out she was a fake. I opened my mouth to answer when my cousin said, "She's a catfish."

"A what?" I asked.

"Ugh," Cyn groaned, "don't you know anything, Fi?"

Oscar smiled in my direction. "A catfish is a fake profile to lure unsuspecting prey. Sometimes they're just looking for a friend or for romance. Sometimes they con money from their victims."

I turned sideways in my seat to face my cousin. "We're not preying on anyone." The guys may have thought I was defending our actions, but Cyn got the message. It was an order.

"Of course, we're not," she said. "It was just for fun while Fiona made her own account."

"So, there's no chance of me hooking up with Audra?" Oscar teased. He winked at me in a conspiratorial way, and I smiled back at him. His flirty words were an obvious joke and instead of making me feel uncomfortable, I felt like I belonged. Like this stranger and I shared inside jokes all the time.

"We can always fake pictures to look like you did," Cyn said.

Oscar laughed a rich, hearty bellylaugh. "I have never had to fake a make-out session. Just so you know."

He parked the car and grinned at us. "Here we are."

It was one of those venues that had an arcade, bowling and laser tag attached to a sports bar. The way we'd dressed, I expected my cousin to throw a tantrum. Instead, she pumped her fist in the air. "Yes! You boys are going down!"

We went inside, and Cyn immediately headed for the bowling lanes. I didn't know if the Danvers knew it, but my family took bowling very seriously. My grandmother had been a fanatic, and every chance she had, she'd taken the whole family to the local bowling alley. Cynthia was the best bowler in the family, and I was the second best.

My cousin gave me a meaningful look. "Boys, you want to make it interesting?"

Oscar casually leaned on the counter. "What are you thinking?"

"If we win, you let us drive your sports car," from the way Cyn said the words, I knew it was something Oscar had refused to do in the past.

"What if we win?" Oscar said.

"Name whatever you want," she answered, "you're not going to win."

Charlie jumped in. "A kiss."

"Uh-uh," Oscar shook his head, "I'm not going to jail for kissing a minor."

Cyn smirked. "Audra is 20."

He tilted his head and examined her. He was obviously suspicious.

I wasn't worried. Unless these guys were pros, there was no way they'd win against us.

"If we win, then I get pics of Audra on my profile," Oscar said.

"I thought you didn't need a fake girlfriend," I said, and Cyn fist-bumped me.

Oscar waggled his eyebrows at me. "Who said anything about a girlfriend? I like hot girls on my profile."

I blushed. Although Audra wasn't real, she had my face and body. I'd never been called hot before. The only hot describing me referred to the heat from my face flushing.

"Whatever," my cousin said. "Let's bowl."

We got our rental shoes and headed to our lane. Cyn sat next to me and whispered, "I'm a little rusty."

I whispered back to her, "I'm not."

She grinned at me, and I grinned back. For the first time in my memory, I felt a connection with her. I wasn't sure how the rest of our time together over the next few months would work out, but I started to have a little hope. Maybe it wouldn't be the nightmare I'd envisioned.

"Ladies first," Charlie said, and I held back my smile.

My grandmother had taught us that the ones who led had the mental advantage over the ones who followed. If you could intimidate them from the start, then you could throw them off their game. I'm not sure if she was right about that, but it's what she'd taught us, and it always seemed to work. Since my cousin's game was a little rusty, I motioned for her to go first. She took her first turn and knocked down only six pins. I was a little nervous about just how rusty she was, but I smiled at her while she waited for the ball to return and said, "You've got this."

Charlie moved closer to her and said, "Good start. I can give you some pointers, if you'd like."

"Maybe later," she patted him on the chest. Her second shot knocked down the rest of the pins.

"So, we didn't exactly iron out the terms," Oscar said. "How do we declare a winner? Highest score? Most strikes?"

I grabbed my ball and tuned him out. It didn't matter to me how they determined the winner. This was one thing I was confident in. I shut out the world, took my aim, and let the ball slide from my fingertips as I glided forward. The ball went fast and straight with a slight curve just before it hit the pins. They all fell down in a beautiful choreographed surrender. I held my smile from my face, calmly walked to my group, sat down and said, "Next."

The boys stared at me in shock, and Cyn giggled. "Oh, did we forget to tell you that our family likes to bowl?"

The guys took their turns and did fairly well. Compared to the average bowler, they were good. Compared to us, they sucked. It quickly became less about the bet with the Danvers and more about a friendly competition between the girls.

I won the first game with Cyn coming in a close second. "So," I asked the guys, "what were the terms of the bet?"

Oscar laughed. "It doesn't matter. You won."

I placed a hand to my chest in a mock surprise. "You mean, me?"

Taking me by surprise, Oscar placed his hands on my waist and lifted me into the air. He twirled us around, and said, "Yes, you. Don't rub it in."

When he placed me back on my feet, I was laughing so hard, I had to lean on him for support. If this was what having guy friends was like, I'd been missing out all these years.

The Danvers demanded a rematch, which was a strategically bad move. Now that Cyn was warmed up, she dominated the game. I came in second, but she far outpaced me.

"Maybe you should give me pointers," Charlie said and Cyn smirked at him.

Next, we went into the restaurant side and shared a pizza. The guys kept us laughing through supper and afterward playing in the arcade. I didn't know if this was the kind of thing Cyn did with her friends all the time. I'd imagined wild parties with kegs and teenagers hooking up with strangers. If this was how she hung out, then I was down with it.

The guys dropped us off with a simple goodnight and no awkward walk-you-to-the-door moment. Cyn motioned me to follow her into her room, and I sat in a plush chair in the corner of her room while she booted up her laptop.

"What did you think?" she asked me over her shoulder.

"Tonight was great."

"Yeah, they're dorks, but they're so much fun." She smiled at me. "My friends don't like them because they're not cool enough. So stupid."

I agreed. I wondered if that meant that her friends were actually what I had assumed they'd be. Instead of asking her, I inquired about her focus on her laptop. "What are you doing?"

"Loading Audra pictures and tagging Oscar."

I got up and stood over her shoulder to see what pictures she had. "They lost the bet. Why are you sending the pics to him?"

"Just thought he'd like them."

I looked at the pictures. He probably would. There was one where he was holding me in the air and we were both laughing, there was another one of me leaning into his side and another one of us sitting next to each other eating pizza. No one else from the group was in the pictures. It looked like we were on a date.

Cyn tagged Oscar in the pictures and posted them with the message *Thanks.*

"That's all you're going to say?" I asked her.

"Sure," she clicked away from Audra's profile to her own. "It's simple and mysterious. Anyone reading it will assume there's some deep, private message between Audra and Oscar. People will wonder what's going on, and they'll ask either you or him. Plus, Oscar knows how to play the game. He'll respond with something incredible. Trust me."

"Have you two done this before?"

"Not the catfish thing. But we've online flirted. Mostly to make other people mad."

"Thanks for tonight, Cyn," I told her and made my way to the door. "I think I'm going to turn in now."

"It was fun," she said.

"Yeah, it was." I left her room, closing the door behind me, and stepped into my room. I booted up my laptop and logged into my social profile. I still had a tiny bit of followers, and compared to the Audra profile, mine was pathetic.

Because I was connected to Audra, I looked at the pictures my cousin had posted. I had to admit, I did look pretty good in those pictures. So much older than my current age. And Oscar looked incredible. If my friends saw these pictures, they'd flip. If my parents saw these pictures, they'd flip—but for a very different reason. A wayward thought entered my head. If they thought I'd gone wild, would they bring me home?

I sat back in my seat and let the concept sink in. They'd be mad at Uncle George for letting me go crazy, but it wouldn't last long. No one could stay mad at George for long.

A comment popped up underneath Audra's post. Oscar had replied *I'd do anything for you.*

The words sent chills down my spine. Mysterious and sexy. Oscar definitely knew how to play the game. I stood from my desk and walked to Cyn's room. I had to know her reaction to what he'd said. Just as I was about to knock on the door, my cousin let out a shrill scream.

I opened the door to see her sitting in front of her laptop. "No! No, no, no! How dare you! You miserable waste of flesh!"

"Cyn, are you OK?"

She looked at me. Tears began pouring down her face, and her cheeks turned bright red. "Nathan," she said and balled her fists. "Just sent a connection request to Audra."

Nathan

Genivive's idea of a romantic date consisted of posing in front of every flower and plant at the arboretum in a vain attempt to fill up my phone's memory card. She'd told me to share them on my social media profile, but that wasn't happening. Word was getting around to our mutual friends about my split with Cyn. Some of them wondered why it had taken so long because we were an obvious mismatch. Others were pissed that I'd hurt her. Flaunting my date with Geni wouldn't make any of them happy. Except Genivive, of course.

The only reason I'd planned to go to the arboretum was the seminar on essential oils. But ten minutes into the speaker's presentation, my girlfriend was fidgeting and whispering in my ear and complaining how bored she was. I endured it a few more minutes but then gave up. The seminar was running for another couple of weeks. I'd just have to attend it later. By myself.

When I'd planned the date with Cyn, I'd originally planned to go out to eat afterward. But once we'd toured the entire 70 acres, I was done. I'd taken my new girlfriend home and told her I'd email the pictures to her.

Then I'd delete them from my phone.

Nic was pouting when I walked through our back door and into the kitchen. He gave me a pathetic, wounded expression, and

I was tempted to tell him he was welcome to steal the girl from me. Instead, I ignored him and made my way to my room, where I watched a replay of a classic football game until it was time to come down for supper.

It was rare for the entire family to be home on a Saturday night, so Mom insisted the whole family pile into our media room and watch a movie. She chose a superhero movie that we all liked, and I sat in the dark for the next couple of hours forgetting all the drama and my brother's supposed broken heart.

After the movie, I watched more sports in my room and then sighed as I saw a notification from social media stating Genivive had updated her status. I dreaded seeing what she'd posted, but it was better to know the damage than be blindsided.

She had posted a few pictures of herself from the afternoon and tagged me in them. Since I wasn't in any of the pictures, it wasn't as bad as I had imagined.

Then I got another notification. Cyn Houghton was with Audra Houghton, Oscar Danvers and Charlie Danvers at Game Station. I clicked on the text, and my screen moved to a picture of Cyn and a pretty blond sharing pizza with the brothers.

Cyn had been my girlfriend for four months. In that time, I'd met her parents, been to numerous family dinners, and had heard a million stories about Cyn's childhood. I knew her Uncle Harry was a flake, her Aunt Jillian was a hippy wannabe, and her cousin Fifi was a loser.

Never once did anyone mention Audra. As threatened as Cyn acted about Fifi, I found it hard to believe she'd be completely fine with a hot, older cousin. So fine that she'd never bother to mention her, ever. Much less introduce her to the Danvers.

I rolled my eyes at the pictures of Cyn and Audra hanging out with Oscar and Charlie. They looked like they were having a blast. I knew Charlie was. The whole time I'd dated Cyn, he'd acted like a wounded puppy. He had it bad for her. I'd threatened Cyn once that if she kept hanging out with him that it was over with me. Instead of dumping me like I'd hoped, she promised to never see them again. I didn't believe she'd kept the promise, but I was never able to catch her breaking it.

Now, I was sure, all these posts were to make me jealous. The only thing it did was make me wonder who this Audra person was.

I found the girl's profile and noticed it had been made today. *That wasn't suspicious at all.* I shook my head. What was Cyn up to? A brief thought crossed my mind about how sad it was that I didn't trust my ex. That I thought she'd manipulate any situation to win me back. Maybe it sounded egotistical, but I completely believed she'd do anything to win me back, including making a fake profile.

The only way to find out if my suspicions were accurate was to call her out. So, I hovered over the profile and sent a connection request. If this was Cyn playing some stupid game, I'd find out.

After a few minutes, the connection was accepted, and I wasted no time using the site's feature to send a video request. The request blinked for a minute, and I wondered if Cyn would accept it. The site said Audra was logged in, and I waited patiently as the call continued to ring. If Cyn answered, then I could challenge her. If no one answered the video call, I could challenge Cyn on that, too. Those were the only two options in my head.

Instead, I was surprised when a wide-eyed blond answered the call. The girl from Cyn's pictures still had the same shirt on. I recovered from my surprise and said, "Hi Audra. You don't know me."

"Oh, I know you," the girl's voice held a tinge of anger. "I'm surprised you have the guts to contact me."

I shrugged. "I thought I'd say hi to Cyn's family."

"You've said hi," she scowled at me. "What do you want?"

I leaned back against my headboard and relaxed. The girl was obviously real. And obviously angry. Even over the poor-quality video call, she was pretty. And obviously related to Cyn. They had the same high cheekbones and face shape. She was real, and she was a relative. Though something didn't add up. "Cyn never mentioned you when we dated."

"Why should she?" the girl glared at me. "It's not like you meant anything to her." The girl's eyes darted above the computer screen. Although I didn't hear anything, I was sure Cyn was in the room listening to every word I said.

I kept the smile glued to my face. If the girl was trying to hurt or insult me, she missed her mark. "So, are you in town or did Cyn leave?"

She stared at the screen for a moment, no expression to give me a clue what she was thinking. "My sister and I are visiting," she finally said.

"Is Fifi your sister?"

"Fiona," the girl corrected, "is my sister."

"So, that means we'll get to hang out," I said.

Audra's eyes narrowed. "I don't play with children."

I placed my hand over my heart. "You wound me," I pouted. Even though the girl was pissed with me, I couldn't help flirting with her a little. Not outrageously. After all, my ex was in the room with her.

"You'll live," she retorted. "I'm not looking for jailbait."

I quickly glanced at my screen. It said Audra was twenty. "I turn eighteen in a couple of months," I countered.

Her faced morphed to a fierce mask of anger. "You. Did. Not. Just hit on me after dumping my cousin."

Raising my hands like I was asking her to slow down, I said, "Whoa. I wasn't hitting on you. I was correcting your assumption." I grinned at her. I wasn't sure who this Audra person was, but she was fun to argue with.

"Let me correct *your* assumption. I don't care about you. You can scurry along and play with your little friends. I'm done with this conversation, and I'm glad my cousin is done with you. She deserves better."

With a click, Audra was gone. I stared at the vacant screen, processed what I'd just experienced. Whoever this Audra-person was, she was definitely real, and she was angry.

And still a mystery.

My phone buzzed, and I glanced down to see another text from Genivive. It was the seventh one today. Maybe if I had been excited about this relationship, I would have welcomed her attention. As it was, I'd had more fun arguing with a stranger than I had spending time with my new girlfriend. She was texting me - this time - to invite me to the water park. Our mutual friends were going, and I assumed that meant Cyn was, too.

My brother passed by my room, and I yelled for him. He still wasn't speaking to me, but he stopped anyway.

"You going to the water park tomorrow?" I asked.

He shrugged.

"Is Cyn going?"

"Yeah," he said.

"Then I think I'm going to bow out. I think it's too soon for us to casually hang out."

"Genivive is going," Nic stuck out his bottom lip. "She'll be upset if you aren't there."

I felt bad for my brother. It would be much easier on him if I didn't go, if he didn't have to watch me and Genivive together. Instead, he was more worried about her feelings than his potential torture.

"I'll let her know I don't want to make anyone uncomfortable. I'll stay home," I said. "You go and have fun."

"Whatever," he said and left.

I grinned at my phone as I texted Genivive my decision. How could she argue that I needed to show up when my excuse was all about protecting Cyn's feelings?

Genivive's next text tried to convince me to change my mind, but I stood firm. I did make a small compromise with her. I'd join the gang at Tucker's diner afterward. If we got a long table, then I could sit at one end and Cyn at the other. We wouldn't have to interact at all. Which was fine by me.

I didn't know what game she was playing with Audra, and until I figured that out, it was best to steer clear.

And maybe Nic spending time with his crush would mellow him out, maybe encourage Geni to go after my brother instead of me.

Maybe she'd dump me and save me the trouble of breaking up with her.

One could only hope.

Chapter Four

Fiona
The next morning, I checked my social media account before heading downstairs to breakfast. It was still abysmally boring with no new requests. Even though I'd been tagged in the Audra picture, no hot boys or cool girls wanted to get to know boring Fiona. I sent a quick text to my little brother, telling him that I loved him, and then I went downstairs.

"Ah," Uncle George sat at the kitchen island sipping hot coffee, "you're an early riser like me."

I didn't think 8 am was early. "I guess so."

"Excellent," he said, and offered me some coffee. When I declined, he told me to help myself to whatever was in the kitchen. I didn't feel comfortable enough to cook in my aunt's kitchen, so I grabbed a bowl of cereal and sat at the island.

"My girls don't get up until noon on Saturdays," he smiled. "So, I usually go into the office for a few hours, and then come back after they're awake."

I sighed, partly because I would have to tiptoe around the house not to wake them and partly because I looked forward to some peace without worrying if I was angering Lisa.

George kissed the top of my head, "Have fun today," he picked up a backpack, shoved his laptop into it and began walking toward the front door. At the door he stopped and pointed to a white envelope on a small entry table in the foyer. "Ash is mowing today. Make sure he gets his check."

I nodded and watched my uncle leave. Ash. That was one of the guys Cyn had rejected as my boyfriend. I relaxed. If he wasn't someone my family approved of, then I didn't have to worry about impressing him.

Back in my room, I changed from my pajamas into some cut-off shorts and a faded t-shirt. I pulled my hair into a ponytail and grabbed my ereader. There was a hammock in the back yard that I'd love to read in, but I'd be in the way when the lawn mower came, so instead, I grabbed a glass of juice and sat in one of the patio chairs on the covered back porch. I really wanted to be in the sunlight, but I figured I could go to the hammock after the boy left.

It was 10 am when a beat-up pickup truck pulled into the driveway. The guy behind the wheel jumped out and immediately began pulling his equipment from the back of the truck. This must be Ash. I popped into the house and grabbed the envelope with his name on it. No time like the present. I'd give him his money now and stay out of his way. Maybe I could convince him to mow around the hammock first so that I could get in it sooner.

I popped over to the truck and held the envelope out to the boy. "Ash? This is for you."

He spun in surprise and stared at me for a couple of seconds. And I stared back. He was gorgeous, in a rugged, outdoorsy way. His dark hair jutted in all directions, not like he'd styled it that way, but like he hadn't bothered to brush it. His deep brown eyes had flecks of amber that seemed to catch the sun, and his skin was a deep, rich brown, the beautiful result of genetics and his time in the sun. He was tall and lean, with a hint of muscles, not bulked up the way Oscar had been. His clothes were wrinkled and torn.

He looked like a hot mess, and I found myself completely charmed by it.

"I usually grab it from the table when I'm done," he said.

I shrugged. "George said to make sure you got it."

"Thanks," he took the envelope from me. "And you are?"

"Fiona."

He lowered his brows and slightly shook his head, obviously not hearing the answer to his question. I smiled at him, silently daring him to ask me.

"I'm Ash," he said.

I motioned to the lawn equipment. "I assumed."

"Yeah," he said and rubbed the back of his neck. "I better get started. I have four houses to do today."

"OK," I said, and as I was about to ask him to start at the hammock, my phone rang. I pulled it from my back pocket and saw that my little brother was calling me. I held up a hand goodbye to Ash and answered the call. "Frank!"

My little brother's sweet voice came on the line. I held it tighter to my ear and sighed with pleasure. It was so good to hear him. "Fifi, come here. I miss you."

"I miss you, too, Sweetie. I wish you were here." I sprinted across the yard and into the house. I went straight to my room and spoke to my brother for a few minutes before my parents took their turns with me on the phone.

With my parents, I hinted that I'd gone on a double-date with Cyn. I wasn't sure how much to share. I'd accepted that I'd be here for the whole year, yet I still hadn't completely let go of the idea to force them to change their minds. The thought was growing in my mind, though I wasn't sure if I could take the risk of making them mad or potentially hurting George's feelings. Lisa and Cyn, I'm sure, would be glad to get rid of me.

I rang off with my family and went back to my ebook. When I heard the lawn mower cut off, I watched Ash load his equipment into the truck and drive away.

"I thought he'd never leave," a groggy Cyn said from my doorway. "Ugh, why does he have to come here so early?"

"Because he has other houses to do?" I said and didn't challenge her on her early statement.

"He could do them first and leave us until last."

I ignored the comment.

"Daddy's taking us to the water park today after he comes back from work," she stretched and then yawned. "You can wear your new bikini."

I really hadn't wanted to wear the thing in public. "Are you sure? There's not much material on that thing. Wearing it at a water park seems like begging for a wardrobe malfunction."

"You'll be fine," she waved away my concern. "After breakfast, I'll help you get ready."

"What's to get ready?" I asked. My hair was already in a ponytail. All I had to do was put on the horrible bathing suit.

"Your hair, your make-up, your cover-up and shoes. Everything?"

"Make-up? To a water park?" She had to be kidding.

"Waterproof," she said like she thought I was as crazy as I thought she was.

She was serious. When she came back upstairs, we spent way more time than I thought was necessary fixing our hair into identical messy buns. Then she outlined my eyes with a plum, waterproof eyeliner and jet black mascara. Next, she highlighted my cheekbones and finished off with a pink-toned gloss. She did a similar look to her own face with the only difference being she'd used a blue eyeliner.

After we put on our swimsuits, she criticized my usual shorts and t-shirt with sneakers. Instead, she pulled a large swath of fabric from her closet and wrapped it into a sarong with a knot tied on my left shoulder. She loaned me one of her thick-soled sandals to complete the look. I stared in the mirror and didn't recognize myself. I wasn't going to the park. Audra was.

"I'm guessing there will be boys there?"

"Of course, there will. It's not a girls-only venue," she laughed.

"I mean," I leveled a look at her, "your friends."

"If you mean Nathan," she scowled at me, "no."

"The Danvers?"

"No," she said, "though we should go with them some time. They'd be fun."

I nodded. "Then who?" The way she refused to share any details made me suspicious.

"Just a few friends."

A pit of tension formed in of my stomach. "Cyn, I'm not ready."

She frowned at me. "Whatever. You're shy and don't talk to strangers. Use that. Whenever you don't have anything to say, just raise your eyebrow like you can't believe they're so beneath you."

"I don't do that," I protested.

"Then hang out with my father, like the rest of us are too juvenile for your attention."

"But, that's rude," I said.

"Do you want to make friends with my friends?"

"I," I didn't know how to answer that question. If they were like Nathan, then no. I'd originally planned not to make any friends at all, but the more I thought about that, the more lonely it sounded.

"Just hang with my father."

That's the way the trip started. Uncle George and I stood in line together for the most extreme rides while my cousin and aunt lounged by the massive pool. As we passed by the pool on the way to the large water slides, I noticed Cyn now surrounded by six teenagers. We waved at the group as we passed them, and one of the boys broke away to walk with us.

"Where are you going?" he said. He was tall and athletic, though on the lean side. He had dark hair and bright blue eyes, and his open expression was a lot friendlier than I had expected for one of Cyn's friends.

"There," George pointed to the slide in the distance.

"Mind if I join you? None of those wimps," he pointed to his friends, "will ride it."

"Sure!" George grinned at the boy. "How are your parents?"

The guy launched into a funny story about his parents traveling abroad. Although he answered George, he included me in the conversation. He was attractive with a bright smile and spent most of the conversation telling us funny stories about his parents and his little sister. At no point was the conversation weird or awkward. He was easy to talk to, and I found myself relaxing and enjoying spending time with him.

The three of us went down the largest slides, and after the fourth trip down, George took a break. Cyn's friend and I climbed up again, and this time, he recommended we go down the slide with the two-seater inner tubes. I figured why not, and we rode together down the slide that had the most turns and twists. When we splashed into the pool at the bottom, he yelled, "Yeah! That was awesome!"

Uncle George met us as we got out of the pool and said, "You were flying down that slide. That looked great. I got some video if you want to see."

We watched the video, and the boy said, "We were soaring! Can I have a copy of that?"

George got his number and forwarded the video to him. Then he noticed a sign and pointed to it. "Let me get your picture next to that."

I smiled at the bright yellow sign that said *I survived the Twisted Trail Water Slide.*

We stood next to the sign, and the boy casually wrapped his arm around my shoulders. Then George had us do another one where he insisted we pose like superheros. He had us laughing as he took several silly shots. "I'll send these to you," he said.

We walked back toward the pool where Cyn and her female friends were sunbathing. As we got near them, a couple guys joined, bragging about their rides on the waterboarding machine. The guy next to me, which I realized now we'd never exchanged names, draped his arm over my shoulder and bragged about our epic trip down the water slide.

Uncle George announced to the group that he and Lisa were leaving the park. The teenagers made plans to go to a local diner for supper, and when Cyn mentioned riding with one of the girls, the group got weirdly quiet.

The tall, slender girl Cyn had spoken to gave my cousin a pitying look. "Maybe it's best if you don't come. Nathan will be there."

My fiery, feisty cousin, who normally would tell this girl where to go, looked completely deflated. Her friends were telling her they didn't want her there, and not even the nice guy I'd spent the afternoon with stood up for her.

"What about you?" the guy asked me, and all eyes turned to me. The nerve of the group to think I'd abandon my cousin for them had me looking at all of them in disgust.

I guess I did do the eyebrow thing like Cyn had said because I found myself taking in every single one of them like I couldn't believe they'd think I'd hang with them. "Not interested," I said with a small laugh.

Most of the group looked at me in complete surprise. I guess they weren't used to being treated this way. I didn't care. They were nothing to me, and I'd communicated that loud and clear. The guy next to me was the only one unaffected by my behavior, maybe because he'd spent time with me or maybe because he had a shred of decency in him. "I don't blame you," he said and winked at me.

I didn't return the flirting. Instead, I headed to the locker where we'd stored our stuff and waited for my family to follow. Within minutes, we were out of the water park and on the way home. Uncle George was his normal, happy self, but I could tell that Lisa and Cyn were furious. It made no sense to me why they'd be angry when I'd stood up for my cousin.

Stepping into the house, Aunt Lisa grabbed my arm and nudged me away from the others. "The way you treated Cynthia's friends is unacceptable," she hissed.

"Aunt Lisa, they were rude to her. I was standing up for her."

Lisa sneered like I was the dumbest human on the planet. "They were looking out for her feelings. They knew it'd be hard for her to face Nathan."

"That wasn't what it looked like to me," I defended myself.

Lisa's weary sigh drew out for several seconds. "You meant well, I guess. But you have a lot to learn. Think twice before you insult her friends again."

"Maybe I shouldn't hang out with her friends if they're going to treat her that way," I said as she began to walk away.

"Maybe not," Lisa called over her shoulder.

I was hot and waterlogged and frustrated beyond belief. All I wanted was a shower and a nap and to forget this afternoon had happened. Instead, I got my cousin blocking my bedroom doorway.

"What do you want, Fifi?" she said. "Are you trying to ruin my life?"

"I don't know, *Cindy,*" I emphasized and pushed my way into my bedroom. "Is it worth the effort? From what I can tell, you don't have a life unless your friends tell you so." I threw myself onto the bed and watched as she stalked to the foot of it and glared at me. "Don't be stupid," she said.

"I'm not the one that ran home like a whipped dog because they said you couldn't join them for supper."

"They didn't want things to get awkward."

"They ordered you not to come because it wasn't comfortable for them." I sat up and raked my eyes over the near-stranger glaring at me. "Where is my cousin that had no problem yelling down a referee at a minor league game because she didn't like his calls?"

Cyn paused. "I was a stupid kid."

"Yeah," I smiled at her. "But you didn't take crap from anyone. Why are you letting them dictate to you?"

"You don't understand," she sat on the edge of the bed, the angry heat leaving her face. "They were Nathan's friends first."

"So what? Either they're your friends or they're not."

She was quiet for a moment, and I wondered if I'd gone too far. "They think you're Audra," she finally said.

"You didn't correct them?"

"They never said it outright. When they saw you with Daddy, they asked who you were, and I said my cousin. Then Genivive found Audra's page and sent a request. The rest of them did, too, except, of course, Nicolaus." She placed her hands over her face. "That's another issue."

"What?"

"You brushed off Nathan yesterday and then spent part of the afternoon hanging out with his little brother." Cyn stared at the ceiling. "He's not going to like that."

"Who cares?"

"He messaged Audra a few times last night, and I never found out what he wanted. If he was trying to get back together with me."

Because he wasn't. I kept the thought to myself. I hated that Cyn had placed herself in the situation. Texting her ex and hoping he had an ulterior motive. "What did he talk about? If he wasn't probing for information about you?"

"Take a look," she grabbed my laptop and logged into Audra's account. I watched the log in and made a mental note.

She showed me the direct messages she'd had with Nathan last night. He asked her questions about Audra, and she made up some answers. Several times she tried to move the conversation back to

Nathan's reasons for breaking up with Cyn, and he deftly avoided answering her questions. He seemed way more interested in learning everything he could about Audra instead of talking about his ex.

I wasn't an expert when it came to boys, but even I could see that Nathan was checking out Audra. Not planning to rekindle his romance with my cousin.

A notification popped up and my stomach sank. "Um, Cyn?"

"Yes."

"Nicolaus just tagged Audra in a post."

She yanked the laptop from me and groaned. "This is a disaster."

I leaned over her shoulder and rolled my eyes. He had posted the picture of us by the Twisted Trail sign. His tag said *had a great afternoon with this beauty @AudraHoughton.* "This is ridiculous." Everyone was focused on Audra. This fake girl had a better social life than I did.

"Nathan is going to hate this," Cyn said under her breath.

"So what?"

"You don't understand," she said and shoved my laptop back to me. "I've got to figure this out." She rushed from the room and left me watching her in total confusion.

Almost the moment she'd slammed my bedroom door behind her, Audra got another notification.

A direct message from Nathan.

I debated whether to call Cyn back, but in a split second decided against it. Maybe if I told Nathan to go away, he would. Maybe if I told him to focus on his new girlfriend and stop making their friends choose sides, he'd listen to reason. Or maybe he was just a top-notch jerk who wanted every girl to fall in love with him.

I blew out a frustrated breath. "There's only one way to find out," I said to myself as I opened his message.

53

Nathan

Sometimes my friends were awesome. Sometimes they were lame. Like today.

Before the whole Genivive-Cyn fiasco I'd created, the gang had planned to meet for supper after going to the water park. My new girlfriend had convinced most of the group that Cyn wasn't ready to see me yet, so Cyn had been uninvited to the meal.

I knew it was Genivive's fault. Just how heartless was this girl? Her best friend had been dumped, and she had banned the girl from eating with us. If anything, I was the one who should have stayed away and Cyn be around her friends to comfort her.

My best friend Ben Wallace and I arrived after everyone else. Since I hadn't gone to the water park, he'd backed out, and we'd spent the afternoon playing racquetball at the rec center. I'd come home to take a shower just as Nicolaus was pulling out of the driveway to head to the diner.

Which was another issue. He was still acting like a wounded puppy over Genivive. Well, if he wanted a chance with her, he might get it sooner rather than later.

When I got there, a seat next to Genivive was waiting for me, and I slipped into it and found myself across from my brother. He was animatedly talking, his hands and arms in high motion as he gushed about the great time he'd had at the park.

My girlfriend glared daggers at him.

"Hey," I said to the whole table. "What did I miss?"

"Your brother," Genivive spat, "and his new girlfriend."

I raised my eyebrows at Nic. That was a fast rebound. If this girlfriend made him happy, great. It just put a damper in my hope that my brother would steal away my current girlfriend.

Nicolaus beamed. "Not my girlfriend. We just hung out."

"I'm surprised you had a such a good time," Geni scowled, "That girl was awful."

I held back a grin. Genivive couldn't hide her flagrant jealousy of this girl. Maybe she'd learn a lesson from this ordeal.

"After the way she treated us," Juliet said, "you should have dumped her on the spot. I can't believe you'd go out with a loser like that."

Nic grinned. "She's hot. Plus, I like that she stood up for her cousin." He glared at me for a second. "Family loyalty is important."

I gave my brother a bored look. I wasn't going into all of this again. Seconds before, he was happy. He needed to stay there. I wasn't going into drama mode with him. I glanced at Ben, who sat a couple seats over from Nic. He had his own melodramatic stepbrother, so he knew exactly what I was going through. Ben shook his head and turned toward the menu.

I followed his lead until Nic's next statement captured my attention.

"If you'd just let Cyn come, then Audra wouldn't have gone off on you."

I kept my eyes glued to the diner menu, not seeing a single item in front of me. Instead, I listened intently to the escalating argument between my girlfriend and my brother. I wasn't worried that it'd go very far. Nic didn't like confrontation, unless it meant whining to me about how he thought I'd wronged him. True to his nature, Nic ended the conversation and pulled out his phone instead.

He tended to be passive aggressive, like our mother. So, I pulled out my phone and checked out his latest post.

What had happened at the water park that my brother now felt completely comfortable tagging this stranger? They had to have had a good time. Otherwise, he wouldn't have that goofy grin returning to his face. He didn't mention Audra again, but everyone knew he was thinking about her.

Cyn had brought this girl to hang out with our friends. Was this coincidence or was she manipulating us?

Without thinking, I typed a quick message to Audra. I'd enjoyed sparring with her during our video chat.

Then, she'd completely surprised when she'd sent me a direct message later that night apologizing for her rudeness. Our texting back and forth wasn't as satisfying. It seemed she'd lost her angry spark and was semi-flirting with me while trying to talk up how great her cousin was. She was still this huge mystery to me, and even though it was probably the worst idea ever, I wanted to figure her out.

You said you don't hang out with children and then you went to the water park with my baby brother?

I pressed my lips together to prevent myself from smiling when she immediately responded.

I hope you're not expecting me to explain myself.

The feisty Audra had returned. This should be fun. I sent a message back. *My humor doesn't translate well online. You'll see when we meet in person. I'm a funny guy.*

She didn't respond. Our waitress took our orders, and the group started planning a small party we'd have next weekend. I barely spoke. After all, they really didn't need my input. This party would be like every other one we'd had this summer. Same people. Same snacks. Same music. Different home. Officially planning the event seemed like a colossal waste of time.

I checked my phone every few minutes and wondered if Audra was ghosting me. I wouldn't blame her. If her profile was accurate, she was a college woman, and I would be a high school senior when school started next month. But she'd spent the day with a sixteen-year-old boy. So, why wouldn't she talk to me?

Just as I was giving up, she sent a message back.

Let me be very clear. Not interested.

But you're interested in my baby brother? I instantly replied.

She didn't respond, and I wondered if she wasn't talking to me because she was messaging Nic. I watched him for several minutes. He remained animated, talking to anyone who'd listen about how fun and cool Audra was, but he never picked up his phone. He was talking about her, not to her.

After a few minutes, I sent another message. It was a little more blunt than I'd intended, but I didn't want this woman screwing around with my brother's feelings. Despite what Nic thought, I did love him.

My brother is here bragging about how much fun the two of you had together. Don't you want to set the record straight?

She responded. *I've had enough playtime with children for one day. I need adult company now. Goodbye, Nathan, I'll leave you to play with your little friends.*

Then she was offline. I stared at my phone for a few seconds. What game was this girl playing? Was she as manipulative as Cyn? Did Cyn know Audra was playing around with Nic's heart? My baby brother might hate me for it, but I had to get the truth. If he was a pawn in the Houghton girls' twisted game. I'd find a way to put a stop to it.

Chapter Five

F iona
      On Sunday, I got some overdue peace. The family attended a local church, and probably because Aunt Lisa was afraid I'd insult more of their friends, she gave me the option to stay home and get settled in. I jumped on the chance.

I liked having the house to myself and watched mindless TV for a while before getting bored. I cleaned up the kitchen while they were gone and then grabbed my ereader to finally get some time reading in the hammock. I'd barely settled in when Uncle George's luxury sedan pulled into the driveway. He parked his car in their 3-car garage, and I heard doors slam.

I glanced at my phone. They were supposed to be gone for another hour. And from the sounds of slamming doors, I knew something had happened. I reluctantly turned off my device and slid from the hammock. One day, I'd get a chance to read here. Obviously, today wasn't it.

Though I really wanted to stay away from the drama, I had to find out what was happening. I entered through the back porch and stepped into the kitchen.

Aunt Lisa banged pots and pans as she yelled at no one in particular. Uncle George sat at the kitchen bar with a totally devastated expression on his normally jolly face, and Cyn stood off to the side with her arms crossed over her chest.

"We've known them for years," Lisa slammed another pan on top of the stove. "That girl has slept under my roof. We made soup for them when the whole family was sick. This," she hit the countertop with every word, "is unacceptable."

I slid next to Cyn and raised my eyebrows, but she shook her head. "Later," she mouthed to me, and I got the hint. When Lisa was raging, we all stood silently and watched.

"No respect," Lisa took the pan she'd just placed on the stove and tossed it into the cabinet for it to crash and clang with the other pans. "And then supporting it? Telling me she was sorry? If Cyn had done something so atrocious, she'd be grounded for life!"

I had a hard time believing that statement. I didn't think my cousin had ever been grounded, and I'd seen her do some pretty outrageous stuff.

Lisa paused in her frantic movements and placed her hands on her hips. She stared at George as if expecting him to answer, though she never gave him the chance to speak. "So condescending," she said, "like she was so sorry my daughter's heart had been broken. Like she cared."

My aunt addressed me, pointing her long, bony index finger in my face. "Just because she was horrible isn't an excuse for us to be rude. To stoop to her level."

I swallowed hard. "Yes, ma'am," I said, like I'd been guilty of making such a suggestion.

I glanced over to Cyn, who stared at the floor, refusing to meet anyone's eyes. Maybe I should've taken my cue from her and did the same thing.

Lisa looked at her daughter, and her chin began to wobble. The heated anger fled from her body, and tears formed in her eyes. "I'm so sorry you had to see that, Darling," she wrapped her arms around my cousin. "If I had known..."

My cousin nodded her head a single time. "I'm so sorry," Lisa said and kissed the top of her daughter's head. "We'll change churches."

Cynthia smiled and hugged her mom back. "You're the best Mommy ever."

Lisa closed her eyes and leaned her head to rest against her daughter's.

"We don't have to leave our church," Cyn said. "I'm sorry that Mrs. Wicker was so awful. But don't worry about it. Nathan won't be with Genivive for long."

My mouth dropped open. Nathan and Genivive? The jerk dumped Cyn for her best friend?

"I know for a fact he's interested in someone else." My cousin pinned me with a stare that made my stomach twist in knots. She had a plan. And I was guaranteed to hate it.

"Well," Lisa said, "that will serve them right. Maybe Genivive will learn a valuable life lesson about staying loyal to one's friends and honoring the sanctity of a relationship."

"Yeah," Cyn said, a smile growing on her face, "I think Genivive will definitely learn a valuable lesson from this. Nathan will, too."

Lisa leaned back and grinned at her daughter, all fury seemingly forgotten. "I can't believe how kind and gracious you've been through all of this. So mature for so young a person. How did I get lucky enough to have you as my daughter?"

My cousin grinned at her mother. "I'm the lucky one. You and Daddy are the best. And," her gaze trained back to me, "I'm so thankful I have Fi here to support me through it. Maybe she shouldn't have been so rude to my friends yesterday, but I know she did it because she wanted to protect me. She really does want to help me get over Nathan and what he and Genivive did to me."

Lisa and George beamed at me, and it was the first time since I'd arrived that I'd had Lisa's open approval. I smiled back at them, though I had to force it. My cousin was plotting, and her words had been more of a warning to me than what they were on the surface.

Cyn was telling me I was going to be part of whatever plan she'd cooked up, even if I didn't like it.

She'd also shown me exactly what it would take to get my aunt's approval. If I was stuck here for the next nine months, having Lisa's approval would make it an easier experience.

But was it worth it? I had an awful feeling I knew exactly what she wanted, and if I was right, I'd be way more involved in this drama than I ever wanted to be. I'd feed into the shallowness of her friends' world and potentially into Cyn's insecurities.

My cousin's gaze said I didn't have a choice. But that wasn't true. There was always a choice.

Just sometimes you had to choose between two really sucky, terrible options. My parents called it between a rock and a hard place.

I called it screwed.

Later that night, Cyn invited me to her room. Once the doors were firmly shut, she motioned for me to sit on her bed.

I gingerly sat next to her and said, "I didn't know Nathan dumped you for Genivive."

"I didn't tell anyone. It was embarrassing."

Embarrassing. Did that mean my cousin wasn't in love with her ex? "It must have been hard seeing them together."

She sighed and leaned against her headboard. "It was going to happen sooner or later. I should have given Mommy and Daddy a heads up that they'd be together. I figured she knew since she read his text, but I guess she overlooked that part. I felt really bad when we walked into the sanctuary, and they saw Genivive practically sitting in Nathan's lap." She sighed. "Then Mrs. Wicker made it worse by saying how sorry she was that Nathan had dumped me for her daughter. Mommy just looked at her like she'd grown a second head, spun around and walked out."

I felt bad for Aunt Lisa. Cynthia was her world, and that must have hurt. The one thing, though, that had been bouncing in my brain was, "I thought Genivive was your best friend. Why would she say yes to Nathan?"

My cousin traced the delicate pattern of flowers on her bedspread. Pink rosebuds and green leaves wove into each other over an ivory background. She ran her fingers over the print as if she could actually feel the petals. "Probably payback," she finally said.

"Revenge? For what?"

"When Nathan broke it off with his last girlfriend, she called dibs," Cyn said with a bored tone.

"You stole your best friend's crush?"

Cyn laughed. "No. She doesn't have a crush on Nathan. She just wanted to date him."

"I don't understand."

She leaned back against her headboard. "There are a handful of guys at our school that every girl wants to be with. Some of them are accessible. They'll smile at you, joke around, flirt. They give you the impression that under the right circumstances you might have a chance with them — guys like Nicolaus, for instance. Then there's Nathan. He's untouchable."

"That sounds horrible."

She laughed. "It's not. He's not a bully or a snob or anything. He's nice to everybody. He just won't flirt or give you much attention unless he's interested." She pinned me with a look, and we both knew what she was thinking. He was giving Audra way too much attention for a guy with a new girlfriend.

It was my turn to trace the pattern on the bed. I avoided eye contact with my cousin and waited for her to continue speaking.

She was quiet for a while. I expected her to press home the point that Nathan had been flirting with Audra. Instead, she went back to her confession. "Anyone who dates Nathan automatically gets respect," she said. "It's not about love, or romance, or emotions. It's about popularity."

Part of me was shocked. But after seeing this group in action, I wasn't as surprised as I should have been. "So you stole Nathan from Genevieve because..." My mouth had trouble saying the thought my brain had formed. My cousin had dated a guy because it made her more popular. And losing him somehow made her less.

"Yes," she said, reading my thoughts.

"Then why were you so devastated?"

"You don't understand," she said, "It's our senior year. I wanted it all. Homecoming queen, prom queen, cutest couple, most popular girl. All of it. If I had Nathan long-term, then I would have done what no other girl in our school has been able to do."

I shook my head in disbelief. "You were using him?"

"It's not like that. Don't judge me. I genuinely liked Nathan. And I thought he genuinely liked me. Not every couple dates because they're in love. And who's to say that given time we wouldn't have fallen in love." She jumped up from her bed and began pacing the room. "We just needed more time. Nathan gets bored so easily. And I was trying so hard to keep his attention. And it would've worked if Genevieve hadn't stepped in."

I had felt so bad for Cyn. I had thought this guy had broken her heart. Instead, he had broken her chance to be Homecoming queen. It seemed so stupid to me. Maybe that's because I'd never been that popular. But still, it seemed so trivial.

I had treated Nathan like scum on my shoes. And maybe he deserved it for dumping my cousin the way he had. But now I realized just how mercenary this relationship was. How mercenary this group of friends was. And I knew beyond a shadow of a doubt

I didn't want anything to do with them. If it meant that I spent the next nine months all alone, I'd do it. I didn't want to be involved in any of this.

Cyn, however, had other plans.

"You see why we have to get him away from Genevieve as fast as possible, right?"

My head snapped up, and I stared at my cousin in open shock. "What?"

"She can't have him," my cousin pulled her desk chair to sit in front of me, our faces inches apart. "She took away my chance to be the top girl in the school. Nathan needs to be out of the equation. If she's single and I'm single, then we have an even playing field. So," my cousin smiled, "she needs to be single."

"Are you crazy?" It was the wrong thing to say, of course. Because my cousin instantly scowled at me and backed away.

"You're so naïve, Fiona," she narrowed her eyes at me. "High school is about playing the game. And if you're not a player, you get played." She lifted her chin in defiance. "And I don't get played," her words edgy and hard.

I stood up from her bed. "I don't want to be played, either. But I don't want to play these games. You and your best friend are fighting over a guy that neither one of you love. Just so that you can get something out of him. And why does he even go along with this?"

"Because we're all playing the game. Genevieve and I get to be popular. Nathan doesn't have to be alone."

I made my way to her bedroom door, but at her words I paused. That sounded so sad. For a moment I felt sorry for these popular kids. Using each other. Entering shallow relationships. Where were their hearts? If wanting to date someone because I genuinely had fallen in love made me naïve, I wanted to stay that way. "Don't you want to fall in love?"

"One day."

We stared at each other in silence, and I tried to put all these puzzle pieces together in my mind. "Popularity first, love later?"

She lifted one shoulder. "Something like that."

I shook my head and stepped toward the door. All of this drama, all the anger and tears and frustration. All of it was political. And I didn't understand it.

"Aren't you curious?" my cousin said.

"About what?" I turned and faced her from her doorway.

"How I'm going to do it."

My throat started to close. Dread washed over me, and my fingers helplessly clenched at my side. I knew what she was hinting at. And I didn't want to hear it. But being ignorant wasn't going to stop my cousin from whatever plan she had hatched. And since I was positive it included me, it was better to know what I was facing. Although I was sure I knew the answer, I asked anyway. "Do what?"

Cyn crossed the room and pulled me in so she could close her bedroom door.

"Break them up."

I shook my head at her. "Can't you just leave them alone? If Nathan is so untouchable won't he dump her soon, anyway?"

"I'm not leaving that to chance."

I leaned against the wall next to her door. Her light switch dug into my back, but I didn't care. The only thing I could focus on was watching the slow smile form on her lips.

"You see, my dear cousin, Nathan's already bored. He's already found another girl who fascinates him. Given the right incentive," her lips stretched wider, "he might fall for someone else."

"The right incentive?"

Cyn motioned to her bed, indicating I should sit back down. I remain rooted where I was and waited for her to continue. When it was obvious that I wasn't going to follow her instruction, she began talking again. "Nathan has everything he could ever want. So naturally, he wants whatever he can't have. That's how I snatched him from Genevieve. I made him think I was as unattainable as he was."

"And he fell for that?" I'd never considered that Nathan was stupid. I couldn't imagine Cyn dating anyone that she didn't completely respect. Though now I was questioning that assumption.

"Obviously." She moved her chair back to her desk and booted up her laptop. She logged into Audra's profile and in a few clicks had pulled up the history of her messages with Nathan. "See for yourself."

Curiosity got the better of me, and I reluctantly dragged my feet over to stand next to her. On the screen before me was a string of messages between the two of them. Cyn flirting shamelessly. Nathan flirting back.

"You see," she smiled at me, "He's doing the same thing with Audra." Her smile turned brittle, her lips hard. "You're a natural at this game. And you didn't even know you were playing."

I sucked in a deep breath of air, but it didn't help the strangled feeling I felt in my chest. "I was defending you. I thought this guy had broken your heart, and I had my cousin's back. I wasn't playing some twisted game to try to get his attention or to make him like me."

"It doesn't matter," she said, "You have his attention now. And we're going to use that." Even though she still had a smile on her face, her eyes hardened, and she reminded me of the hard-core cousin I'd known growing up. The one who didn't take crap off anyone. A part of me was relieved to see that she was still in there. That she wasn't anyone's doormat. But that was a very small part of me. Because the rest of me knew that I was in trouble. Because she was laser focused on me.

"Genevieve is going to be infamous," Cyn said. "And not because she's going to hold on to Nathan longer than anyone else ever has. She's going to be his shortest relationship ever."

I backed away from her. As if putting physical distance between us would separate me from her plan. "I don't want any part of this."

"That's the beauty of this all. You're not. All I need is Audra. And thanks to you, I can be her anytime I want."

"You can't video chat with him."

"I won't need to. Often." Her message was loud and clear. She was going to take over the Audra profile, and she expected me to play along.

"I'm not doing this. You can't force me."

"If you think you can get out of this by refusing to play, I have news for you, Cousin. You video chatted Nathan. And Nicolaus thinks that he spent an afternoon with you. You're already neck deep in this."

"And that ends now." I placed my hands on my hips. I was serious. Whatever she was going to do, I couldn't stop her from using that profile. But I didn't have to play along anymore. No more Audra. I was done with her. I opened my cousin's door and turned around and faced Cyn. "I can't stop you from doing whatever it is you plan to do. But that doesn't mean I have to play. This is your game, your friends, your ex. I don't want any part of it."

I turned to walk away and froze in my tracks. Aunt Lisa stood in the hallway glaring at me, and I knew she'd heard what I'd said to her daughter.

Any goodwill that I'd hoped to get from her was a distant dream.

If I was punished and tortured for doing the right thing, then that's what I do. I wouldn't live with my family forever. But I'd have my conscience always. And I was going to make my conscience happy.

Nathan

My girlfriend wasn't a nice person. Not that that completely surprised me. After all, she had screwed over my brother and her best friend just to get me to agree to be her boyfriend.

But just how mean a girl she was became apparent when she laughed at the Houghton family leaving church after seeing us together. Apparently Cyn hadn't told her parents about Genevieve and me. And apparently Genevieve thought it was hysterical.

I had been watching for Cyn and her family, wondering if the elusive Audra would show up. When she wasn't there, it added more questions to the list I already had.

Genevieve had invited me to join her and her family for lunch after church, but immediately after we'd eaten, I made the excuse that I needed to go.

I'd spent all afternoon researching essential oils and fragrances. The more I learned, the more I realized I didn't know. If my business partner and I were going to be successful, then I had a lot to learn. We'd divided up our pet project with him taking the manual labor while I handled the business side. Until this point, our little business had been relatively easy. Now, I was hitting a roadblock, and I needed to figure this out. My partner was depending on me.

After I'd had my fill of research, I searched for something else to do. I was bored out of my mind and tried to fill my time playing video games. But since my brother was still giving me the silent treatment, playing them by myself wasn't much fun. I could have challenged my little sister. Even though she was only eight years old, she was pretty good at the games her older brothers played. She was currently spending a month with our grandparents out of town on their farm. At this point, I almost wished I was with her. Even though it meant days of farm life and farm chores. I'd trade all that in a heartbeat rather than being stuck in my current situation.

I found myself later that night cruising around social media. Even though I didn't want to admit it to myself, I kept searching particular profiles to see if they came on board. I'd been on there almost an hour and was ready to click away when a particular indicator light popped up. I didn't waste any time sending Audra a message.

It's late. Having trouble sleeping?

Taking a break from studying. Her reply was almost immediate. I frowned and looked at the message. Was she too tired to freeze me out? I had completely expected her to ignore my message instead of replying immediately. I narrowed my eyes when she sent me a follow-up message.

What are you doing up so late?

I tapped my fingers on my desk and examined every single letter, as if something in that message could answer the biggest question in my head. Which Audra was I getting tonight? Sometimes she treated me like I was the biggest jerk on the planet, and sometimes she was flirty and sweet. There was no consistency at all.

Are you so tired that you forgot you hate me?

Again her response came instantly. *I don't hate you.*

I frowned. Something wasn't right. Where was the girl who challenged me? No matter which Audra I typically got, she always pushed back. This was a new side of her.

You don't like me, I typed back.

This time her answer came after a few minutes. *We don't really know each other, do we?*

I frowned at the message. This conversation felt real. Not like two random strangers talking. Something definitely wasn't right.

No, we don't. I typed and waited to see if she took the bait. In my experience, this was where girls hinted that we should get to know each other. It wasn't egotistical of me, just a fact. Being rich and relatively attractive made girls throw themselves at me and my brother. Nic didn't seem to mind, but I did. I wasn't a trophy for a girl to win. The problem was, I hadn't found a girl yet who understood that.

I was a little relieved when Audra didn't immediately respond. It was a couple of minutes before she said *I need to get back to studying. Good night.*

Good night.

I saw the indicator light go off, but I stared at the words. This girl confused me. I totally expected her to nail me for the Houghtons running out of church earlier today. Not that it was my fault. But, the fun Audra was fiercely protective of her cousin. I expected her to echo what had been rattling around my brain for hours. I should have kept my distance from Genivive at church. I should have known Cyn would see us together for the first time and been a little more sensitive.

So should Genivive.

As if she knew I was thinking about her, I received a text from my girlfriend and cringed. Her parents were going out of town on Wednesday and would be gone the rest of the week. She'd also gotten permission for people to sleep over if the party went too late.

There was no way I was staying at her place.

I need to work this week, so I can't stay late.

Everyone assumed my job was working for my Dad at his brokerage. I didn't bother correcting their assumption. I wasn't afraid of Genivive prying. It was obvious she didn't have a genuine interest in me. She wouldn't ask.

I quickly told her good night and then crawled into bed. I hadn't lied to her. I did plan to work, and part of that was going back to the arboretum. I had more questions than answers about essential oil scents.

Chapter Six

Fiona
          The next morning Lisa put away her breakfast dishes and asked, "What do you girls have planned for today?"

My aunt worked part time at a realtor office during the summer, so I hadn't been surprised to find her in the kitchen when I'd come down for breakfast. I had been surprised to see my cousin already up and dressed.

"I'm going to Genivive's," Cyn said.

My mouth dropped open. She had said it like it was no big deal. Like yesterday hadn't happened. And although Cyn's announcement had shocked me, my aunt's reaction surprised me even more.

She calmly nodded and then asked me, "Are you going?"

I slowly shook my head, mostly in disbelief that my aunt had calmly accepted her daughter's statement. Where was the indignation from yesterday? I knew the woman could hold a grudge. She still hadn't forgiven me for my innocent statement to my little brother. Where was her outrage that Cyn was still spending time with the girl who'd stabbed her in the back?

My aunt stared at me, expecting an answer. "I thought I'd swing in the hammock and read."

"All day?" Lisa didn't approve. "You can't sit around the house all day, every day. Why don't you walk to the library? I'll leave you directions and the spare house key." She ripped a sheet of paper off the notepad by their home phone. After scribbling directions, she slid the note to me. "Here. Go get a schedule of events for the next month. They are always hosting unique programs."

I wanted to suggest that the schedule of events would be online, but I knew that wouldn't go over well. Instead, I accepted the paper and the fact that I was going to spend part of my day at the library.

The walk was three miles, and I enjoyed looking at the various houses I passed. There was one little house in particular that caught my eye. At first because it had a beat up truck parked in the driveway. I immediately thought about Ash and then chastised myself. I was sure he wasn't the only guy in town who drove an old truck. Still, I wondered if that was his house. It was a cute little home. Nothing like my uncle's massive house. It had charm to it, and I wondered about the family who lived there.

The library was an old Victorian home that the city had transformed into a public gathering area. Wrought-iron tables and chairs dotted the lawn on one side of the building, and visitors casually strolled around. This place practically demanded that you take your time and soak up the atmosphere. Inside, it was the same. No one seemed in a hurry, and I found myself leisurely strolling from room to room, taking in the rows of books housed in dark, rich bookshelves and large overstuffed chairs in sunny window nooks. It felt like stepping back in time until I found the very modern coffee bar where I imagined the house's original kitchen had been.

I bought an espresso and found a sunny corner to sit and read. If coming here every day made my aunt happy, then I had no problem spending my time here.

I spent a couple of hours reading and then decided to walk home before the afternoon heat came in full force. On my way out, I grabbed a schedule of events the library was hosting. There was a book signing by a local author, reading groups for elementary children and various demonstrations by local craftsmen. One particular demonstration grabbed my attention. Handmade soap. It was the type of thing my mother would love. Maybe I'd attend and share what I learned with Mom when I saw her next.

I was thinking about the soap class as I walked home. Maybe if I signed up for it, Lisa would approve.

I approached the quaint little house and saw that the truck was still in the driveway. As I passed by, Ash stepped onto the front lawn carrying a foreboding-looking machine that I had no clue about.

"Hey Ash," I said and waved to him.

He placed the equipment into the bed of his truck and leaned against the tailgate. "HI Fiona," he said. "What are you doing?"

"Walking home from the library. Is this another yard you mow?"

He wiped sweat from his forehead, leaving a trail of dirt from his work gloves. "Among other things. Want to see inside?"

"Are you sure the owners won't mind?"

He grinned at me. "Positive. It's being renovated and flipped. Tell me what you think."

"OK," I followed him into the house. Inside were the standard beige walls with coordinating hardwood flooring. It was small and cute, but nothing really special. I walked from room to room, and Ash told me all the changes that had been made to the place.

We ended the tour in the kitchen, and he said, "Well? What's your verdict?"

"It's nice," I said. "A lot of hard work went into this house."

"But?" he leaned on the kitchen bar and waved his hand for me to continue.

"This is such a cute little house. I wish there was something special that when I walked in I felt like I'd discovered something really unique."

"Like what?"

I searched how to explain my thoughts without insulting him. "I don't know. When I see this house, I think of a little country cottage, so I guess I'm looking for something cottagey."

"Cottagey?" He walked to the sliding glass doors that led to the back yard.

I followed him. Outside was a nice-sized back yard. There was a patio that connected the back door to the outside wall of their garage.

"What if I built a planter and a trellis along the garage wall? I could plant some flowers and maybe something that would grow up the trellis." He stood next to the wall and stretched his hands as if painting the picture for me.

"That would be great! You could plant a climbing jasmine, and they could sit on the patios in the evening and smell the flowers."

"Not a bad idea," Ash said.

We walked back to his truck.

"What about out here?" I pointed to the front of the house. "Maybe you could plant a few flowers in front of the house, too."

"Yeah," he said. "I like that. I can get Reed's Nursery to recommend what to plant. Thanks, Fiona."

I smiled. "My pleasure."

"Do you want a ride back to your house?"

I was tempted. Ash was the first person in this town that felt like a normal, nice guy. Plus, he was super cute. But I didn't want to risk Cyn seeing me and report it to her mother. There was no telling how Lisa would react. "No, thanks. It's a nice day, and it's not far."

He nodded. "Well, your great ideas mean more work for me, so I guess I'd better measure out the planter."

"I didn't mean to cause you more work." I hadn't thought about who would do all the work to make my suggestions a reality. I felt bad that I hadn't thought it all through.

"No, you're right. The house needed something. I just didn't know what." He winked at me, "But if you're really feeling guilty, you can always lend a hand."

"I'd love to," I said. "Are you sure your boss won't mind?"

His lips twisted as if I'd told a joke and he was trying not to laugh. "Not at all. We want this property on the market as soon as possible, and if you help, I can have it all done tomorrow."

"Then count me in," I agreed. It wasn't until I was almost home that I considered my aunt's reaction. If she didn't like it, then I'd have to call and cancel. I assumed that Uncle George has his number somewhere.

When Aunt Lisa came home from work, I offered to help her make supper. I figured this was as good a time as any to bring up my plans for tomorrow. I dreaded telling her, because I figured she wouldn't approve. But maybe the fact that it got me out of the house would work in my favor.

"So, you were right about the library. There were some interesting classes."

"Hmm," Lisa barely responded as she pulled some vegetables from the fridge and washed them before placing them next to a cutting board.

"I think I'll take the soap-making one. It sounds like fun."

"Of course that's the one you'd choose," she said under her breath.

I assumed I wasn't supposed to hear her statement, so I pressed on. "And on my way home, I ran into Ash."

"Yeah?" Lisa focused on chopping the bell peppers in front of her, and I got the impression she wasn't paying close attention to what I said.

"He's working on this house renovation, and I offered to help him plant flowers."

"Better you than me," Cyn said, coming into the room and grabbing a drink from the fridge. "Why did you volunteer?"

My stomach tied in knots. I was hoping to tell my aunt about my plans without my cousin's interference. I had a better chance of Lisa accepting my spending time with Ash if Cyn wasn't around to disparage it. "The house needed some curb appeal, and it'd give me something to do." I left out the part that I also liked spending time with him.

"That's a great idea," Lisa said. "It gives you something to do besides reading all day. Maybe you can help me with my flowerbed. " She stopped chopping the bell peppers and slid them into a mixing bowl. "I'll tell you what I want, and you can go to the nursery and plant them while I'm at work."

"Tomorrow?" I crossed my fingers that she wouldn't say yes. If she insisted on tomorrow, then I'd lose my chance to hang out with Ash.

"Any time this week is fine," she added more ingredients to her bowl and began stirring. "You can help Ash tomorrow and then plant my flowers after that."

I agreed. Whatever it took to get on Aunt Lisa's good side.

"And hopefully you won't find my flower choices boring," she said.

It was going to take a lot of work to make the woman forget my unintentional insult.

After we'd helped Aunt Lisa clear the supper dishes, Cyn dragged me into her bedroom. I didn't know what to expect. I guess I'd hoped she and Genivive would bury the hatchet, that they'd make amends for the boyfriend fiasco and vow not to let a guy come between them.

That didn't happen.

My cousin returned home more determined than ever to make her best friend and former boyfriend pay for their betrayal.

Cyn waited for me to sit in her desk chair before she paced the room with excitement and laid out her plan. She talked about how her best friend had passive-aggressively gloated about her new boyfriend and how happy they were together and how much it bothered Genivive that her own happiness came at Cyn's expense.

"Maybe she meant it," I said. I didn't believe my statement any more than Cyn did, but I was hoping it would calm her down. With each sentence she said, my cousin was getting more and more worked up.

Her only response was to take one of the decorative pillows off her bed and throw it at me. It whizzed by my face, and I grabbed it from her desk and held it in my lap, thinking it might come in handy if Cyn threw anything else at me.

She continued her tirade, ending with, "So, after Audra steals Nathan from Genivive, then she'll break his heart."

I grabbed the pillow in my lap and covered my face. "This is crazy," I said into the pillow.

"No," she said, "it's brilliant. It's perfect."

She walked to my side, placed her hands on the armrests of the chair and leaned in, her face inches from mine. "He already likes you," she said, "and if you keep playing hard to get, he'll become obsessed. It's how I stole him from Alexis. Just start hinting that you don't get involved with other girls' guys. He'll drop Genivive in a heartbeat." She leaned back with a satisfied grin.

I wasn't going to do this. Cyn had to see how stupid this was. "It's not going to work. He's not going to dump his real life girlfriend for someone online. Plus, he could say he did, just to make Audra happy, but keep dating Genivive anyway." I sat up and watched my cousin, hoping she understood how pointless this was.

A wide smile stretched across her face. "That's the beauty of this scheme," she said. "He knows that you're my cousin. If he doesn't dump her for real, you'll know."

I sighed. We'd been talking about this for the last 30 minutes, and I didn't feel I was any closer to getting through to her. "But Cyn, if we did this, it would make us just as bad as them."

"No, it wouldn't. Because we're teaching them a lesson."

"And what lesson is that?"

My cousin paused a moment. I knew what was in her head. *To learn not to mess with me.* But if she said that out loud, it would convince me even more to refuse to go along. She finally said, "Not to play with people's hearts."

"Isn't that what we're doing?"

"But we're not doing it to be mean," she said. "We're doing it to prevent them from treating others like that. Think of it as a public service to Nathan's future victims." She stood taller and straightened her shoulders like she'd just morphed into some bizarre super hero.

"Even if we break them up, it won't stop Nathan from hurting someone else." I pointed out, hoping to pierce whatever delusion she had running through her head.

"That's why you have to break his heart. So he understands."

I groaned. "Cyn, I've never dated. I've never even kissed a guy. How am I supposed to be this femme fatale that lures him in and breaks his heart? This plan is ridiculous. It will never work."

"We'll do this together. I'm an expert when it comes to Nathan. I know exactly what it takes to lure him in."

I didn't point out the obvious. She might have lured him in, but she didn't keep him. Make him fall in love? I wasn't sure it was possible. Then a horrible thought formed in my head.

"Then what?" I asked my cousin.

"What do you mean?"

"After we break his heart? Then what happens?"

Cyn didn't speak, and I had my answer. "You want him back."

She stood in front of me. "It's not like I'm in love with him."

"Then why? He's a jerk and a cheat, and he's not worth your time. Why take him back?"

"I'll be a legend."

I sighed and shook my head. "You can't be serious. You're willing to put up with his abuse just to be popular?"

Cyn frowned at me. "You make it sound like he's violent or something. It's not that bad."

"No," I said, "I won't go along with this. It ticks me off that you're willing to put up with him just because you want to be popular. Whatever else you have planned, you can forget about it."

I opened her laptop and was happy to see she'd left it unlocked. I pulled up the Audra account. "We're ending this now."

Cyn rolled her eyes. "If you deactivate the account, I can make a new one. I have all your pictures, so I could do it in a few minutes."

I stared at the deactivate button flashing red in front of me and dropped my shoulders in defeat. "Fine," I said, "I won't delete the account. But let's give it a rest for a couple days. Promise me that you won't log in until Wednesday or Thursday. I won't either. Let Audra go radio silent."

She shrugged one shoulder. "Fine with me. It's only going to work in my favor. Nathan will go crazy if he doesn't hear from her for a few days."

My stomach sank. I hadn't spoken to Nathan since Saturday. That meant Cyn had. She had been playing this game all along. "So, we agree," I said and watched for any hints that she was lying to me. "No Audra for a few days."

"Agreed," she said, reached over me and logged out of the account.

I hoped she meant what she said.

If she stayed off the account, it would give me time to come up with a plan. My cousin was the most stubborn person I knew. I could only hope that she'd come to her senses over the next couple days. Because there was no way I'd talk her out of this stupid plan.

The chance of her giving up her road to popularity was just as unlikely. I needed to come up with a plan. Something that would appease my cousin and keep her away from Nathan. I wished I could just step away from this whole mess and let her deal with it. But this was my face she was using, even if it wasn't my name. So, like it or not, I was in the middle of this.

And I hoped that in a few days' time, I'd figure out how to escape.

Nathan

Immediately after breakfast my brother went to Genivive's house to help her plan her party. He took great pleasure in telling me that she'd asked him and showed a fake surprise that she hadn't asked me.

I had a hunch why my current girlfriend kept her clutches hooked into my brother. And that reason had a name.

Audra.

Ever since Nic had begun bragging about his time with the other girl, my girlfriend had begun making snide comments about Cyn's cousin. She had done it at lunch yesterday with her family, and she'd even sent me a text asking if my brother was out with Audra because he hadn't returned her text.

If I'd been romantically invested in Geni, I would've been offended. She either didn't know her jealousy was obvious or she didn't care.

I was perfectly fine with her chasing after my brother. He liked her, and it seemed she liked him. Maybe I should encourage Audra to spend time with Nic, as long as she didn't get serious with him. I didn't want her to break his heart. Only encourage Geni to make her move.

I hated all this high school drama. It made me even more grateful for my business.

My dad was always pressuring me to take an interest in his business. He'd learned the stock market as a teen and by the time he had been my age, he'd been making ten times more money than his friends at their fast food part-time jobs. Not that he needed the money. My grandfather was the richest man in town. But Dad had wanted to prove he could outdo his old man, and he expected me to have the same drive. He wanted me to carry on the legacy of building wealth for the family.

Like we needed it.

But he kept pressuring me because we both knew Nicolaus didn't have the killer instinct, and my sister Beka was too young for us to know whether she'd be good with money. So, all Dad's hopes and dreams rested squarely on my shoulders.

And how did I fulfill my so-called destiny?

I held back a smile as I pulled into the gravel parking lot of a tiny store that looked more like some kid's playhouse than a storefront. I'd invested in goats.

The Vega farm was a small acreage on the outskirts of our town, and I'd discovered it when my mother sent me on an urgent errand to get some face cream she swore she couldn't live without. When I'd stepped into this tiny shed for the first time, I'd thought my mother had lost her mind.

It had been nothing more than a tiny warehouse where the Vega family sold their organic beauty products. All from goats' milk.

I'd purchased my mother's face cream, along with a bar of soap for my sister. Later that night, when Beka gushed on and on about her stupid rose-scented soap, I came up with an idea. I spent the next few weeks researching and then finally pitched my idea to my dad.

It wasn't the stock broker route he'd wanted me to take, but since it was an investment opportunity, he'd given his blessing. And his financial backing.

The next day, with my business plan in hand, I'd gone back to the farm and made a deal with the owner.

My money and marketing ideas. His family's products.

That was last summer. We'd begun with the renovation of the outside of the building and a small marketing campaign. It had taken longer than I'd hoped, but almost a year later, we were starting to see a profit. This summer, we'd renovate the inside of the store and hold a grand opening. With, hopefully, a new line of products using organic essential oils. Then I'd prove to my father that I had what it took to follow in his footsteps. I'd tell him about my secret project; where I had invested my earnings from the tiny beauty products store and hoped to see an even bigger profit come in.

Then I'd pay him back his initial loan and maybe he'd get off my back.

I stepped inside the building and greeted Ceara Vega. She was in the grade below mine and while she was kind and had a lot of friends, she wasn't part of the crowd I normally associated with. She was pretty, with rich caramel skin and thick black hair, and I'd briefly considered asking her out when I first started working with her family, but her heart was set on someone else.

"I'll let Dad know you're here," she said and sent a quick text. She helped the one customer in the store and then came back to me.

"So, I hear congratulations are in order."

I laughed at the sarcastic tone in her voice. I didn't have to guess what she was referring to. Wildwood was a small town, and I knew it wouldn't be long before everyone knew I had a new girlfriend. "You don't approve?"

"Why can't you date a decent person? There are plenty out there, you know."

"Like you?" I teased.

Her eyes grew round, and her lips parted in surprise. She blinked a couple times as she tried to form a nice way to reject me.

With another laugh, I let her off the hook. "Don't worry, Ceara. I know you're not interested."

She'd never told me she was crazy about Ash Ellis, but she knew I had guessed. I never directly brought up her crush, and over time we'd reached an understanding that the subject would remain unspoken.

I examined the shelves displaying their items while I waited for her dad. I wanted to review our budget for the renovation of the shop's interior. We'd start it in a couple of weeks, and I wanted to make sure we had everything in order. Increasing the profits from this shop was integral to paying back my dad.

Ceara rung up the customer and as soon as the older lady had left, she said, "So, um, did you break up with Cyn before you met her cousin?" There was a hesitation in her voice, a story behind her question.

"Audra?" I asked and picked up a lavender-scented body lotion. I'd get it for my mother when I left the store.

"No. Fiona."

I heard the caution in her voice and glanced at the girl. She was staring at the cashier counter and refused to make eye contact with me. "No," I said. "I haven't met Fiona. I've spoken to Audra."

Ceara raised her head and frowned. "Ash never mentioned Audra."

I hid my smile. One of the things I liked about this girl was her complete transparency. Even when she thought she was being subtle, I saw through it. "And he mentioned Fiona?"

Ceara blushed. "Yeah. He said she seemed nice."

"Well, she's related to Cyn," I said sarcastically.

The girl laughed. "That's what I thought. But Ash would have said if she was a snob. Right?"

Ceara didn't care if the girl was friendly or not. Ash had met a new girl, and my friend was threatened. "What else did Ash say?"

She casually shrugged and turned her back to me to fidget with some glass jars on the shelf behind her. "She's cute."

I held in my smile. "You don't have anything to worry about," I said. Ash was as crazy for Ceara as she was for him. If only one of them would get the guts to tell the other.

"She's not cute?" She still had her back to me.

"If she looks anything like her sister, then I'm sure she's cute." Fiona was probably hot, but I wasn't going to feed into Ceara's insecurities by saying so.

"There's two of them?" she faced me with a big pout on her lips.

"Don't worry about them. Nic already has Audra in his sights, and no one is talking about Fiona. Which means the girl either hasn't left her cousin's house or doesn't socialize." I put the lavender cream on the counter and placed my hand on my friend's shoulder. "They're not a threat."

She sighed. "If you say so." She didn't look convinced.

"I'll see what I can find out about Fiona. Just to prove to you that I'm right."

Then her father walked into the store and all talk of crushes was over. Time to get down to business and forget about the upheaval Cyn's cousins were causing.

Chapter Seven

F**iona**
    Ash picked me up the next day and handed me a coffee and a bag of donuts before he drove us to the house. "I work best on caffeine and sugar," he said.

"Works for me." I didn't need the caffeine. I was pumped about working with him on the yard. I didn't know a lot about gardening, so I was hoping he didn't expect great skill from me.

He yawned and took another swig of his coffee. "Sorry," he said. "I was up late last night."

"Oh?" I said, hoping he'd volunteer why. He remained quiet, and I watched the houses fly by on our short drive.

At the house, he had a flat of flowers sitting in the front yard. "I figured you plant in the front while I build the planter box in the back. Once that is ready, then we'll stain it and finish planting the flowers."

"How many do you want planted in front?"

"All of those. I have more in the back."

I did some quick calculations. "There are 36 flowers here. Where do you want them?"

"I don't know," he said and waved toward the yard. "Just make it look good." He walked to the back and left me to figure it out.

Just make it look good? I wasn't a landscape architect. I had no clue how to make it look good. I searched the Internet for landscapes and after a hundred or more images, I found a design I liked. There were already some bushes in front of the house, so I used the tiller machine Ash had left me and churned up the grass and dirt in the pattern I wanted to create.

I heard a saw start up in the backyard, signaling Ash had begun building the planter.

After I tilled the yard, I went into the house to get a glass of water. Ash had told me to stay hydrated and had brought plenty of water for us to drink while we worked. From the kitchen, I watched him place lumber over a couple sawhorses and begin staining the pieces. On the edge of the patio were a handful of the same flowers I had out front, as well as two larger plants in containers.

I gulped down my water and went back to my project. I had gotten ten plants in the ground when Ash walked to me. "I changed plans slightly," he said, "I stained the wood, and I'll let it dry while we plant out here."

He examined the pattern I'd made from the tilled soil. "Clever," he said. "This will look great. We need to get something to border the flowerbed, but that shouldn't put us back much."

I showed him the picture I'd found online. "I'm going for this."

"Perfect," he said and started planting on the left side of the front door while I did the right. Once we were done, Ash pulled a couple bags of mulch from his truck bed, and we spread it out amongst the flowers.

"This is awesome," he said. "Exactly what the house needed. Now, let's get the backyard done."

We worked side-by-side, assembling the planter box and then filling it with dirt. "We'll plant these first," Ash handed one of the larger plants to me. "Climbing jasmine, just like the lady said."

He had already attached a trellis to the garage wall, and we planted the jasmine, intertwining a few of the branches with the trellis. We planted the smaller flowers next, and it looked as charming as I'd hoped.

"This is amazing," Ash said. "Way better, thanks to you." He fist bumped me. "We should celebrate."

Motioning to our dirty clothes with my filthy hands, I said, "Like this?"

"I don't mind," he said, "but anywhere we go might not appreciate us tracking dirt into their building. How about tomorrow afternoon?"

His suggestion was a little disappointing. Not that I'd expected him to ask me on a date. I had hoped he'd suggest celebrating tonight. "Lisa wants me to plant flowers for her. I thought I'd do it tomorrow." I figured the sooner I got it done, the better.

"OK," he said, "then I'll wrap up here tomorrow. You get your flowers planted, and maybe we can meet up later in the week."

"OK." I hid my disappointment. I liked making this house look inviting. However, I hadn't discovered a hidden desire for gardening. Once in a while was fine. I didn't want to do it all the time. Plus, I wanted to get to know Ash better. Right now, all I knew was he mowed lawns and helped renovate houses. And that I was developing a little crush on him.

"Great," he said. "I'll drop you home and then run to the nursery to get a border. Then, our cottagey house will be ready to go on the market."

He smiled at me, and I returned it, even though I wasn't completely happy. I wanted to spend time with him. Obviously, he wasn't thinking the same thing. Otherwise, he would have asked me to go to the nursery with him. Instead, in minutes, he'd dropped me off and pulled away with only a quick, "See you later."

Later, I told myself. He'll be back to celebrate finishing the house. And we'll get to know each other better. Being with him had been fun. Easy. Granted, we were working side by side, not actually hanging out like friends. But I was hopeful. Maybe he could be my first real friend in Wildwood. Maybe he could be more.

Nathan

"Heard from Audra lately?" I asked my brother after he'd come back from Genivive's. He'd spent all day with my girlfriend yesterday and gone back again today.

He'd claimed there was a lot for them to do to prepare for the party and that Geni needed him. I'd tried not to laugh at his statement. Our friends' parties consisted of hanging around, playing music for anyone who wanted to dance, and having plenty of drinks and snacks. It wasn't like there was a lot of planning to do. But, if it kept Genivive and my brother together, then let them plan all they wanted.

I'd spent the morning trying to fulfill my promise to Ceara and find out more about Fiona. I'd found her social media account and realized it had been created the same day as Audra's. Weird.

Fiona's account was small. Less than twenty friends while Audra's had grown to ten times that size. There were a few pictures that were public, but her posts were private. Very different from Audra's whose whole account was wide open. The public pictures were random, and none of them showed Fiona's face. I searched for her on other social media accounts and found nothing.

Fiona barely existed online.

I went to Audra's account. People had been tagging her in posts, but she hadn't responded in the past couple of days. I wondered about her other social media accounts and found her on other platforms with just as many connections. All the accounts had gone live in the past couple days.

I'd hoped to talk to Audra. I'd planned to ask her why Fiona wasn't hanging out with Cyn and her friends, not that I expected to get a straight answer. But I was hoping for some information. It'd be awesome if Audra said something like Fiona was spending all her time texting and talking to her boyfriend back home. That would put Ceara's mind at ease.

But Audra wasn't logging into her account.

So, against my better judgment, I sought out my brother.

"Why?" Nic plopped himself on the couch and flipped on the TV. He grabbed one of our game console controllers and handed me another one.

I sat in my dad's recliner and faced the screen as Nicolaus chose a combat game. "Team mode?"

"Yeah," I answered.

"I saw on Tuck's livestream how to get past the canyon," my brother said, referring to a popular online gamer.

"Cool," I said.

Nic showed me the trick he'd learned, and as we navigated our characters into uncharted territory, I tried again. "Are you bringing Audra to Geni's party?"

My brother grinned. "I hadn't thought about it. That's a great idea. Maybe Cyn can bring her."

I waited for a few minutes and then casually said, "What about Fiona?"

"Who?" Nic said and then entered into a heavy battle.

I dropped the question and continued playing with my brother.

Something weird was going on. I had assumed that Cyn's cousin Fifi was Fiona, and that Audra was the extra family member I'd never heard of. But what if the opposite was true? What if Audra was Fifi? Then who was Fiona and why did Ash know her?

It struck me that the people who knew Audra hadn't heard of Fiona and the people who knew Fiona hadn't met Audra.

Maybe because the girls had very different tastes in friends. After all, if I asked Nic about Ceara Vega, he'd have no clue who I was talking about. Still, it was weird.

If Audra came to Genivive's party tomorrow night, I'd get some answers. For Ceara and for myself.

Chapter Eight

Fiona

Uncle George was awake when I came downstairs Wednesday morning. "Good morning, my dear," his big, happy voice greeted me. "Can I make you some breakfast?"

"No thanks," I didn't want to take advantage of his generosity. I hated the way my aunt and cousin seemed to take him for granted. Maybe one morning I'd get up early enough and make breakfast for him.

Lisa came into the kitchen wearing a sleek, navy suit and kissed her husband's cheek before grabbing a muffin. "I've got a big meeting today," she said. "I might be home late."

George smiled. "No worries. The girls and I can fend for ourselves, right Fiona?"

"Sure," I smiled at my aunt, "I'm happy to help with whatever cooking or cleaning you want done around the house." I hoped my offer went a little way to mending bridges with her.

But somehow, I had the knack of always saying the wrong thing. "You're not an indentured servant here. Just have a normal summer, like Cynthia." She narrowed her eyes at me like she needed to drive the point home through my thick skull.

"Certainly," George softened the blow from his wife's words, "you girls work so hard during the school year. You should enjoy your summer."

"Thanks," I said, not really knowing how to respond.

Soon after, George and Lisa left, and I was faced with figuring out how to spend my day. Who knew how long my cousin would stay in her room. So, I grabbed my eReader, a glass of lemonade, and finally got time to hang out in the hammock. I spent the entire morning there, but as it got closer to lunch, the air temperature became more unbearable, so I went inside to cool off.

As soon as my cousin was awake, I'd get her to drive me to the nursery to buy Lisa's flowers. She hadn't asked for a lot, and I figured I could get the chore done this afternoon.

Cyn was on her phone, sitting at the kitchen counter, sipping a coffee. "I'm not sure that's the best idea," my cousin said. As soon as she saw me, she placed a finger over her lips and put the phone on speaker so I could hear.

"What's wrong?" the female voice said. "You're always up for a party."

"Well," Cyn's words exuded a fake sweetness I'd heard her use whenever she wanted to insert her superiority over someone — mostly me. "Audra's not exactly into partying with high schoolers. She's twenty, you know."

"She didn't look twenty to me," the girl's voice matched Cyn's snotty tone. "She looked so much younger."

Cyn released a fake laugh. "What can I say, we Houghton women have great genes. My grandmother always said we might age, but we'll never look older."

"Oh, my grandmother says that, too. Right before she visits her plastic surgeon." The girls both laughed, and I sat on the other side of the counter and raised my eyebrows at my cousin. Surely there had to be a reason why she wanted me to hear her conversation.

"Will you ask her?" the girl said.

"Sure, Genivive. Just don't get your hopes up. Audra probably won't agree." Cyn motioned to me, and I had no idea what she wanted.

I raised my shoulders to question her, but my cousin, in a very convincing voice, said, "Oh wait. Here she is. I'll find out."

I expected her to pretend to talk to me. Instead, she held the phone away from us and said, "Hey Audra, how was class?"

My mouth dropped open. I had no idea what she was talking about, so I did a noncommittal, "Fine." I hoped that was good enough.

"So," Cyn brought the phone closer to us to ensure that her friend heard. "We were thinking it might be fun to throw a little welcome party for you. What do you think?" She violently shook her head no.

I gave her a thumbs up to confirm I understood. "Who would be there?" I asked, and my cousin glared daggers at me. I realized she'd wanted me to flat-out refuse, but I had a different idea.

"My friends and I. Maybe some other people from our school," my cousin narrowed her eyes at me, and I grinned back.

"Sorry," I said. "Not my scene. Maybe you should invite Fiona. I know she's awkward and a dork, but she's a high school kid like you. They would be more her kind of people than mine."

Cyn's eyes rounded with surprise. "Um, I don't think Fi would be interested. She's not exactly popular."

Her words hurt. They were true, but that didn't make them hurt any less. "Yeah, not really her scene, either. Thanks for inviting me to your little party," the words came out a littler harsher than I'd meant them. But really, what did Cyn expect when she'd put the fake me on the spot and then insulted the real me.

"Your cousin is a jerk," Genivive said as soon as Cynthia said she was back on the phone.

Instead of sharing the thought that Genivive was the jerk for stealing her friend's boyfriend, I waved goodbye to my cousin and ran upstairs.

I sat on my bed and looked out the window. Across the street sat a familiar truck and seconds later, Ash walked around the side of the house pushing a lawn mower. I watched him for several minutes and wondered what he was like. I knew Cyn and Aunt Lisa thought he was off-limits, and despite what my cousin said, I really didn't want to break my parents' rules and start dating. But still, he seemed nice. And anyone not good enough for my cousin and her friends sounded like my kind of people.

I toyed with the idea of going wild. If I was out of control, my parents would have to get me. I wouldn't be stuck here with my aunt's hatred, my uncle's oblivious attitude, and my cousin's drama. I could be enjoying my summer with my family, building sand castles on the beach with my brother and getting ready for my new school. This situation was unbearable, and I wanted out.

Several minutes later, Cynthia barged into my room. "Well, you got your wish."

I blinked in surprise at her. "And that is?"

"You're invited to the party."

I laughed. "How are we having a welcome party for Audra when I'm going to show up?"

"Oh, she only invited Audra because she wanted to size up the competition."

"She said that?"

Cyn sneered. "Of course not; it's a move I would've made." She frowned. "So, Fi, I guess it's time the real you met my friends."

My stomach dropped. I knew I'd only been invited to the party because I'd opened my big mouth. Now, I wished I could take it all back. From my short exposure to the group, I hadn't had been impressed. "I don't know if that's such a good idea."

She narrowed her eyes at me. "Then you should have kept your mouth shut. We don't have much time to get you ready."

"I thought you said they were meeting the real me. I can't get glammed up. I'll look just like Audra."

Cyn chewed on her bottom lip as she thought about my words. "I guess you're right. But if you go looking like that," she motioned to my faded t-shirt and cut-off jeans, "then don't expect me to hang out with you."

I didn't answer her. I never expected her to hang out with me. I wasn't cool or popular and being surrounded by a large group of strangers triggered my introversion to a painful level. "I'll probably sit in the corner by myself the whole time. It's OK," I said more to myself than her, "I like to people watch."

She rolled her eyes at me. "Until they realize you're not Audra, you won't be alone." She smirked. "You might have to be extra Fiona tonight."

I let out a nervous laugh. "I don't think that's going to be a problem."

Cyn sighed. "You'll be fine. I'll keep the girls away, and as long as you're not flirting, the guys will leave you alone."

"Trust me. I don't know how."

"Then, I guess I'll leave you as is and get ready myself. Just be yourself."

A few hours later, I had those words running through my head. My hands shook, and I shoved them into the pockets of my shorts. I did change out of my cut-offs into something a little nicer, but it in no way compared to Cyn's sundress or the designer clothes the other girls wore.

As soon as we stepped into Genivive's huge, picture-perfect home, I thought I was going to be sick. A little over ten feet away from me stood Nathan, Nicolaus and some other boys I didn't recognize.

I hadn't mentally prepared to see them. Which was stupid. Of course, they'd be here. Nathan and Nicolaus were part of Cyn's friend group. They had more right to be here than I did.

But seeing them brought my nerves to an excruciatingly painful level. Panic was racing through my veins, and I fought the urge to run out of the house. But I had to remain cool. If I was here when school started, I'd probably see even more of them. I had to get a grip on my nerves and pretend I hadn't walked into a room with complete and total strangers who were ruthless social climbers.

Nicolaus was the first to spot me, and he rushed over, arms outstretched like he was going to hug me. I cringed and slid behind Cyn, and that was enough to stop the boy in his tracks.

My cousin said loudly, "Hey Nic, meet my cousin Fiona."

Confusion clouded his face as he drew closer to me and examined me intensely. "Fiona?"

I stuck out my shaking hand. "I-it's nice to meet you." I was so scared he'd call our bluff that my whole body was practically shaking. Why did I agree to this? This was way more risk than I was comfortable with. I wasn't used to lying or acting or any kind of subterfuge. I seriously questioned my ability to pull this off. "If, if you want, you can call me Fi."

Nicolaus shook my hand, and when he felt it tremble, he covered it with both of his own. "It's great to meet you, Fi. I'm sure you're sick of hearing this, but you look a lot like Audra."

My mouth grew dry, and my tongue stuck to the roof of my mouth. I couldn't say a single word.

"Audra and Fi are sisters," Cyn said the lie so convincingly, I would have believed her if I hadn't known Audra didn't exist. "Fi's 16. She'll go to school with us next year."

"Cool," he said and slid his arm around my shoulder. "Let me introduce you to everyone."

He led me to the group of guys I dreaded talking to. Nathan's eyes immediately narrowed as we approached and didn't lose their suspicion, even after Nicolaus had shared the lie Cyn told him.

"I've never heard of identical siblings unless they were twins," Nathan's voice drawled. "I suppose it's possible."

Nicolaus laughed, and in that moment I could have hugged him. "Considering Audra and Fi are living proof, I'd say it's definitely possible. Besides, people say we look alike. Of course, those people are overdue their next optometrist visit."

The guys around them laughed, though Nathan's eyes only narrowed more. I felt like some bug he was examining under a microscope, and the more he stared, the more nervous I became. I was relieved when Nicolaus finally steered me to where the girls were congregating in the kitchen.

He did the round of introductions like he'd been the one to bring me to the party, his arm firmly in place across my shoulders. Most of the girls said polite hellos and then proceeded to ignore me. Genivive, however, glared at me like I'd crashed the party and trashed the furniture. I practically felt the hate emanating from her.

I knew this was the moment in the party where I found a quiet corner and waited until Cyn was ready to go home. I'd make myself so unobtrusive that everyone would forget I shared any space with them.

Fortunately, this gathering was small, and the only alcohol present was a few bottles of wine and several six-packs of beer. It wasn't the raging wild orgy I'd seen in all the teen romcoms, and I wasn't sure if I was disappointed or relieved.

Nicolaus offered me a glass of wine, and I politely declined. It wasn't that I hadn't had alcohol before. For all my parents' crazy rules, I was actually allowed a glass of wine or champagne whenever we had special occasions. But alcohol made me relax, and that was the last thing I needed to do. I needed to stay nervous and remain Fiona the Shy. The last thing I needed was to show any resemblance to my fake older sister.

I accepted the soda Nicolaus offered instead and dipped out of his arms. I walked over to a small sofa set in the corner of their living room where I could stay on the perimeter of the party but not be actively involved.

To my surprise and utter disappointment, Nicolaus followed me and sat by my side.

"So, you're going to Hill High. What grade?"

"Junior," I said and sunk deeper into the corner, trying to add a little space between us.

The boy wasn't deterred and stretched his arms along the back of the couch, effectively placing his arm on my shoulders again. "Same," he said. "Know what classes you're taking yet?"

"No," I shrugged and tried to subtlety push his arm away from my back. "My parents might change their mind. I'm just hanging with Cyn for now."

"And Audra," he added.

I sighed. I didn't want to talk about the fake girl. "No," I said, hoping to send Audra into social Siberia, "she started taking online college classes, and they're really tough. She'll spend most of her time studying this summer."

"That's too bad," he said. Nicolaus frowned. "But she came to the water park."

"That was before her classes started."

His lips twisted in thought. "But you didn't come."

My heart raced. Was he figuring out our deception? "I wanted the house to myself," I said and avoided his eyes, terrified that he'd see the truth. "They have a hammock that's a great reading spot."

"Oh? What do you read?"

My stomach tied into more knots. "Why are you asking so many questions?"

"I'm getting to know you," humor laced his words, and I looked up to find him staring at me. Laugh lines surrounded deep blue eyes, and even though I knew he was laughing at me, it wasn't mean.

"Can we talk about you, instead?" I felt like an idiot for saying it, but he had me so nervous I struggled to remember how words were formed.

His lips stretched into a wide grin. "My favorite subject. What do you want to know?"

I hesitated. I wanted to tease him and ask if he was as self-centered as his words sounded. But that was something Audra would say. After a really awkward silence, I finally said, "What's your favorite subject in school?"

If I had been trying to impress this boy, I would have mentally face-palmed myself at the ridiculous, embarrassing question I'd just asked.

The boy scrunched his face like he was holding in a laugh, like he knew how mortifying the question was and had tried to spare me the crippling humiliation. It was a nice gesture, but totally unnecessary. He needed to think I was the true me - socially awkward and inexperienced with boys. I was showing him that spectacularly.

So, as much as I didn't want to be embarrassed, the fact I was successfully distancing myself from Audra made me a little proud.

"Does it make me a dumb jock if I answer athletics?" His self-deprecating grin charmed me. Nathan might be an egotistical jerk, but his little brother seemed more approachable, more down-to-earth.

I smiled. "No. If I had a single coordinated bone in my body, I'd probably answer the same thing. So, do you play sports? I mean, are you on a team?"

"No," he said and lifted his hand in a helpless gesture. "I played football with Nathan, but I got hurt last year. No more football for me. Now I work out with the team to keep in shape. You like working out?"

I shook my head. "I like reading."

We sat there in silence for a few minutes. Someone had started up a sound system and dance music floated to where we sat. Three couples had moved to the makeshift dance floor, and we watched them for a few minutes. "Want to dance?" Nicolaus said. He slid his arm away from me and scooted to the edge of the sofa, seconds away from standing up. He assumed I'd say yes, and I imagined in any other circumstance I would. But tonight I had a mission, and swaying to music while this boy held me wasn't part of the plan.

"No, thank you," I said. "But you can ask someone else. Cyn might want to."

Nicolaus turned to fully face me. "No?" he asked in surprise. I was sure he didn't hear that word often. He might not be the most popular guy in their school, but he was just as handsome as his older brother.

"I'm, uh..." How did you tell a guy to go away without being rude? "I'm comfortable here. But you can dance."

His brows drew together. "It would be rude to leave you alone," he said and slowly stood up. I didn't know if he was trying to gently force me to dance with him or just trying to be polite as he made his escape.

"It's not your party," I pointed out. "So, you're not responsible for me."

He stood over me for a moment, probably still in shock that I'd turned him down. "The offer stands," he finally said. "If you want to dance, come find me."

"Thanks. That's really nice, but I'm not comfortable dancing in front of strangers."

"You're comfortable here," he motioned to the couch.

"Yeah."

He nodded and then walked away. He stopped once to look back at me before joining a group of guys drinking beer and watching a sports game in the next room. He never came back to talk to me, and I never sought him out.

Overall, I'd say Mission Awkward Fiona was a raging success. No one would want to spend time with me after that. Now, I just had to find a way to separate Audra and Nathan and thwart Cyn's revenge plan.

N athan

I didn't have to search for Fiona Houghton. She found me.

And Ceara had competition. Fiona was beautiful, just as beautiful in her minimal makeup as Audra was fully glammed. She'd spent half the night looking like a frightened fawn who would bolt into the wooded park behind Geni's house at any second.

Then, when Nic left her to sit alone in the corner of the room, she seemed to relax. No one, not even her cousin, bothered to include her. The party happened all around her, and she simply sat there and played on her phone.

Although my bet was she preferred to be alone, I felt bad that everyone was ignoring her. I reluctantly stood from where I'd been watching sports with the rest of the guys and walked to the kitchen. Genivive sat there glaring off into the distance, and I realized she was staring at my brother. Apparently his stunt with introducing Fiona hadn't gone over well with her. Even though I was her official boyfriend, she hadn't noticed I'd stepped into the room.

I grabbed a couple sodas and walked to where the shy girl sat all alone. She scooted to the extreme edge of the couch, even though I hadn't tried sitting next to her. I sat down on the couch with her, making sure I kept plenty of space between us. I didn't want to scare her more than she already was.

I held out one of my sodas. "Here, I thought you could use a refill."

She reluctantly took it and squeaked out a "thanks".

"So, you're not into parties, huh?"

Her cheeks flushed, and she whispered, "No."

"What do you like doing?" I half expected the shy girl to shrug and not open her mouth. I wondered if this was the reason none of us had heard of her before. That she had social anxiety.

She swallowed a couple times before saying, "Reading."

I nodded. Maybe talking about her favorite subject would put the girl at ease. Get her to relax. "What do you like to read?"

Her face flushed a little more. "Romance."

Smiling at her, I said, "I'd pegged you more the intellectual type. You know, classic literature."

She shrugged. "I like some classic literature."

"Let me guess," I smiled at her. "*Pride and Prejudice.*"

"Everyone likes *Pride and Prejudice*." Her voice came out slightly stronger, more confident. If I wanted this girl to open up, I was on the right path.

"Not them," I motioned to my friends just as they yelled in victory when their team scored a point.

Fiona smiled, and I gave myself a mental high five. "Maybe not everyone," she said.

"Do you know what my issue is with *Pride and Prejudice*?" I softened my words, so she'd know I was teasing her.

"You have an issue with the book?" She raised her eyebrows at me and shook her head as if she couldn't imagine anyone having an issue with the classic tale.

"I do." I flipped the top of the can open and took a swig of soda. "It's Mr. Darcy."

"What's wrong with Mr. Darcy?" She leaned forward, and I held in my smile of victory.

"You expect me to live up to him. Do you know what kind of pressure that is for a guy?" I took a sip of my soda and watched her reaction.

"I don't." She placed her hand over her chest as if she was ready to defend herself against my accusation.

"Not you personally. Girls in general. They want this rich, handsome guy who's somehow brooding yet kind. Prideful yet romantic. The complete package." I smirked at her, hoping to make her laugh. "I've got the rich and handsome thing, but how am I supposed to get the rest?"

She sucked in her bottom lip in an attempt not to laugh. "So, you think you're handsome?"

I sat stunned for a second. Not that she was insinuating I was ugly, but that she was teasing me. I'd hoped to crack this girl's armor a little, but I hadn't expected this level of success. I wanted to keep the conversation light-hearted, so I answered, "My mom said I am, and I don't think she'd lie to me."

The girl turned her head to hide her smile. When she faced me again, she had a stoic expression. "Moms are nice like that."

I grinned at her. Complete success. She was comfortable enough to tease me back. "Yeah, they are." I motioned to her sitting in the corner of the couch. "So, are you doing OK? Need anything?"

She raised the soda I had brought her. "This is great. Thanks."

I stood up and said, "Nice to meet you, Fiona."

She nodded, and I walked away.

I'd wait until tomorrow when I saw Ceara at the shop before I gave her the bad news. Fiona was beautiful, she didn't fit in with the popular crowd, and worst of all, when she got comfortable, she had a wicked sense of humor. She was exactly the type of girl Ash liked. Beautiful, sweet and funny.

If Ceara wanted her man, then she needed to make her move. Now. Before Fiona Houghton stole his heart.

Chapter Nine

Fiona

I opened my laptop before breakfast the next day and logged into my account. I had a new request. Ash Ellis. My fingers trembled in anticipation. Ash had searched and found me on social media. That was a good sign, right?

I quickly accepted the invitation like it would disappear if I didn't snag it immediately. Ash had said we'd celebrate, and I hoped he'd tracked me down to make plans. Even though I wasn't supposed to date, my parents had reluctantly given their permission. As long as it didn't affect my grades - which couldn't happen since it was summer.

I had planned to plant Lisa's flowers today, but that could wait if Ash wanted to hang out.

Even though it was early, I saw that Ash was online. He apparently saw me, too, since he immediately sent me a message.

The boss loved the flowers.

Great. I sent back and waited for him to say more. As an opening line, it wasn't the most promising. But maybe he'd used it as an excuse to talk to me.

I told him that you'd come up with the idea.

You did? He'd told his boss about me. What did that mean?

Ash took several minutes before he replied. *Well, not you exactly. I said a friend stopped by and suggested it.*

A friend. My hope that this conversation was a lead-in to a date was dwindling. When Ash didn't say anything else, I figured he was waiting for me to respond. *What did your boss say?*

I didn't care what his boss said. I wanted to plan our celebration. I wanted to spend more time with Ash.

That's why I wanted to get in touch. We have another project we're working on, and he said I could bring you along, get your thoughts. If he likes what you come up with, then maybe he can hire you.

Hire me? I wasn't looking for a job. Having spare money would be great, of course. But I wasn't interested in landscaping for a living.

Isn't that great? Ash said.

Great. I replied. Because what else could I do? *He knows I'm not a professional, right? I'm just a high schooler.*

Yeah. How does Saturday sound? At noon?

That works. I waited for him to elaborate. Maybe he'd want to celebrate afterward. Though, the middle of the day on Saturday didn't really scream romance.

When he signed off without mentioning anything else, I groaned in frustration.

"What's your problem?" Cyn walked into the room.

"Nothing," I said. I wasn't ready to tell her my feelings about Ash. I probably never would. She thought he was a loser.

"I'm bored," she said. "I thought it would be fun for Audra to post more pics. Let's go through your clothes and have a fashion show."

I quickly closed my laptop to hide my communication with Ash. "You're not going to find anything really exciting. I wear jeans most of the time. I have two dresses for special occasions, and that's it."

"You're kidding me," she flipped through the few clothes I'd placed on hangers and began rummaging through my suitcases where everything else was. "How can you only have four pairs of shoes? And ugly ones, at that?"

"They're not ugly. I don't need any more shoes. Those work," I defended.

Cyn walked to my bedroom door and yelled down the hall, "Mommy! Come here!"

Within seconds, Lisa appeared. "What's wrong, Baby?"

She pointed to where she'd stacked my shoes on my bed. "Look at this. Those are her shoes." Lisa crinkled her nose, apparently not liking my taste in shoes, either. "*All* of her shoes."

Lisa looked horrified. "All?"

"It's fine, really," I said. "That's all I need."

"White sneakers, black pumps, black sandals, white flip flops. Where are the slides and wedges and boots and booties and high heels and everything? Where are the fashion colors and whimsical and fun ones?" Cyn shook her head in disbelief. "How can her parents do this to her?"

I expected Lisa to laugh. I wanted to laugh. She acted like not having a crazy amount of shoes equaled child abuse.

"I'm completely shocked," Lisa said. "You want adventure, and your shoes look like this?"

"I don't want adventure," I insisted to people who refused to hear me. I ignored her premise that adventurous people wore adventurous shoes. "I'm fine with what I have."

"At a minimum," Cyn said, "she needs a pair of wedges and a pair of slides."

Lisa nodded. "When it gets colder, we can look at boots." She glanced at her watch. "I have one appointment this morning, and then we can go shopping."

"No," I said, "that's not necessary. This isn't urgent."

"There won't be time this weekend," Lisa said.

I sighed. "I'd hate for you to take off work just for me. We can do it some other time."

"I won't have anyone accusing me of neglecting you," Lisa crossed her arms over her chest.

With the stubborn tilt of her chin, my aunt said she wouldn't tolerate arguments.

"Thanks, Aunt Lisa," I said. At least if we got this shopping trip out of the way, I could work on her flowers tomorrow and then see Ash on Saturday. All I'd wanted, besides staying with my parents, was a summer of reading and going to the beach. In the two weeks I'd been here, I had already been shopping, gone on a double date, been to a party and gotten entangled in my cousin's drama with her ex.

I was ready to slow things down. An easy day of shopping and a low-key weekend was just what I needed.

Shopping was a disaster. Cyn invited her friends to come along, and they invited the guys to meet us at this upscale shopping center Lisa insisted we visit. Because Lisa was going to be there, Cyn and I agreed that I had be Fiona. No make-up, no fancy clothes, no flirting with boys.

None of that was a problem for me.

Except for the fact that we weren't the cozy, intimate group I had hoped. In addition to my aunt and cousin, Genivive and three other girls planned to join us. Before Cyn called to invite them, I'd worried that they would mention Audra in front of Aunt Lisa. My cousin didn't share my concerns. She concocted some stupid story about Audra making her mad and repeated the story to every girl she invited. She said it was a guarantee that no one would expect Audra to join us, and no one would risk making her angry by mentioning the girl.

I thought it was really risky until I saw the plan in action. When the girls met us at the first store, Cyn led them away from her mother and gave a convincing performance of struggling to shed her anger with her imaginary cousin. If Cynthia wasn't in the drama club at school, she needed to be.

The girls shared their sympathy and then all was forgotten as they focused their energies on the latest fashions.

I was finally beginning to relax when an uninvited group joined our shopping party.

I cringed inwardly as I realized Nicolaus and Nathan were with the group. I saw them before they saw me, and I pulled Cyn behind a display for a mini-freak-out session.

Cyn laughed at my fears. "Just look at them with that wide-eyed terror, and they'll have no doubt that you're Fiona."

I felt insulted, but not enough to cover the fear. If they insisted I was Audra and Lisa noticed, it would be one more strike I had with the woman. Cyn read my mind.

"Listen, I'm serious about the fear. Audra has never acted afraid. I'm going to distract my mom the moment they notice you. That way, you can tell them you're Fiona without her overhearing."

"You're going to leave me alone?" My heart raced to my throat.

"Yes," she smiled. "The more terrified you are, the better. Trust me. No guy wants to be around a nervous, freaking-out girl. They're drawn to confidence. Just don't be confident."

"N-not a problem." My throat felt like it was closing as Cyn led me back to the group. Almost instantly, Nicolaus saw me, and Cyn led Lisa to the other side of the store to check out a purse she'd seen.

"Audra," Nicolaus came to my side and began to hug me.

When I took a step back, he smiled. "Sorry, Fiona. You two really do look identical. Maybe when I see you together, I can figure out how to tell you apart."

I breathed a small sigh of relief. "Yeah," I said, amazed at how easily the lie slipped off my tongue. "When we are side-by-side, you'll be able to see."

He smiled and slipped his arm over my shoulders.

I let him lead me over to where Genivive and some other girls were standing, still distanced from Lisa and Cyn.

"Find anything good, ladies," he said. I expected him to drop his arm, but he kept it over my shoulders.

"Oh, Nicky," Genivive said, "how did you know we were here?" She glanced around the women's clothing store. "Or were you here shopping yourself?"

The girls around him tittered, and I frowned at them. I wasn't fooled by Genivive's supposed joke. She'd meant to insult him. That fact confirmed when she added, "I found a cute tartan skirt I think you'd love."

I narrowed my eyes at her. I usually didn't tangle with the mean girls, but I couldn't stand to see anyone bullied. Even if it was a popular guy who could stand up for himself.

Without thinking, and totally forgetting I was supposed to act scared, I said, "If you're talking about the blue one over there," I waved my arm toward the back of the store, "I'd pay good money to see Nicolaus in it. He'd look like a Scottish warrior."

His lips twisted with humor, and his arm tightened, pulling me closer into his side. "My mouse has claws," he whispered to me.

Genivive's smile turned brittle. "I suppose," she wrinkled her nose at me. "If you're into that kind of thing."

I widened my eyes in mock surprise. "Are you saying you're not? Don't you follow fashion trends? Did you not see Sarden's collection during New York Fashion Week?"

Genivive scoffed. "Of course, I did."

Somehow I kept my face neutral and didn't break into the laughter bubbling in my chest. I'd made the whole thing up. And Genivive and her insecurity played along rather than admit I might know more than she did about fashion.

The popular girl twirled on her heels and flounced away from us, forcing her entourage to follow.

When they were out of earshot, Nicolaus said, "So, this designer is bringing kilts into fashion?"

I grinned at him. "I'm sure he would. If he existed."

He burst into laughter. "Yeah, that's what I figured. I'm surprised Genivive didn't call you out. She's supposedly Hill High's fashion guru."

I stepped out of Nicolaus's embrace and faced him. "Are you going to tell her?"

"Pfft," he grinned at me, "After you came to my defense? That wouldn't be very grateful of me, now would it?"

"I suppose not."

His smile widened. "I think such heroics should be rewarded. Don't you?"

"As in?" I asked. My nerve ending fired up my spine. The nervousness that had previously disappeared was back full force. I couldn't imagine what he planned to say, but the intense gleam in his eyes made my whole nervous system fire warning shots.

"Dinner? Movie?"

My heart stopped beating, and I struggled to force air into my lungs. Was he asking me out on a date? No way. He knew I wasn't Audra. I was plain, simple me.

"That's not necessary," I said to save my pride. I didn't want to look like some desperate girl who turned a boy's harmless flirting into an awkward situation and force him to explain he was kidding. That wasn't going to happen.

His smug, flirty smile left his lips, and a stunned expression crossed his face. "No?" He blinked rapidly for a few seconds. "Is it me?"

"Is what you?"

"You don't like me? Did I come on too strong? Not strong enough?"

Maybe it was possible he had meant to ask me out. Not likely. But possible.

I grinned at him. "I don't know you. How could I say I don't like you?"

"Um, you just turned me down. That usually tells a guy that a girl doesn't like him."

"You weren't serious," I said.

"No?" He studied me for a moment. "How is this?" He grabbed my hand and led me to where my aunt and cousin stood by a purse display.

"Mrs. Houghton," Nicolaus said, "if I asked Fiona out, do I have your permission to take her on a date."

Aunt's Lisa's shock almost rivaled mine. She stared at me as if she'd never seen me before. Then she turned to Nicolaus and stared at him. "You want to take Fiona on a date?"

"Yes," he said, ending all doubt that he meant what he'd said. I still didn't trust him or his motive for asking me out, but I had to accept it was a genuine offer.

"I'm," Aunt Lisa chocked out, "I'm not the one you need to ask. Mr. Houghton makes those decisions."

"Then, may I stop over tonight and ask his permission?"

"Certainly," she said, her voice having a decided lack of certainty. "In fact, why don't you come for supper?" Her words grew stronger and surer. "Seven?"

He grinned. "Yes, thank you. I'll be there at seven."

"Lovely," Aunt Lisa recovered and gave him her typical charming smile. "We'll see you then."

Nicolaus pulled me a few feet away from my relatives. "Believe me now?"

"I'm starting to." I pulled my hand from his and crossed my arms over my waist. "But why?"

He laughed. "Because I want to. Why else would I ask?"

"This isn't some haze-the-new-girl scheme, is it?"

He laughed harder. "You've watched too many movies. No one's forcing me to ask you out, I didn't make or lose a bet, I don't expect you to change your clothes and hair and become my Cinderella. Don't buy what those movies are selling you. I'm just a regular guy who wants to take a beautiful and interesting girl out on a date. I want to get to know you better." He paused and smirked at me. "Is that OK with you?"

I wasn't sure. My parents had said it was up to Uncle George whether I dated. I hadn't seen one instance where Uncle George turned down whatever Cyn and Lisa wanted. So, I knew he'd be thrilled to say yes to this boy. Did I want to break my parents' rules on a guy I really didn't know? That was the real question. After all, I didn't have this concern when I thought about dating Ash. So what was the issue? I didn't know.

The boy waited patiently for my answer. "I guess it's OK if we hang out. Though I have to warn you. I'm not cool like—"

I'd planned to say Cyn, but he jumped in with "Audra."

I blinked a couple of times. "I'm definitely not Audra. I'm not anything like her."

"I didn't ask out Audra, now did I?" he smirked at me.

A million thoughts raced through my head. Was he using me to get to her? Did he ask me out because he knew he'd never have a chance with the older girl? Was I his consolation prize? Could he actually prefer me over the sexy, cooler version Cyn had created? There was only one way to find out. "Assuming George agrees, what were you planning for this date?"

Nicolaus's shoulders dropped, and it was the first indication I'd had that he might be nervous. "I want to surprise you."

I wasn't big on surprises. Surprises usually meant uncertainty and risk. He read my reluctance accurately.

"Don't worry. It will be fun. I promise."

"OK," I said.

Our shopping trip continued for another couple of hours. I felt awful that I'd agreed to go on a date with Nicolaus when I was interested in another guy.

But Ash hadn't hinted that he was interested in me. I tried to remember that and push away my guilt. It didn't work very well.

As soon as we got home from shopping, I checked my social media messages. I had one single message from Ash that simply stated he'd see me on Saturday and to wear casual clothes.

I had been tagged in one of Nicolaus's posts that hinted we had spent the day together, though it was really vague. I didn't know if Ash had seen that or if his comment was just a general statement.

If he had, I wanted to set the record straight. I wanted him to know that I wasn't interested in the other guy. I quickly typed a message stating that I was free Saturday or any other day. I hoped it wasn't too subtle, and then I worried that maybe it was too bold.

Liking guys wasn't easy.

His answer was immediate. *Are you free tomorrow?*

My fingers hovered over the keyboard. Should I make plans with Ash, knowing that in a few hours I'd be making plans with Nicolaus? I wanted to spend time with Ash. Even if he was only interested in being friends. I'd have some time with Ash before Nicolaus and I went on our date. If there was any hint from Ash that he was interested in me, then I'd call off the date and find some excuse to give Uncle George and Aunt Lisa. I wouldn't lead Nicolaus on if I thought I had a chance with the guy I liked; I didn't want to treat him the way I'd seen Cyn's friends treat her.

Let me talk with Aunt Lisa, I messaged him. *Just to make sure she hasn't planned anything else for me.*

It was the truth. Not the whole truth. But a little true. I needed to make sure no one had anything planned for me before I committed to Ash.

OK was the only thing he said.

I stared at those two little letters, hoping they'd tell me if he was angry, resigned, happy. I had no clue. I guessed I'd learn more when I told him whether I was free.

I had a couple of hours before Nicolaus was expected to arrive, and although I could use the solitude to quiet my mind, I was too restless to rest. I went downstairs and saw my aunt in a frenzy of activity getting supper ready. This was no ordinary meal. She was going overboard.

"Can I help?" I asked.

Lisa was too busy to even throw me her usual scowl. "Yes," she pushed a bowl at me. "Mix those ingredients until they're smooth and then pour them into that pan."

I did what she said without question. I had no idea what she was creating, and as frazzled as she seemed, I figured it was best just to take orders and obey. We worked that way for the next thirty minutes. She barked orders. I followed.

That is until Uncle George ambled into the room. "So, you have a young man coming over. How exciting. I thought you'd dress up for the occasion, but going casual is good, too. Keep him guessing."

Aunt Lisa paused as she placed a pan of au gratin potatoes in the oven. "For crying out loud, Fiona," she said, "You look like you've been rolling yourself in flour. Get upstairs and get ready. I'm not going to all this trouble so that you can show up looking like you've put in four days of hard labor."

I quickly nodded and raced upstairs. When I saw myself in the mirror, I laughed. My hair was sticking out in all directions. I had a smudge of flour across my cheek, and my shirt had a large wet stain over my collarbone. I looked like a hot mess, and there was a part of me that wished I could show up to supper like that.

Lisa would lose her mind, Cyn would probably look down her nose at me, and Uncle George would crack up. I wondered how

Nicolaus would react. Because that would tell me everything I needed to know about this boy. Could he be a potential friend? I guessed I'd find out soon enough.

Nathan

After being dragged by my brother and friends to meet the girls for shopping, I disappeared as soon as I could get out of it. Basically, after we'd all had lunch. In the short time I'd been with my friends, I'd watched Nic flirt with Fiona and my so-called girlfriend lose her mind with jealousy.

I'd had enough and went to the Vega farm to run some ideas by Mr. Vega. The new storefront had brought more revenue to the little store, and I hoped once the interior was redesigned that we'd generate even more sales. I'd finally gotten to the essential oils exhibit at the arboretum and had more ideas of how we might expand the product line that Vega Farm's store offered.

Right now, it was too small to start selling online, and they didn't have a way to easily or cheaply scale up their production. But once the renovation was done and sales increased, then maybe I could talk the Vega family into taking a risk and aiming for a larger market.

My other business project, the one only a handful of people knew about, had reaped a large profit for me much faster than I had anticipated. I'd spent the last hour talking options to reinvest my profit with my mother. She knew how important it was for me to impress my dad, and she wouldn't risk causing any drama by telling him what I was doing. She'd let me face him and the consequences, good or bad, of what I had done. That didn't mean she wasn't willing to give me advice. Dad might be the finance wizard of the family, but Mom had run her own successful business for years. She knew how to make a profit, even if she hadn't grown her business into the juggernaut my father had done with his own ventures.

With Dad at work and Nic hanging out with friends, it gave us dedicated time to pour over my finances and my options. Things were looking up for my businesses. I was slowly getting results, and if my luck held, I'd be able to repay my dad before I left for college next summer. That was the goal.

I'd just have to get through senior year with him nagging me. I could do it, though. Because shocking my father with a lump sum repayment would be worth every little complaint he had.

If only my personal life was as promising. In that regard, all I had to look forward to was dumping my current girlfriend and remaining single. My current girlfriend who was obviously using me to increase her popularity status. Because ever since Nic's attention turned elsewhere, she'd had little interest in me.

Walking to my bedroom to play a game before supper, I passed by our bathroom and saw Nic standing in front of the vanity mirror, shaving the tiny amount of dark hair that dotted his jawline.

"Where are you going?" My brother had changed from his usual summer attire of old, faded t-shirts and shorts to a nicer pair of jeans and a button-down shirt. Something I'd expect him to wear on a date.

"The Houghtons," he said over his shoulder as he brushed his hair.

"Seeing Audra?" My neck and shoulders tightened. The girl had sent me a flirty message almost every day. If she was toying with my brother while coming onto me, she'd have to answer for her actions. She had no business leading on a guy four years younger than her.

"No," he said, "she's taking online college courses. She doesn't have time to hang out."

I relaxed a little, realizing the older girl had brushed off Nic.

That still didn't explain why he was going to Cyn's house. I waited silently, hoping my brother would share what he was doing without my asking. Apparently not.

"Then why go over there?" I gave up waiting.

"Stupid Houghtons are making me meet them before they approve me taking Fiona on a date. Like they haven't known me since I was a baby." Nic scoffed.

I ran over in my mind what he'd just said. "Fiona?"

I didn't like this scenario any more than when I thought Nic was interested in Audra. I didn't see them together. Nic liked adventure and parties and anything social. I had trouble imagining my brother digging below the surface to discover the fun side of the shy girl. She wasn't his type, and I worried he was using her to make Geni jealous.

"What?" he smiled. "Don't tell me you didn't notice her. I saw you hitting her up at Geni's party. Not cool, man. Flirting with a girl in front of your girlfriend."

"I was being nice," I said. "She is new to town, and I was saying hello."

Nic rolled his eyes. "Whatever. Just know that I called dibs. She's going out with me, so you need to back away."

I held my hands up like I was defending myself against a weapon. "I'm not going after the girl."

"You better not. You stole Genivive from me, so I'm claiming Fi."

His words crawled over me. It felt more like marking his territory rather than a genuine interest in the new girl. "What do you mean claiming Fi? We're not fighting over girls. I'm not trying to steal any girl you like."

Nicolaus frowned and then said, "Whatever. You have Genivive. Worry about her and not whoever I'm going out with." He straightened his clothing and then dabbed on some cologne. "When are you, by the way?"

"When am I what?"

"Taking out Genivive. I thought you'd be going out more."

I shrugged. The truth was I didn't want to take her out, and ever since Audra and Fiona had arrived, Genivive seemed less focused on me. She had started our relationship with texting me all the time. Now, I heard from her once or twice a day. And sometimes those texts centered around her searching for my brother.

Curious about Nic's reaction, I said, "I'm not sure Geni and I are compatible."

My brother scowled at me. "You can't break up with her. It will crush her."

I sighed. "I don't want to hurt her. But she seems way more interested in you than she does me."

Nic's eyes widened slightly and a ghost of a smile crossed his face before he reigned in control of his reaction. "It doesn't matter. You can't dump her."

"But then you could go out with her," I said.

He took a step back. "What game are you playing? Are you only interested in a girl if I want her? Are you going after Fiona next?"

"Of course not," I scoffed. I hadn't imagined dating Fiona, though based on our conversation at the party, I knew we'd have fun hanging out. "I didn't even know you liked Genivive. If I'd known," I leveled my gaze to emphasize whose fault that was, "I wouldn't have agreed to go out with her."

"You wouldn't have agreed? You make it sound like she asked you out. You're a liar, Nathan. Get out of my face."

Then he slammed the door and shut me out. I had all the answers I needed when it came to Nic's feelings for Genivive. My little brother was in love. Too bad the girl didn't deserve his devotion.

Chapter Ten

F iona

Nicolaus patted the porch swing seat next to him. We'd finished supper and gotten George's permission to go out — no surprise there. Then, my uncle had suggested we sit on the back porch and make plans while the rest of the family cleared the dishes and prepared dessert.

I sat next to him, glad Cyn had talked me into wearing my new sundress. Maybe this routine typically happened whenever my cousin brought a new guy home. Although the sun had set, the heat of the summer night still raged on, and if I'd worn jeans, like my original plan, I'd have been burning up.

I left a space between us, one because I wasn't ready to get cozy with this boy and two, it was way too hot to cuddle. Maybe that's why George sent us outside. Or maybe he was as clueless as I thought. Loveable, but totally clueless.

"So," I turned slightly to face Nicolaus, putting a little more space between our bodies. "What were you thinking?"

"That you look amazing."

My face heated beyond the sweltering night air. "I meant," I had trouble looking him in the eyes. I felt this strong shyness overcome me. Boys didn't compliment me. And Nicolaus's attention was way more than I was ready to handle. "About the date."

He laughed. "You're welcome," he said sarcastically, and I realized how rude I'd just been. I'd been so caught up in being uncomfortable that I'd lost my manners.

"I'm sorry. Thank you for the compliment. I guess I'm just nervous about this surprise you have planned. I'm not big on surprises."

He nodded. "Yeah, I picked up on that. But don't worry. I'll tell Cyn what I have planned so you'll be dressed appropriately."

I let out a sigh of disappointment. It was stupid. I had no right to expect him to understand me. So, I had no right to be disappointed when he misunderstood my concern. "Thanks," I said.

Nicolaus grinned, and I realized he'd misunderstood me again. He thought I was relieved. The boy didn't have telepathy, and I couldn't expect him to read my mind. I wasn't like the girls he hung out with, and if they were his only experience with the opposite sex, then of course he'd come to those conclusions.

Maybe on our date he'd see the real me. Then, we'd both know if there was any chance of a friendship. I didn't hold out for romance. Having a romance with someone here meant staying, and a strong part of me still wanted to leave. I hadn't been here a month yet, and I still felt like I was drowning in a sea of the unknown. If I had to face the unknown, then I'd prefer it to be with my parents and brother - the people who'd support me no matter what. Not the relatives I felt could turn on me at any moment.

"When do you want to go out?" I asked, trying to pull my brain from the depressing trajectory it had taken.

"Saturday," he said. "I'll need a little time to get it all set up."

I breathed a sigh of relief. "Saturday sounds great." That meant I'd have my time with Ash tomorrow and have plenty of time to cancel on Nicolaus if I needed to. It was a relief that, for once, I'd have a little control of the situation.

Nicolaus moved closer to me. "There's your smile. I was beginning to wonder if you even wanted to spend time with me."

I hadn't realized I was smiling. There was no way I'd tell him that I was glad I had time to break our date if things looked promising with Ash. That wasn't the type of thing a guy wanted to hear after he'd asked out a girl, I was sure.

"I'm not big on surprises," I told him, "but I do want to know you better." If I was stuck in this town when school started, it would help to have a few friends.

He reached over and played with the tip of my hair where it laid across the back of the swing. "Same. So, while we're waiting on dessert, tell me something about yourself."

I leaned my head back to think and inadvertently pulled my hair from his fingertips. What was there to tell about my life up to this point? Not much. "Well, we moved from Cedarville, and I attended an all-girls private school."

His eyes widened. "All girls? That must have sucked."

I shrugged. "The school was fine. I liked my classes."

"But no dances. No guys to flirt with. No prom."

I shrugged again. "We had social activities. Founder's Day Tea. Father-daughter dances. Just no boys."

"I'd die if my parents sent me to an all-boys school. Girls are my favorite part of the day." He wryly smiled at me. "Not that I'm a player or anything."

"Yeah," I gave him a teasing smile, "I'd never think you're a player."

"Hey, I've got game," he sat up taller. "Girls find me attractive."

At that, I started laughing. "I agreed to go on a date with you. Do you really want to point out that I'd have competition if we started liking each other?"

He slouched back. "That wasn't my smoothest move, huh?"

"Not exactly."

We rocked in silence for a moment. It was comfortable, and not awkward the way I was afraid spending time with him would be.

"You know," he said as if thinking out loud, "I don't think I've ever had that type of conversation with a girl before. Flirting, definitely. But that felt..." he trailed off and didn't finish his thought.

I knew what he meant, though. It was comfortable and fun and friendly. I'd felt more like my true self in the past couple minutes than I had during any other interaction with him — except at the water park, which he thought he'd spent with Audra.

Without meaning to, I released a deep sigh. How did that saying go about deception and tangled webs? Before I had a chance to remember it, Nicolaus spoke, "That sounded bad."

"What?"

"Sighing like that? It wasn't exactly a happy noise."

I spoke the truth. "I was thinking about you and Audra at the water park."

"What about it?" When I didn't answer, he grabbed my hand. "Are you worried I'll compare you to your sister? I would never. People compare me to my brother all the time, and I hate it."

It was the first time I felt I'd seen the real Nicolaus. Not the mask he wore to meet his friends' expectations. "Then let's make a deal." I wanted to put his mind at ease. And gain a little peace of mind in the bargain. "You don't compare me to Audra, and I won't compare you to your brother. How does that sound?"

"Perfect." He shook my hand. "You have a deal."

"Dessert is ready," Cyn called from the doorway leading into the kitchen.

We stood up and began walking into the house. I noticed the curious and guarded expression my cousin wore as I passed by her. No doubt when we were alone she'd want an explanation of what deal I'd made with Nicolaus. I could have told her right there that it wasn't important, but before I opened my mouth, she turned from me and stalked back to the dining room table.

She sat across from me and raised one eyebrow. Her message clear.

We'll talk later.

"My father talks way too much," Cyn said as she closed her bedroom door behind me. Seconds after Nicolaus had said goodbye, she'd dragged me to her room.

I sat at her desk and watched as she paced. I didn't have to wait long before she got to the point.

"What deal did you make with Nicolaus?" Her tone clearly stated she thought I'd double-crossed her.

I narrowed my eyes at her. I hadn't played any games. I'd been completely upfront about where I stood with the whole Audra campaign. The only thing I'd done that she might not like was talking to Nathan without her there. I hit the space bar on her keyboard, and the Audra profile popped up. I raised one eyebrow at her. "Have you been chatting with anyone lately?" Two could play the accusation game.

"Don't change the subject. What were you two talking about?"

I laughed. "Nothing to warrant your suspicion. I promised not to compare him to his brother as long as he didn't compare me to my sister."

She sat on her bed, her eyes never wavering from mine. "And that's it?"

"That's it."

She drummed her fingers on her bedspread. "Why would that even come up? Why were you talking about Audra?"

"We were just getting to know each other. I warned him that I wasn't anything like her."

Cyn rolled her eyes. "You *are* her."

"Not really. She's popular because you know how to be popular. I don't know any of that stuff. I know how to be awkward, and if he's looking for someone like Audra, then it's a waste of time dating someone like me."

She absently nodded. "Why is he taking you out, anyway?"

"I have no clue," I laughed.

Instead of joining me, my cousin stared at her computer screen. "We could make this work, you know. Get insider info on Nathan and Audra's relationship."

"No," I said. "I won't have my very first date ever being a spy mission for you."

"Yeah," Cyn reluctantly agreed. "That would be pathetic."

"Thanks," I dryly said. "Now that we've established I'm pathetic with no ulterior motives with Nicolaus. What about you?" I pointed to the screen.

She twisted her lips in frustration. "I don't get it. He should be panting after Audra. We've done everything to get his attention. Why hasn't he been in touch? This doesn't make any sense."

"Maybe he's not interested," I offered.

"No," she said and pulled the laptop off the table. "He needs a little encouragement."

She sat on her bed and quickly typed off a message.

I rushed over to see what she'd sent him.

Your brother seems like a nice guy. If this is an act, and he breaks my sister's heart, he will be sorry.

We waited for a few minutes before Nathan replied.

I could say the same thing.

Fi is harmless. Cyn typed.

I frowned at her. What did that mean, anyway? That I was a nice person, or that I didn't have the skills to break a guy's heart?

I waited for Nathan to respond, to assure Audra that his brother had good intentions. The longer he waited, the more nervous I got.

Let her get to know him and find out for herself.

"What?" I stared at Nathan's cryptic message. "Is that a warning or something?"

Cyn waved my concern away. "Nic is harmless. I don't know why Nate said that."

"Then ask. Audra would want to know."

She laughed. "Really? Audra would?"

I nudged her with my elbow. "Just do it."

Cyn typed. *Are you saying he can't be trusted?*

Nathan's response was almost immediate. *I'm saying tell your sister to take her time and get to know him. Then she can judge for herself.*

"Give me that," I said and pulled the laptop from my cousin.

Then your brother can have the same advice about my sister.

For once, I wished we were video chatting, so I saw his expression, to interpret if he was hiding something.

This weird conversation left me less than excited about my future date.

Nathan

This thing with Genivive and Nic and the Houghtons was getting out of hand. After my brother left, I'd spent way too much time thinking about the whole situation. I needed to think about my business and taking it to the next level.

But I did feel guilty about ignoring Genivive, so I sent her a text and asked if she wanted to grab a burger at Tucker's. She said yes, and I picked her up thirty minutes later.

She was uncharacteristically quiet as we drove to the diner and after we'd ordered our food, I asked, "Everything OK?"

She forced a smile on her face. "Sure! Why wouldn't it be?"

"You're really quiet tonight. I thought maybe something was bothering you."

An annoyed expression flashed on her face and was quickly replaced by the fake smile. "Nope. I guess I'm just tired. Shopping isn't as easy as it looks, you know."

I smiled at her. "You looked like you were having fun."

"How would you know? You abandoned us. You don't know what happened."

"What happened?"

"We found this amazing sale, but this old woman grabbed the last pair of wedges in my size. Then Cyn found the cutest skirt and grabbed the last one on sale."

I tried not to laugh at her complaints. The girl was seriously aggravated and once she began airing her grievances, she didn't stop. "Then the smoothie place was out of guava. Who runs out of guava?" she continued, and I nodded my head, agreeing with whatever she said. Not that I actually cared that she didn't get her guava mango smoothie. But she was upset, so I was trying to be supportive.

"And Nic was hanging all over that girl. So annoying," she said and motioned to me, "When we're in public, we don't act like that. You and I have more class."

"What girl?"

"Fiona," she spat. "She acts like this poor, little socially awkward girl. But she swooped in fast and scooped Nic up. It's all an act, and sweet Nicky is going to be played."

I didn't agree. If Geni had spent even five minutes talking to the girl at the party, she would have seen how genuinely uncomfortable the girl was. I carefully watched her expression as I said, "Nic seems happy. Maybe he'll forgive me for stealing you from him if he falls for someone else."

My girlfriend frowned. "He doesn't like her that much."

"He's at her house right now getting permission for them to date."

She slammed her fist on the table. "He is not."

"Didn't you know that they're going out?"

Genivive took a sip of water and stared out the window. "No," she said under her breath.

I unwrapped my silverware from the paper napkin coiled around it. "Why did you want to go out with me?"

She quickly turned to me. "What?"

I was tired of the charade. It was time to get this all out in the open. "You're obviously crazy about Nic. Why dump him and go for me?"

She didn't deny her feelings, which earned a little respect from me. Her lips twisted to the side, and she winced. "Were you in love with Cyn?"

"No."

She dropped her shoulders. "I hoped you weren't. I don't think Cyn loved you, either."

I shrugged. It didn't bother me that Cyn hadn't loved me. It was actually a relief, since I'd worked so hard to dump her without hurting her feelings. That hadn't worked, but it was good to know I hadn't broken her heart.

"I just got tired of hearing how she was going to be Homecoming queen and the most popular girl in school, all because she was dating you." She looked me directly in the eyes as she confessed, which earned more respect. "I just wanted to shut her up."

"And be Homecoming queen?" I added.

"Who doesn't want to be Homecoming queen?" She wryly smiled at me.

I smiled back. "Why don't you go after Nic? He's crazy about you."

She rolled her eyes. "So crazy that he's dating another girl."

"You're taken." I hesitated before speaking again. It was the right thing to do, but despite how open we had been, I wasn't sure she was ready to hear it. "Unless you don't want to be."

Her eyes narrowed. "Are you dumping me?"

"No," I grabbed both her hands and held them. "I suggesting you follow your heart. We both know I'm not the Hollingsworth you want to be with. Go after my brother. He wants you just as much as you want him."

"He has a funny way of showing it."

"So do you," I teased and held up our joined hands.

"Fine," Genivive said. "We're over. But you can't tell anyone. I won't have Cyn looking down her nose at me because I lost both Hollingsworth brothers."

"That works for me," I said. "I won't tell anyone you know that we broke up. As long as you pursue my brother. When it's time to go public that our relationship ended, you can tell people you dumped me."

Her eyes rounded in excitement. "Seriously? I can tell people that I dumped you for your brother?"

I lowered my brows. I'd get some serious ribbing about that, and Nic would gloat about it all the time. But, if the rest of my summer was drama-free, it was a fair trade-off. "Yes," I said. "We're officially over. And when you're ready, you can tell the whole world you dumped me for Nic."

She grinned. "Thanks, Nate. You're the best."

I smiled back. Too bad break-ups weren't like this all the time. I'd never imagined I'd make Genivive so happy by letting her go.

Not long after I returned from my break-up, my brother came home from the Houghtons.

"For a guy whose got a date, you don't look very happy." I said as my brother plopped down on the sofa next to me. He leaned his head back on the couch and stared at the ceiling.

Nic shrugged. "It's fine."

"Fine?"

He sighed and rubbed his hand over his face. "I don't know. She's a little weird."

"Weird?"

"I can't explain it. She's gorgeous, but I feel like I'm dating my sister." He frowned. "Why am I even telling you this? It's not like you care."

"Believe it or not, I actually want you happy."

"Yeah, I can tell," he said sarcastically. "Nothing says *love you, Bro*, like stealing a guy's crush."

I'd promised Genivive I wouldn't tell anyone she knew that we'd broken up. I was torn between keeping my word and making my brother happy. But if I told him, I had no doubt he'd shout it to everyone he saw. As hard as it was, I needed to take a step back and let Geni figure out what she wanted to do. Besides, if I told him now, he'd probably cancel his date with Fiona. It would be cruel for the girl to be dumped her first month in town.

"Just go on the date and see what happens," I said. "Maybe you'll have fun."

He rolled his eyes and didn't respond.

Taking my clue that he wanted to be alone, I went to my room and got online. I was shocked when seconds later, Audra messaged me warning that my brother better not break her sister's heart.

If only she knew how close to the truth she was. The best I could do was try to subtly warn her that Fiona needed to take it slow.

Then she threw my advice back to me. I stared at the words for a minute. What did that even mean? Was Fiona not into Nic?

I hit the video chat button. Why play the guessing game when I could get my questions answered directly?

She accepted after some hesitation, and when the video activated, both Audra and Cyn's faces popped up on the screen.

"Good evening, Ladies," I said immediately. It was awkward facing Cyn. Sure, we had seen each other at the party and during the girls' shopping trip. But we'd had plenty of people between us.

"Did you need something?" Audra cut to the chase. Now that I had met Fiona, it was eerie how alike the girls looked.

I raised one eyebrow at her directness. The girl still seemed hostile toward me, even though a few days ago, our texting had evolved to more of a truce. "Just clarification," I said and watched the girls' reactions. Audra remained suspicious while Cyn had a small, satisfied smile on her lips. That made no sense. What was my ex up to?

Audra tilted her head as if studying my image. I imagined she had a similar expression when she was taking her online classes. When she didn't answer, I said, "Are you worried Nic will break Fiona's heart?"

Cyn pursed her lips. I recognized that look. She was trying not to laugh. She wasn't worried. In fact, she looked triumphant for some reason.

Audra wasn't so easy to read. "Are you worried Fi will break Nic's?"

I chose my words carefully. "Nic likes her. But he's not in love yet. He's currently in rebound mode."

Cyn's smile dropped from her face. She knew Nic hadn't dated anyone in several months. "Who?" she demanded.

I wryly smiled at her. "Not at liberty to say."

"So, you're saying Nic won't fall for my sister," Audra brought us back to the topic.

I sighed. "I'm saying Fiona needs to take it slow. If she's the type to fall instantly in love, she'll be frustrated with my brother."

Cyn frowned. "Don't act like you care about her feelings," she said, "What's in it for you? Why do you want them apart?"

I laughed. "I don't want them apart. Just trying to be a nice guy."

Audra blinked a couple times while Cyn's expression turned cynical. It was funny how they'd switched positions so quickly.

"That's all I wanted," I said. "Good night."

We rang off.

After a few minutes, I received a message from Audra. *Maybe you're not evil.*

I laughed. Was this an actual peace offering from the girl? I debated how to answer. Definitely not flirting, though a part of me wondered how she'd react if I did. But I had made progress breaking through her hard exterior. At least when we texted back and forth. In person, she still didn't trust me.

My fingers hovered over my keyboard as I debated what to reply. Finally, I settled on *Maybe not* with a wink emoji.

Maybe I like this side of you. How could a guy who cares about my sister break my cousin's heart? You're a mystery to me.

I examined her words and felt guilty that I immediately distrusted them. If I were in Audra's shoes would I have said the same thing? Giving her the benefit of doubt, I answered, *You don't know the whole story.*

Then tell me, she responded immediately.

Warning signals went off in my head. Was she still sitting next to Cyn and asking me these questions? Was Cyn pulling the strings and Audra was the puppet? I wasn't falling into the trap where I insulted Cyn to her family.

I responded the only way I could. *I don't think that's a good idea. It's getting late. Good night.*

Then I signed off.

Even though I'd broken up with Cyn, I still felt tied to this family. Now, through her cousins. I seriously needed Genivive to make her move on Nic so that I could make my escape. Free and clear of Cyn, free and clear of Audra.

Free and clear of the only innocent person in this whole drama.

Poor Fiona Houghton. She was stuck for life.

Chapter Eleven

Fiona

Ash picked me up the next day. I was grateful Aunt Lisa hadn't formed any plans for me, and I didn't bother telling Cyn what I'd planned to do. I figured it would easier to get out of the house before she woke up than risk her disapproval and stopping me from going.

As I strapped on my seatbelt and looked at the house, it was hard not to shake my head in disappointment. I'd always been an open book, and in the matter of a couple weeks, I'd kept secrets, told partial truths and pretended to be someone else. It felt good to sit in this truck and be myself.

"What are we doing?" I asked as he pulled out of the driveway.

"My partner on the house is working on this farm outside of the city. He's been renovating the shop at the edge of the property, and I thought you might like to be part of the consultation." Ash smiled at me.

"Really?" I was a little disappointed that this was a business trip for him, but I was honored that he'd included me. Plus, I was fascinated by the prospect of renovating a building. I'd only seen renovations on TV. To see one first hand was exciting. "What kind of shop?"

"Bath and beauty," Ash said. "They make all-natural goat milk products. Which is why I need you. What would I know about a beauty store?"

I laughed as I tried to imagine Ash poking around the kind of high-end beauty stores my mother liked to visit. Not that she was big on make-up. But she loved organic cleansers and anti-aging products. I might not be a fashionista or beauty queen, but I knew about skin care.

Ash motioned to the bag on the seat between us. "Help yourself," he said.

I grabbed a sausage roll from the bag and dove in. "These are incredible," I said.

"My mom made them."

"Mind if I have another one?" I asked after I had devoured the first.

"Help yourself," he said.

Minutes after I'd finished my second sausage roll, Ash parked the truck in a gravel parking lot in front of a small wooden structure. There was one large window and one door, and the building looked more like a little cottage than a store. It was quaint and sweet, and I liked it instantly.

Inside, though, was a different story. There were rows of metal shelves along the walls and two tables that had random products on it. It looked like someone's garage and lacked all the charm the exterior held.

Ash introduced me to Mr. Vega, the owner of the farm, and his daughter Ceara, the maker of their products. Ceara was stunning. Tall, willowy with honey-brown skin and the deepest soulful brown eyes I'd ever seen. Soulful brown eyes that never strayed far from Ash. I didn't blame her. I'd been staring at him myself. I gave the girl my best smile. She looked to be my age, and with any luck, she might be a future friend. However, the girl was either shy or unfriendly. Her lips stretched into a returning smile that never quite met her eyes.

Unfortunately, Ash didn't notice the strain between us. Probably because his eyes never strayed far from her face. He obviously liked her, though his awkward one-armed hug with her said he hadn't made his move yet. Any romantic hopes I had in that direction were useless. I held my disappointment in as I focused on the project before us.

Mr. Vega talked about what he'd like to do with the shop. Basically, make it more functional than it currently was. He wanted a place to store their products so they could produce in bulk, and he wanted ways to display complimentary sets that could be bought together when someone found a particular scent they liked.

The guys were talking stats and measurements and logistics, and I felt like they were missing the whole point of a remodel.

"Do you mind if I share my opinion?" I broke into the conversation during a lull.

Ash encouraged me with a wave of his hand.

"The outside of this building is adorable. It makes me want to come inside. But when I'm inside, I want to leave. I feel like I walked into someone's warehouse. The inside needs more charm. You want patrons to linger. The longer they stay, the more they'll buy. At least that's what happens when my mom shops for these products."

"Exactly," Ceara said at my side. "Our typical shopper is female, and trust me, women want a shopping experience, not an order delivery."

Mr. Vega placed his hands on his hips. "Did my daughter pay you?" he asked me with a playful smirk.

Ceara laughed. "I've said this a hundred times. Thanks for having my back, Fiona."

I grinned at the girl. "Any time." Maybe we could bond over the store's renovation. It would be nice to have a friend outside of Cyn's circle.

"Fine," Mr. Vega said. "Ash and I will work out functionality, and you girls work out style."

Ceara clapped her hands. "I'll show you my sketch book," she said and motioned for me to follow her. Over her shoulder, she called out to her father, "We're going to the house. Meet us there when you're done. I'll heat up Mom's cookies for you."

I got into a small silver sedan, and Ceara drove us down a gravel path to a small white house set amongst a tree grove. The exterior was worn, but welcoming, and I found myself charmed as much by their home as their little store.

Ceara led me inside to a large farmhouse kitchen. She motioned to the kitchen table and ensured I had a serving of milk and cookies before she raced to her room to get her sketchbook.

"Thanks for back there," she said as she placed the book between us. "My dad still sees me as a baby. Sometimes he needs a second opinion before he listens to me." She smiled indulgently and continued. "This is what I was thinking," she said and opened the book to a page where she'd drawn a shelf with a linen liner, silver bowls containing round and square objects, which I assumed was soap, and small jars displayed next to them. It was really pretty, but I felt like there was something missing.

"You use all natural products, right?"

She nodded.

"Why not have some ingredients displayed? You could have rosemary sprigs here," I pointed to one area of the shelf. "Vanilla bean pods over here. And show pictures of your goats who produce the milk."

The other girl pulled out a pencil and roughly sketched in my suggestions. "What do you think?"

"I love it," I said. "You have some really great ideas, Ceara. You really didn't need my input at all." I flipped through the book and found more pictures of her vision for the check-out counter and the tables in the center of the room. "This is going to be so cute. I can't wait to show my mom."

"Invite her over any time." Ceara reluctantly smiled at me. Whatever had caused her initial hesitation, I was hopeful I had overcome.

I sighed. "I wish I could. She and my dad moved out of state. I'm staying with my aunt and uncle."

"Oh," she gave me a sympathetic smile. "It's tough being a way from your parents. My mom travels a lot for her job. The only good thing is when she's going to be gone longer than a week, she makes guilt cookies."

"Guilt cookies," I laughed.

"Yes, she feels guilty for leaving us, so she makes a ton of cookies." Ceara pointed to one on my plate. "And they are incredible."

"They are," I said. "You should sell them in the shop. Encourage people to linger around while they're sampling your products."

She snapped her fingers. "That's not a bad idea."

"So," she said after she'd had a bite of cookie. "You're staying with Cyn?"

"You know her?" I said surprised. "I guess this really is a small town."

"Yes," Ceara's tone spoke volumes. She knew Cyn and didn't like my cousin. She wasn't rude enough to say it. She didn't have to.

I smiled at the girl. "My grandmother always called her a force of nature. Cyn can be tough to handle sometimes."

"That's one way of putting it." She pulled her sketchbook towards her and held it against her chest like a shield.

I could see my opportunity for making a new friend dwindle before my eyes. I quickly said, "It's OK if you don't like her. That's between the two of you. None of my business."

Ceara nodded, her guard still firmly in place.

I had no idea how to move us forward. We sat in uncomfortable silence for several minutes until I couldn't stand it anymore. "So, your drawings are great. If I'd tried to draw anything like that, it would be a disaster. I mean, it would look like a stick store for stick people." I laughed, and she reluctantly smiled back.

"Thanks," she said. Then she sighed, and her shoulders dropped like she had surrendered some internal battle. "Ash said you did a great job with the flowers at the little house."

I was flattered he'd mentioned me, but after seeing him stare at Ceara, I had no hope of getting his attention. "It was fun," I said, "not something I want to do all the time, but fun."

"How did that happen?" A slight blush formed on her face. "I mean, how did you start working with him?"

I shared with her my forced trip to the library, and when I mentioned the soap making class, she winced.

"Wait," I said and smiled at her, "you're teaching the class, aren't you?"

Her face flushed deeper. "Dad thought it would be a good way to advertise our products. But I completely dread it. What if no one comes? What if everyone comes?"

I understood exactly what she meant. "I'll be there. Sometimes it helps to have a friendly face cheering you on."

"Thanks, that's nice of you," she said, her smile a little deeper, though still not reaching her eyes.

The guys finally showed up. If they noticed something was wrong, they didn't act like it. They ate their cookies and listened attentively as Ceara shared her drawings.

"You ladies have a great plan," Mr. Vega said.

"I don't deserve any of the praise," I rushed to tell him. "This was all Ceara."

"You had some ideas," she said and smiled as Ash draped his arm over her shoulders.

"Please," I brushed away her words, "it was nothing. You have all the talent here."

Mr. Vega smiled. "Sounds like you girls had fun."

"We did," I said. "This was a blast. I hope I get to come back and see it come to life."

"Of course you can," he said.

I smiled at Ceara and hoped she received my message. I'd love to come back, but only if she wanted me there.

She didn't say anything, and the guys wrapped up their business as they polished off their cookies.

Back in the truck, Ash proved he hadn't been as clueless as I'd thought. "Did anything happen between you and Ceara?" He sounded genuinely confused. "I thought you two would hit it off."

I stared out the passenger window as we passed trees and rural streets. "She's really nice," I said. "Maybe we just didn't click right away." I heard how final that sounded and quickly added, "I guess we just need to get to know each other better."

Ash kept silent for a moment. "I bet she's worried you'll turn out like your cousin," he said. "I told her you were cool, but I guess she didn't believe me."

"I take it she's not a fan of my family," I said.

"Yeah," he said. "Cyn publicly embarrassed Ceara when they moved here a few years ago. Ceara was new and sat at the wrong table in the cafeteria. Cyn yelled at her and told her to eat where no one could see her. No matter what I did, Ceara wouldn't eat in the cafeteria the whole year."

"That's awful," I said. "She was new. She didn't know. Besides," I grew angry on Ceara's behalf, "No one has the right to treat someone like that over a stupid table."

Ash raised one eyebrow at me. "You really believe that?"

"Of course, I do."

He shook his head at me and frowned as he stared at the road ahead.

"What? Did I say something wrong?"

"Nope," he answered. "Just sweet. And naïve. I hope your cousin doesn't run you out of the cafeteria for the whole school year."

I bit my bottom lip and watched as the trees became fewer and stores, houses and structures popped up more. The closer we got to the city limits, the more Ash's words weighed on me.

I was a guppy swimming with sharks. I lived with a shark, and I was going on a date with a shark.

And I had no idea how to keep myself from being eaten alive.

But even worse than that, Ash had shown no interest in me at all. Maybe I would have had a chance except for one inconvenient fact. Every time I looked at him, he was looking at Ceara.

Nathan

"You just missed Ash," Mr. Vega said when I stepped into the shop.

"And Fiona," Ceara gritted her teeth.

I felt like a bad friend. I had planned to talk to Ceara about Fiona and warn her that the girl might be a threat. I'd been so wrapped up in the Cyn and Genivive drama that I hadn't fulfilled my promise to my friend.

"Yeah," Ceara read my mind. "You were so spot on about her," she said sarcastically. "Nothing to worry about."

"Ash brought her here?" I leaned against the counter and made eye contact with the girl.

She pulled on a bright, sarcastic smile. "Yes. To get her opinion on our renovations." She scowled. "I've shown him my drawings a dozen times, and he brings a random stranger to give her opinion."

I blew out a frustrated breath. "That's my fault, too," I said and wryly smiled at her. "He said a friend helped him plant the flowers at our flip, so I said to bring the friend over here to get a second opinion." I placed my hand on her forearm. "I didn't know it was Fiona." In fact, I was shocked it was her.

Ceara pulled her arm away from me. "She worked on your house flip? The one that Dad co-signed so you could buy it?"

I shrugged. "It would seem so. She did an amazing job. The house sold the same day we listed it with an agent."

"That doesn't make me feel any better," my friend pouted.

"It made us lots of money," I teased.

"Still not helping."

I pulled Ceara into a quick hug. "I'm sorry. I had no idea I was putting you in an awkward situation. But," I leaned down to meet her eye level, "I know something that might help."

"That's she's leaving town tomorrow?" Ceara batted her lashes at me.

I laughed. "No. That she's going on a date with my brother tomorrow."

Ceara's eyes widened. "No! Are you serious?"

"Completely."

The girl smiled. "That's terrific," she said, "if Ash hears she's dating Nicolaus, he'll lose interest. There's no way she can like a guy like him and be interested in Ash."

I wondered how true that statement was. I didn't dare tell Ceara that the relationship wouldn't last. She'd find out soon enough. Assuming that Nic and Fiona's date played out the way I expected. And when Genivive finally went after him, Fiona might not be the only girl upset.

"You need to make your move," I told her as soon as her father left the building. "If you like him, let him know."

"What if he likes her?" Ceara bit the corner of her thumbnail.

"He likes you more," I insisted. "Do something."

"I don't know. If he doesn't like me back, it could ruin our friendship."

"What if Nic and Fiona don't work out?" I challenged her. "What if Fiona gets her heart broken and looks for a shoulder to cry on?"

My friend frowned. Then she pointed her finger at me. "Fine," she said, "but if I get my heart broken, I'm going to slug you in the arm."

I laughed. "Deal. And when he says he likes you back, I'm going to say I told you so."

"Deal," she said.

Then Mr. Vega came back into the room with a sketch book. Ceara walked us through her drawings with the suggestions Fiona had made.

The girl was savvy when it came to business.

I wondered just how savvy she was when it came to dating a guy like Nic.

Chapter Twelve

Fiona

I was glad that Cyn wasn't home when I arrived.

I loved my cousin. Just because she and I had never bonded and hadn't been friends didn't mean I didn't love her.

It pained me to learn that she bullied strangers and didn't care.

I sat on my bed and stared out the window for who knows how long. This wasn't the way my time here was supposed to be. Sure, I hadn't had high hopes for my experience, but I wasn't supposed to be embroiled in the popular crowd's drama, and I wasn't supposed to be tainted by my cousin's actions. I really liked Ceara, and I could see us becoming friends. But not if I was painted with my cousin's reputation.

I pulled up the Audra account and stared at the mirage Cyn had created. I'd wanted to protect my cousin. I'd tried so hard to keep her from doing something bad. I didn't want her hurting other people, but my primary goal had been protecting her from herself.

Now I felt like a naïve idiot.

Maybe I should just walk away from all of this and let it implode. If Cyn got hurt, it was her own fault. Was that the right thing to do? Was there even such a thing in this situation?

I could delete the Audra account. It would show her I wasn't her puppet. It wouldn't stop her. She'd have a new site up in no time at all. I couldn't stop that. I thought I'd have some kind of control if I allowed her to continue on her path under my supervision. But who was I anyway? I had no power. No friends. And most of the time —

unless you made me mad — I was afraid to rock the boat, to willfully enter into conflict and drama.

I needed a friend, but all my old friends at my old school wouldn't understand. They'd give me the same advice I was giving myself — walk away and let Cyn defend herself. I wished I could call my mother, but her advice wouldn't help, either. Family was forever. That was her motto. Stand by Cyn's side. Help her to be a better person.

Mom wouldn't understand, either.

A ding sounded on my laptop, and I absentmindedly clicked on it. I didn't realize what I'd done until I heard Nathan's voice.

"Are you OK?"

I stared at his face. There was no way to know if his concern was genuine. There was no way to know what the truth was. "Do you need something?" I asked. Cyn would have called my voice weak and pathetic. I was just tired. Emotionally drained.

"What's wrong? Something is obviously wrong. Talk to me." He leaned closer to the screen.

I wondered what he'd do if I poured out my guts to him, if I shared my problems. He'd probably run the other direction. My lips tugged at the corners. "You don't care, so don't ask."

"I have a heart, you know."

"There is no evidence of that," I said. The calm, dispassionate words barely left my lips, but he heard me.

His brows knit together. "Now I know you're upset. You can't even insult me correctly. I'm coming over. I'm going to make you tell me what's wrong."

Did he truly mean that? It was hard to imagine he actually cared that Audra was upset. Was this the act of a friend or a way to come onto the fake girl? I hated the doubts swirling in my head, and at this point, I was too drained to care. I'd spit it out and let whatever happened happen. "It's Fiona. And Cyn," I said and waited for his reaction.

He sat there for a few heartbeats and right as I was going to tell him that I knew he didn't care, he said, "And?"

"I'm worried Fi is very naïve about hanging out with Cyn and your friends. I think she's in over her head."

Nathan pressed his lips together. "We're not exactly the kindest people."

"Why is that?"

He looked to the right as if the answers were just off screen. "I want to say that's just who we are, but I'm not sure that's true."

"Then why?"

"I don't know."

"I don't think Fi hanging around your brother is good for her."

"What happened? Why are you saying this?" his fingertips touched the screen.

"Fi tried to make a friend today and was rejected because she was a Houghton." I watched his expression closely. He didn't seem surprised.

"I started dating Cyn because she was so assured. So confident. And sexy as hell." He grimaced. "Shallow. I know."

I didn't correct him.

"But once we started dating, everything was calculated. We had to go to certain parties because of who would see us there. We had to dress a certain way because we didn't want to be out of style. Everything we did had a motive, was a competition. I didn't care how popular we were. I just wanted to have fun and dating Cyn stopped being fun."

"Why are you telling me this?" I leaned back. I didn't trust him, even though I believed he was telling the truth.

"If Fiona isn't cutthroat, Cyn will chew her up and spit her out."

"That still doesn't explain why you're telling me this. After all, you're the guy who dumped my cousin to date her best friend. Why not leave Cyn and be single for a while?"

"I tried. But she wouldn't listen. I didn't want to hurt her. I just wanted to escape." He rolled his eyes.

Something in his voice drew me in, told me there was more behind his words and his attempt to casually brush off his confession. "You didn't, did you?"

"No," he sighed, "Geni is almost as bad. That's why I like talking to you."

I rolled my eyes at him. "Yeah, because you think I'm going to rescue you from your girlfriend."

He laughed. "No. Although I wish you would." He lifted his shoulders in a helpless gesture. "I just like talking to someone who isn't afraid to tell me the truth."

I laughed. If he only knew. "You like me because I'm mean to you. What does that say about you, Nathan?"

He grinned at me. "I have no idea, but I'm sure you'll tell me."

"Nope," I said. "I think you need to figure it out for yourself. And while you're at it, maybe you should stay single for a little while. If you're unhappy with Genivive, just tell her that you need a break."

Nathan shook his head and a corner of his lips twitched upward, as if he was trying not to smile. "That I can't do."

I sighed. "You have to break up with her. It's not fair to either of you. What if she falls in love with you? You'll only break her heart. That's not right."

"You're very big on right or wrong, aren't you?"

I thought about it for a minute. "Yeah, I guess I am. It was the way I was raised."

"I'll think about it."

"Doing the right thing?"

One side of his mouth lifted higher in a self-deprecating grin. "Breaking up with Geni."

I shrugged. "Your choice."

He nodded. "Are you feeling better? You know, now that you've had a chance to insult me again?"

I bit my bottom lip trying not to laugh but failed miserably. "Yeah. Insulting you did the trick."

He smiled at me. This time it wasn't a teasing or flirty expression. He seemed relieved. "Any time you need to insult me, I'm here for you."

Oddly enough, he sounded sincere. "I appreciate that."

He said goodnight, and then we hung up.

I closed my laptop to see Cyn standing in my doorway.

"Next time you video chat with my boyfriend, you better let me know," she said and walked into the room. "And shut the door!" she slammed it behind her.

"You're lucky my mother didn't follow me up the stairs!" Cyn said through gritted teeth. "Why are you talking to Nathan without me? You don't know what to say or do!"

I examined my cousin from head to toe. Her dyed black hair, the designer clothes, the laser focus on getting a boy back that she never loved and didn't love her.

"He's not your boyfriend."

"He will be," she said. "At least you didn't screw up the plan. He's going to dump Genivive."

"And then what?" I asked.

"And then we're breaking his heart."

"He didn't break yours," I said. "I told him he needed to stay single. Stop jumping from girl to girl."

Cyn sat on my bed. "Whatever you're trying to do. Stop it."

"I spent the day with Ash Ellis." I'm not sure why I told her that. I knew it'd make her head explode. It wasn't like me to pick a fight, but I was fed up. I'd had my fill of all the lies and manipulation. It was time to make a change, no matter how uncomfortable it was.

"As Audra?" She narrowed her eyes.

"As me."

"Ugh! What are you doing?" she yelled. "You have a date with Nicolaus. You're going to ruin everything."

"It wasn't a date," I said. "I am allowed to have friends, you know."

"Not those kinds of friends. Not him."

"What's wrong with him?"

"He mows our yard?" She said like the answer was obvious.

"So what? Did you also know he renovates houses? That he's forming his own business? That he makes more money than you do?"

Cyn refused to answer and crossed her arms over her chest.

"So, what's your complaint against Ceara Vega? What's wrong with her?" I mocked her stance.

"Who?"

"Ceara Vega. She goes to your school. You ruined her first day because you yelled at her for sitting at your lunch table."

Cyn shrugged. "Don't know her."

"Well, she knows you. I don't care if you're embarrassed because I spent time with a nice, hard-working guy. You know why? Because I was totally humiliated that my cousin is a stuck-up snob who attacks innocent people. I always looked up to you because you were so tough. Now I know the truth. You're not tough. You're a bully. And I'm ashamed to be your cousin."

"Girls," Uncle George stood in the doorway, "sounds like you're angry. Is everything OK in here?"

Cyn narrowed her eyes at me. "Fiona was video chatting with Nathan," she said, her bottom lip quivering.

Uncle George's eyes widened, and he stared at me like I planned to kill kittens. "He called me. Not the other way around."

"Fiona," he frowned, "I don't think that's appropriate. You know how Cynthia feels about him. Plus, you're dating his brother. I don't think that was a wise decision."

Cyn turned her back to her father and smirked at me. I wanted so badly to defend myself or to tell him how guilty his precious daughter was. Instead, I felt a burning behind my eyes and knew my face was growing splotchy as I tried to hold back my tears.

If I'd had any doubt that Cyn was the vicious girl she'd been accused of. I didn't now.

"I need to talk to your aunt," he said and scuffed his foot along the carpet. "I think we might need to ground you." The thought of grounding me was obviously killing him, but forcing everyone to leave me alone while I was confined to the house sounded like the best news ever.

"Oh Daddy," Cyn rushed to her father and wrapped her arms around his waist. "Don't do that. This is Fiona's first date. If you cancel it, who knows when she'll get another one. Besides, Nicolaus is so excited. And you did already say yes." She batted her large eyes up at him.

Uncle George practically melted. "How did I ever get so lucky? You are the best, sweetest girl in the world."

She kissed him on the cheek. "I have an idea. How about I tag along as her chaperone? That way she can still go on her date, but she won't get any alone time with Nicolaus."

Uncle George grinned. "I think that's a great idea."

"Then it's all settled," she flashed a triumphant grin at me. "I'll call Nicolaus and let him know we have a little change of plans."

She bounced out of the room, leaving Uncle George to give me the worst look of disappointment I'd ever seen.

"I promise you, Uncle George. He only wanted to talk, and he called me."

"That may be true," he said, "but you knew it would hurt your cousin. And that's what is breaking my heart."

"I'm sorry," I said. Not for doing what I had done or for standing up for myself. But that the most innocent person in this whole crazy situation was the one I'd hurt.

He nodded and left me alone.

The moment he was gone, Cyn popped back in. I gave her a slow clap.

She rolled her eyes.

"That was quite the performance," I said.

Cyn raised one eyebrow. "You think that's impressive. Just wait until you see what I do next. Thanks to you, by the time this weekend rolls around, Nathan will be single again. And then Audra will swoop in and break his heart."

I glared at her. "Only if you can do it without me," I said.

She glared back. "I can make your life miserable," she said.

"You already have," I shrugged back at her. I wasn't the kind of person who liked risk, who took chances. But now, with Cyn taking control, I felt like there was nothing to lose. If I was stuck here the next nine months, I couldn't live it by obeying her every command. And if I made a complete disaster of the whole situation and it got worse, then I'd force my parents to get me. Right now, I felt like I didn't have anything to lose. And if my cousin thought she was in charge, then she was in for a rude awakening.

N athan
Can we forget our last conversation?

I read Audra's message a couple times. She wanted to forget the only conversation where we'd both been ourselves. Where we'd formed a type of truce, if not the beginnings of a friendship.

Why? I sent back.

I was weak. I hate being weak. I'm strong and independent, and most of the time I'm not a pathetic, blubbering loser.

I shook my head, glad she couldn't see me. *You weren't a loser. You were vulnerable.*

Don't remind me. Seriously, can we forget it ever happened?

Sure. I sent back, totally confused by this girl. And if I was honest, disappointed. I enjoyed fighting with her, but seeing her without her guard up had been refreshing and sexy.

What are you doing tonight? she asked. *Did your girlfriend leave you all alone?*

I read the words over and over. The problem with messaging is you couldn't hear tone. Was this concern, flirting or snark? Was she starting a fight or hitting on me? I hit the video chat button and waited for Audra to answer.

Instead, she messaged me back.

I'm not looking my best right now.

An hour ago she had answered a video call while she was crying. She had been real and vulnerable and, even though she'd insulted me, sweet. Now she refused to answer because she didn't look good. She'd never struck me as vain. So, not answering because of her looks? I didn't buy it.

Don't worry about your blemish breakout. I promise I'm not looking at it.

I waited for Audra's usual snark, to call me out for insinuating she had a zit on her face. Especially since our last conversation never mentioned her skin, especially not the slightly blotchy complexion from her tears.

Her response came a little longer than I had expected, and when it did, I leaned back in my chair surprised and yet not surprised.

I'm glad you can't see them, but I know they're there. So, don't be shocked if I don't always answer your video calls. I still want to talk to you. I don't want to disgust you when I'm looking less than perfect.

I drummed my fingers on the arm of my desk chair. This wasn't Audra. It explained so much. Why her messages didn't have the same spark that Audra and I had when we video chatted. But if I was right, and the person who was messaging me wasn't Audra, then who was this?

I could set another trap, but I didn't want the liar to get suspicious. Instead, I answered back *You could never look less than perfect.*

It was a simple flirtatious note to give me more time to think.

Who was this? It was easy to accuse Cyn. This type of manipulation was right up her alley. But what if it wasn't her? Could Fiona be capable of the deception? I didn't want to believe it, but right now, I wasn't sure which way was up. Maybe they were all in it together. Maybe Audra and her family were all liars, were all playing me.

I ran my hands over my face. I hated this. All of it.

Audra, or whoever it was, had typed something back, but I didn't bother to read it. Instead, I sent a quick message that I had to log off and I'd talk to her later.

I signed off without waiting for her reply and paced around my room. All I'd wanted was a drama-free summer to focus on my business. Instead, I had an ex-girlfriend who was in love with my brother and an ex-girlfriend who might be conspiring with her cousins to catfish me.

Geni was an easy problem to solve. I'd pressure her to make a move on Nic as soon as possible. The Audra situation? Technically, that was easy to solve, too. I could ghost the entire Houghton family and be done.

But what if Audra was innocent? What about Fiona?

Audra could handle herself. She was tough and snarky and didn't need a bunch of high schoolers.

The image of Fiona sitting by herself at Geni's party came to mind. If she was innocent, then I'd be doing exactly what Audra was worried about. I'd be the kind of guy she wanted to keep away from her sister.

I didn't want to be that guy. Some of my friends were cutthroat, but I'd never considered myself or Ben to be like them. Now was the time to prove it. Somehow I'd figure out who was real and who wasn't, and if Fiona was innocent, I'd stand by her against the guilty party.

And if she wasn't?

A heaviness settled in my chest. If Fiona was guilty? My brain refused to believe she was capable of deception.

Either way, I would find out.

Chapter Thirteen

Fiona

Nicolaus stopped by the house the morning before our date. My family was out shopping, and I'd declined going. After the incident with Uncle George, I couldn't bare to see the disappointment on his face again. So, except for meals when I was required to attend, I remained in my room and interacted with the family as little as possible.

"Cyn told me that you're grounded," he said as he stepped into the house. "That she has to come along with us. That really sucks. How are we supposed to get time alone when she's breathing down our necks?"

I had no doubt she'd do exactly that. My cousin would do everything in her power to ruin my first date, which was why I had to distract her. And I knew exactly how.

"I'm sorry," I said. "Cyn and I got into this stupid fight, and her dad took her side. At least we can still go out."

I motioned to the couch, and Nicolaus sat down. "Can I get you anything? A soda or water or something?"

"No," he smiled at me. "I just wanted to see you. Confirm we were still on for tonight."

"Definitely." I took in a deep breath of air and shored up my courage. He wasn't going to like my suggestion, but I had to figure out a way to make him see my side. "You know," I said, "if you brought someone along, then maybe Cyn would hang out with him instead of us."

"You mean, like a double date?"

"Not exactly," I smiled. "Like a double chaperone. He'd bother her so that she wouldn't bother us."

Nicolaus tilted his head to the side and considered my words. "What exactly are you thinking?"

I held up my hand like I could stop him from rejecting my idea before I said it. "Hear me out. What if you brought someone guaranteed to distract Cyn? Someone who knew how to get her attention and keep it. He could keep her busy, and we could have some privacy because she wouldn't be paying attention to us."

Worry lines formed between his eyebrows. "And you know of someone who fits that description."

"I don't. But you do."

Nicolaus grimaced as he realized who I meant. "No. I'm not inviting my brother. Besides, even if I did, he'd never agree to it."

I sighed. "Then, I guess it will be just the three of us hanging out."

"I could ask one of the other guys," he offered.

"Would they be able to distract her, or would she convince them to gang up on us?" We both knew the answer to that. My cousin was tough. The only guy who seemed able to handle her was her ex.

He groaned and rested his head on the back of the couch. "You couldn't have played nice with Cyn?" he teased, though it felt more like an admonishment.

"You mean be a doormat."

"No," he grabbed my hand, "Of course not. I just meant there was no other way to avoid her?"

I wasn't looking for Nicolaus to be my knight in shining armor and slay the dragon - um, cousin — for me. But it would have been nice if he had taken my side. Had my back. I sighed. "Can't change the past."

"Yeah," he said and squeezed my hand. "Just try not to make the same mistake next time."

I wanted to pull my hand from his grasp and tell him to forget about the date. Not make the same mistake next time? Even if he was kidding, it wasn't funny.

I almost canceled the date. Almost. But I wanted to show my cousin I wasn't a doormat more than I wanted away from this boy. I didn't answer him, and as if the silence was more pressure than he could bear, he finally said, "Fine. I'll ask him."

"Thanks," I said and squeezed his hand with both of mine. "We really will have a great date."

He sighed. "I hope so."

Then I shooed him out the door before my family came home. Now that Nicolaus had agreed to ask. I needed Nathan to agree to come. I'd keep my fingers crossed that he'd say yes, and if he didn't, then he'd have a little visit from Audra. I just hoped that wasn't necessary. But, if I had to, I would. I was in too deep now.

By some miracle, Nathan agreed. Nicolaus texted me within the hour, and I had a video call from Nathan not long after that.

This time, I made sure my door was shut and locked.

"You'd be proud of me," Nathan said.

I raised one eyebrow at him. "For what?"

"I'm doing Fiona a favor."

"Really? What is that?"

Nathan smiled. "I'm sure you know all about Cyn barging in on her date with Nic."

"Yeah," I said.

"Well, my brother asked me to tag along. Distract Cyn so that he can enjoy his date." Nathan waggled his eyes.

I held back a smile. "You know that's my little sister you're talking about."

He laughed. "I wish you were coming instead of Cyn. I could distract you."

"Really?" I asked in a bored tone. "By telling me stories about you and your girlfriend?"

"Who says I won't do that anyway?" he asked and sat up straighter.

I laughed. "That would be mean," I smirked at him, "even for you."

Nathan held his hand over his heart. "Was that? Could that have been? No! Not a compliment."

Raising one eyebrow at him, I drolled, "Only you would find a compliment in an insult."

"Uh, uh," he said and grinned, "you're not taking that from me. You don't hate me anymore. We're making progress."

"Progress?" I scoffed. "Progress toward what? I'm too old for you, remember?"

His smile stayed firmly on his lips. "I have friends of all ages. I'm a likable guy."

"A self-proclaimed likable guy." I tapped my chin, "Maybe the problem is you like yourself too much."

"Maybe the problem is you don't hate me as much as you claim," he said. "Read our chat history, my friend. The evidence is there."

"Whatever," I said and did my best to hide my surprise. Had Cyn been chatting with him? Of course she had. How else would she get her plan to work if she wasn't using Audra to get close to Nathan?

I heard a car door close and knew I needed to hang up fast. "I have to go. But for the record," I took a deep breath, "I'm grateful you agreed to go on Fiona's date."

Then I hung up before I could get his response.

I made plans with Nicolaus to meet him at a local diner. That way, Cyn couldn't refuse to stay with us once she saw our guest. We both agreed that a public surprise was the best way to guarantee her cooperation.

Cyn drove us to the diner, grumbling the whole time that Nicolaus should have picked me up. When we arrived a couple minutes early, we got a booth, and I ensured that she sat with her back to the door while I watched for the guys. After a couple of minutes, Nicolaus and Nathan walked through the door.

They both looked stunning in their own way. Nicolaus wore a button-down shirt over dark jeans, and his hair was slicked back. Nathan was more casual in a fitted t-shirt that showed off his muscular arms and made his blue eyes look like laser beams. They were both handsome, and even though they favored each other, they were gorgeous in their own distinct ways.

I waved at them, ushering them to our booth. As they made their way to us, I said to my cousin, "I have a little surprise for you."

She narrowed her eyes at me, and I smiled back, signaling that her distrust was completely warranted. Seconds later, Nathan slid into the seat next to her.

Cyn's mouth dropped open, and her face turned red. "What are your doing here," she furiously whispered to Nathan.

"I heard these crazy kids had company on their first date. So, I figured I'd join the fun." Nathan grinned at us before turning his full attention to my cousin. "So, Cyn, what's new?"

I watched in delight as my cousin barked out a rude comment to him and then turned her fury to me. "This was your idea, wasn't it?"

"Maybe," I said and smiled.

Nicolaus sat motionless. He hadn't even said hello to me yet. It was like he was afraid Cyn would explode. His brother didn't have that problem.

"Now, Cyn, we both know she wouldn't have done this if you hadn't intruded on her date." He winked at me, and I appreciated his open support. "And I had to ask myself, why would Cyn go on

Fiona's date? I only thought of two answers. One, she wants Nic for herself, or two, she wants my attention. Either way, I needed to be here, too. Because if you steal Nic, then Fiona will need a ride home, and if you're trying to make me take notice. Well," he motioned to his body, "here I am."

"I'd never steal my cousin's date," she scoffed at him. "What kind of person do you think I am?"

He raised his eyebrows, telling the whole table how he'd answer that question.

Nicolaus leaned over to me and whispered, "Looks like you were right. She won't be focusing on us at all. Now the issue is, how do we look away from this train wreck and focus on us?"

I laughed. He had a point. It was extremely entertaining watching my cousin and her ex spar. If you'd told me days ago that I'd be plotting against my cousin with her ex, I wouldn't have believed it. "You're right," I turned to Nicolaus. "So, what's good here? What should I get?"

He pointed to a few items on the menu and showed me his usual selection, a huge burger with a side of onion rings. Then he winked at me, "So, are you one of those old-fashioned girls who don't kiss on the first date? Because if you are, I'm getting the onion rings. If you aren't, I'm getting fries."

I laughed. "Why don't we both get onion rings and leave our options open?"

He leaned back in surprise. "That's a bold suggestion from my shy girl."

"I guess I'm feeling a little bold tonight."

Nicolaus winked. "Then I hope the feeling lasts."

We ordered our food and ate in silence. Cyn, it seemed, was giving Nathan the silent treatment, and after a few minutes of him trying to draw her out, he lapsed into silence and ate his food.

It was awkward trying to have a conversation with my date while we had two silent onlookers staring at us. After the meal, however, we got a chance to distance ourselves from the other couple.

Across the street from the diner was a park. The sun was nearing the horizon, so there was plenty of light as we took a walking trail and strolled through patches of trees and flowerbeds. It was pretty and quaint, and the dimming sunlight was enchanting.

Cyn and Nathan sat on a park bench, and soon we'd left them far behind us.

Nicolaus and I started with the easy questions. Things like favorite music and movies and foods. Least favorite things and pet peeves. He was sweet and charming and never once crossed any lines. He flirted, but it was light and funny. At one point, we even shared the worst pickup lines we'd ever heard — mostly from jokes or social media. Not that either of us had ever used them. He was easy to talk to as long as we kept it light. It was when we ventured into serious topics that I felt the familiar sting of disappointment.

"Who is the last person you dated?" I asked him. "You know I've never been on a date before."

"I don't know how that's possible," he teased.

"All girls school, remember?"

"Oh yeah."

"You didn't answer my question," I nudged him with my elbow.

He shuffled his feet as we strolled. "The last person I dated?" he asked, "or the last person I asked out?"

I grinned at him. "Considering how surprised you were when I didn't immediately accept you, I imagine the last person you asked is the same as the last one you dated."

"Not exactly," he sounded like he'd forced the words through his gritted teeth.

"Now you really have me curious," I teased.

Nicolaus released a long, deep sigh. "If I don't tell you, I'm sure someone else will."

"Exactly," I said. "So, tell me."

"I asked out Genivive," he said. "And she said yes."

"OK, I don't see why you were so reluctant to share that."

"She canceled the next day because she was my brother's girlfriend."

I stopped walking. "What? You asked out your brother's girlfriend?"

"She wasn't when I asked her."

"Wait," I shook my head, totally confused. "I don't understand. You asked her out. She said yes. Then your brother asked her to be his girlfriend, but they weren't already going out. He just asked her out of the blue? Is that right?"

"Yeah," he continued walking, his feet shuffling more.

"And she agreed to be his girlfriend and then canceled your date?"

He nodded.

I felt bad for the guy. That had to suck. "I'm sorry."

He didn't answer.

How rude of Genivive to do that to anyone, much less brothers.

"What is wrong with these people?" I asked. "Don't they have consciouses?"

Nicolaus gave me a weak smile. "I'm thinking not."

"I agree."

We walked silently for a few more minutes. My cousin and his brother came into view. They were sitting at a park bench together, talking. We couldn't hear them, but their body language looked relaxed, like they were having an actual conversation and not trying to kill one another.

"What would you think if Cyn and Nathan got back together?"

Nicolaus raised his eyebrows at me. "That's not likely to happen, is it? I mean, Nathan's never dated the same girl twice."

"But what if they did? Would you think it was weird that we were dating when they were dating?"

He scrunched up his face. "That would be awful," he said. "Can you imagine the jokes people would make about us?"

I sighed. After having such a great date, a part of me had hoped he would be a little deeper, care a little less about his popularity and what other people thought. I'd had high expectations, or that is high hopes, and it was kind of sad to see that he didn't live up to them.

"Then, I guess it's a good thing Nathan doesn't date the same girl twice."

"Yeah," Nicolaus agreed. "It's like dating someone who isn't on the same level. Everyone talks."

"What do you mean same level? Are you talking about money?"

He shrugged. "Money, popularity, social standing. All it does is create gossip."

"But what if those two people really loved each other?"

"How could they?" he asked. "They will never understand each other. They can't relate. One person will expect the finer things in life while the other person will feel guilty if they accept expensive presents because they can't return the favor. It just gets messy."

"You sound like you're talking from experience."

"Not personal experience. I've seen it happen. It's not worth the trouble."

I walked a few more steps, thinking about what my date had said. "So, if my parents were poor, then we couldn't date."

"It wouldn't be practical."

"Love isn't supposed to be practical."

"But it should. It has to be if you're not going to get hurt."

I didn't think it was possible to avoid hurting others. That would mean people didn't care enough. And I wondered if that was this popular group's philosophy. Don't care enough to get hurt.

"This date was about getting to know each other, right?"

He smiled. "Yeah."

"Then I have to be honest," I said. "My uncle is rich. My father isn't. My parents are in another state, using their life's savings to start a new business. They don't have a safety net, and if this business fails, they won't have anything left. I'm afraid, even though I'm Cyn's cousin, I fall into that category you just described."

Nicolaus stopped walking and faced me. "But you're living with Cyn. People will assume you're rich. I did."

"But, I'm not. And when school starts and I'm not wearing the latest fashions or a different pair of shoes ever day, people will know I'm not. I won't pretend to be something I'm not." The guilt hit me full force. I had been pretending to be Audra. Even though I hadn't bought into Cyn's plan, I'd still chatted with Nathan as the fake girl. A bitter taste filled my mouth, and I opened my lips to say more, to confess that I had been the girl at the waterpark, that Audra wasn't real.

"Are you saying we can't date?" Nicolaus asked, and it hit me that he almost sounded happy. Wasn't he even a little disappointed? Or was he so relieved to get out of dating a poor girl that he'd let me think I had called off our relationship?

"I thought that's what you were saying to me," I cautiously said. My ego wanted him to deny that he'd found an easy-out clause with me. My heart was ready to walk away.

"I didn't know you were poor."

"Would you have said something different if you knew?"

"Probably not," he reluctantly said.

That's what I thought.

As we got closer to the other couple, we grew quieter. There were a million little red flags saying it wouldn't work out with Nicolaus, but it was still a little sad to have it thrown in my face for something I had no control over. During my first date.

By unspoken agreement, we left the walking trail and headed toward the others. As soon as we approached, Cyn grinned at me. She was going to get me back for my trick, but I didn't care.

"Genivive is having a party," Cyn announced. "Do you want to go Nicolaus?"

The sadness left his face immediately. "That sounds perfect."

"Do you want to go, Fiona?" That question should have come from my date, not his brother.

I glanced at Nathan and blinked a couple of times. I hadn't spoken to him all evening, so it was weird being addressed directly by him.

"She can't," Cyn spoke for me. "She's grounded. She's only on this date thanks to me. I'm sure my parents wouldn't approve of her attending a party."

She was right. My uncle had only let me keep the date because Cyn had begged. Going to a party wasn't part of the bargain. I faced Nicolaus. "I'm sorry. If you want, we can end our date here so that you can go."

"Yeah," he said. "I'm glad we got to know each other better."

I nodded. It was an obvious goodbye. Not a goodnight, let's do this again some time. Goodbye. We weren't dating again. I knew what he meant, and the grin on my cousin's face said she did, too.

We silently headed toward the parking lot, and as I neared Cyn's car, she had one more surprise for me. "Oh no, Fi, you're riding with Nathan."

We all stared at her. I glanced at Nathan to see his reaction. His stiffened posture said he hadn't expected her statement, either. At least he had the composure not to look like it was the worst idea he'd heard.

My cousin ignored our reactions and continued, "Nathan isn't invited to the party, either. So, he might as well take you home. I'll take Nicolaus to the party and bring him home when it's over."

He wasn't invited? To his girlfriend's party? I slowly shook my head, trying to process what we'd said. It didn't make sense, and I wondered if Nathan was as stunned as I was. Nathan and I stood there and watched my cousin and my date climb into her car and drive off.

"Well, that answers my question," he said. "She was here to steal your date."

Nathan
     "Are you OK," I asked Fiona. She had been quiet on our drive to her house, and I felt bad that my brother had ditched her for Geni's party.

"I'm fine," she said and continued staring out the passenger window.

"I'm sorry my brother is a jerk sometimes. If he had known you couldn't go..."

She cut me off. "He'd have left, anyway. He was ready to escape our date."

Escape? Her voice held no emotion, no passion. Did that mean she didn't care, or that she was so hurt she was numb? "Sounds like you didn't have a good time."

"Oh no," she faced me. In the darkness, her face was illuminated by the dashboard lights, and though it might have been an optical illusion, there were no tear tracks down her cheeks, no blotches from crying, no disappointed frown. "I had a nice time. Nicolaus was a good first date. We just realized that we weren't compatible."

The way she said *first date* sent warning bells ringing in my head. "First date?"

She ducked her head and stared at her hands knotted in her lap. "Yeah. That was my first date. Ever."

I held my groan in. Sometimes my brother was a complete moron. "Did he know that?"

Her laughter echoed in the car's interior. It wasn't bitter or angry or any other emotion I had expected. She genuinely sounded amused. "Yes."

Her laugh was so similar to Audra's. I hadn't noticed that before. Even though Fiona seemed fine, her sister would be furious about this date. I was furious. "So, are you ready for your second date?"

"Not with your brother," she said, though there wasn't any heat to her words. "He's a nice guy, but I'm not interested."

"Not with him," I agreed. "With me."

She sat in stunned silence, and I didn't blame her. We didn't know each other, had never flirted, had never shown an interest in each other. I rushed to explain. "I hate what my brother did, and you still have some time before your curfew, right? Let me salvage the mess Nic made."

"I don't need a pity date. Besides, you haven't asked my uncle, so I don't think I'm allowed."

"OK," I said, surprised she cared about her uncle's rules. Cyn never seemed to care about the restrictions her father set in place. "Not a date-date. A friend date."

"We're not friends," she pointed out.

I smiled. "True. But any girl who can landscape a yard is a girl I want to know more about."

"What?" She sat up straighter in her seat. "This really is a small town," she said to herself, and I laughed.

I had never planned to mention the landscaping to her. To do so meant I might have to tell her about my business arrangement with Ash.

"Who told you?"

I could have lied to her and protected my secret, but I didn't want to play games. I wanted to be completely honest. "Ash," I said and glanced sideways to gauge her reaction.

"Why would Ash tell you?"

"Have you been to Sally's Chicken Shack?" I said as I pulled into their parking lot. "I know we've already eaten, but how about dessert? They have the best apple pie in the world."

"Sure," she said and stared ahead.

As soon as I shut off the car, I rushed to her side to open the door for her, but she'd already opened it and stepped out.

"After you," I motioned to the entrance.

She hesitated and then gave a quick nod and walked inside.

We were shown to a worn-out booth in the corner. I admit the place didn't look like much. In fact, it made Tucker's diner look upscale. But I loved the homey atmosphere. Plus, the waitresses loved me.

"Natey," Mabel, an octogenarian who had more spunk than some people half her age, greeted us. "You brought a date? To this place?" Her expression said she thought I was crazy.

I didn't correct her on the date, because she wouldn't have believed me. "I have to impress the lady, don't I? What better way than Margaret's homemade pie?"

"Ah, flattery is it?" She winked at Fiona. "You know what he wants, don't ya?"

Fiona shook her head. "What?"

"A bigger slice." Mabel said with certainty.

My pseudo-date smiled. "He did say it was the best pie in the world."

"Ack," the woman raised her hands in the air, "you, too? Fine. You both have twisted my arms off. Two extra large slices of Margaret's pie coming up."

As Mabel walked away, Fiona said, "She didn't ask what kind."

"Margaret only makes apple," I shrugged. "Don't know why." I had a brief flashback of when I'd brought Cyn here. I'd made a similar comment, and she had made fun of the woman's mental capacity. I hadn't planned to test Fiona, but I waited for her answer as if I had set her up.

"Probably why it's so good. She's perfected the recipe over the years. She specialized in apples."

I leaned back in my seat. "I hadn't thought of it that way."

Mabel came back with two huge slices of pie with an extra-large scoop of ice cream on top. She asked our drink orders, and returned seconds later with a coffee for me, and a diet soda for Fiona. Then she hovered over us as we took our first bites of pie.

Fiona closed her eyes and moaned in pleasure. "This is incredible, Mabel. Tell Margaret she's ruined me for all other pies."

Mabel laughed. "Your sweet-talking gets you nowhere, girly. You don't get any more."

Fiona widened her eyes and motioned to her dessert plate. "I don't think I can finish this one, much less more."

The older woman grinned and then said to me, "I've done my part in impressing your girl. Now it's your turn." Then she flounced away to help another customer.

"She's awesome," Fiona said and then dove into her pie.

I watched her for a moment before I tackled my own. She wasn't flashy like her sister, her confidence was understated, and I bet people underestimated her. My brother sure had. He'd missed out on getting to know her because he was hung up on Genivive.

Fiona seemed nice. And kind. Traits I hadn't associated with the other Houghton girls. I felt the tug to open up to her, to trust her. I had no idea why, but the way she'd treated Mabel, along with Ash's approval had me willing to risk being truthful with her.

"Ash isn't a gossip," I said, "in case you were wondering."

My statement caught her off guard, and she halted her fork mid-way to her mouth. "Sorry, what?"

"He said a friend helped him with the landscaping. He never said your name."

"Then how did you know it was me?"

"Because he brought you to the Vega farm to review their renovation plans."

"And you know all of this, how?"

I hesitated. This was the moment. I either opened up to her or I found a way to downplay my involvement. With a sigh, I blurted out, "I'm Ash's business partner."

She blinked several times and then set her fork on her plate without taking a bite. "Now I'm really confused."

"Ash was looking for some extra work, and I wanted to try some business ideas I had."

"Flipping houses?" she interrupted.

"Yeah," I shrugged, "I was already working with Mr. Vega on his store, and Ceara and Ash were involved in that. So, I asked Ash if he'd be the muscle and I'd be the money."

Fiona's eyes dropped to my arms. "Why couldn't you be the muscle?"

She wasn't flirting with me, but I was flattered, anyway. I patted my bicep. "You noticed these, huh?"

Fiona pursed her lips in disapproval. "It wasn't a compliment. Just an observation."

I grinned at her. "And I feel complimented that you observed."

The corners of her lips lifted slightly, though she kept the stern expression on her face. "Why make Ash do all the manual labor when you're capable of helping?"

Sighing, I said, "Because I don't know what to do. Ash has taught me a few things, but mostly whenever I try, I slow him down."

"Oh," she said and picked up her fork. My honesty seemed to surprise her, and she slowly nibbled on her dessert as she contemplated what I'd said.

I dug into my pie and let her think. I needed to do my own thinking. Fiona wasn't what I had expected. She wasn't mean-spirited like Cyn, she seemed to care about others. Most of my friends would have blindly accepted that Ash Ellis was my paid manual labor. They wouldn't have questioned why I was willing to sit back and let him do all the work while I threw around my money.

Only Ben would have expected me to lift a finger on the project. In this moment, I felt like this stranger knew me better than most of the people I'd known my whole life.

"You could choose one task and learn it well," she finally said. "That way you could contribute more."

With one statement, I felt like this girl knew my soul. That she saw beyond what others typically accepted. She saw through the smokescreen of wealth.

When I didn't answer her, she said, "You don't strike me as the kind of person who's willing to let others do everything for you. You're a take action kind of guy."

"What makes you say that?" I totally agreed, but how she saw it, I had no clue.

She motioned to the table where our barely eaten pie sat before us. "You decided to fix your brother's mistake, make my first date one I want to remember. You were willing to distract Cyn in the first place. You," she cut off her words and blushed. "I just think you like being part of the solution."

Now it was my turn to be stunned. I blinked a couple of times and then said, "I've never thought of it that way. But I think you're right."

She smiled and took another bite of pie.

This girl blew me away. It wasn't her looks, though she did look beautiful tonight. It was the way she saw through what everyone else assumed. Like she saw the real me, when I hadn't even given myself credit. She was open and honest and kind, and I found myself totally fascinated by the girl. I could completely see her hanging out with Ash, Ceara and me, working side by side, laughing. My heart picked up its rhythm. I wanted that. I wanted her as part of my inner circle. I wanted her to get to know Ben. I wanted her to know me. The revelation surprised me, and I focused on my pie. For the first time in my life, I wasn't blown away by the flavor of Margaret's concoction. All of my senses were too focused on examining why I felt so connected with Fiona.

We ate in comfortable silence for the next ten minutes. We didn't talk, but we didn't need to.

When Mabel set down the paper check on the table, she asked Fiona, "Did my boy do good? Impress you?"

Fiona smiled. "Beyond my expectations."

Mabel patted me on the shoulder. "Good job, Natey. This one is worth the effort."

I smirked as Fiona blushed. "Thanks, Mabel," I said, "I always want your approval."

"Smart aleck," she playfully popped my shoulder. "You always want pie."

"That, too," I winked at her, and Mabel walked away laughing.

I reached for the check, and Fiona laid her hand over mine. "No," she said, "my treat."

"Did you not hear the story about my business?" I laughed. "I have money."

"Yes, and I also saw that you paid for the whole table's meal earlier. Nicolaus and Cyn didn't even pretend to try to pay." She frowned. "Just because you have a business doesn't mean people should expect you to spend your money on them."

My heart slowed its pace, and I leaned forward, searching for any other meaning than what she'd said. I couldn't determine one. I heard my voice say, "They don't know about my business."

This time Fiona leaned forward in confusion. "Then why? Why did they do that?"

"My dad gives us a generous allowance. People expect me to pay." I shrugged it off like it wasn't a big deal, even though I was realizing it kind of was.

She slid her fingers between mine and squeezed my hand. "You will never pay for anything else of mine. Ever."

I laughed and squeezed her hand back. "Of course I will. I like doing things for other people."

She sat back and tugged her fingers away from mine. I firmed my grip and didn't let her pull back. She sighed. "Nicolaus was right. Rich people and poor people can't date."

"My brother said that?" When she nodded, I said, "What an idiot."

"No," she said, "We're just hanging out, and money's getting in the way. You insist on buying things because money isn't a big deal to you, and I refuse to accept because money is a huge deal to me."

I released her fingers and let her arm retreat back to her side of the table. She saw this as a real obstacle to our friendship. All because my brother was a moron.

She may have had an insight into the real me, but she didn't know how determined I was when I wanted something. I rarely questioned my instincts. It's what made me a great player on the field.

And my instincts were telling me not to give up so easily on this girl. "Then let's get money out of the way," I said. "You were spot on with the landscaping, and you're right about the small touches you added to Ceara's design for the store. You take what we've done to the next level. So, you can be our finisher or stager or whatever you want to call yourself."

"You're offering me a job?" she asked.

I nodded. Though it wasn't the complete truth. I was offering more than a job. I was offering a chance to be part of my closest group of friends, to hang out with the people who knew me better than anyone else. Others who saw beyond the dollar signs associated with my name. I was offering the real me.

My throat tightened as I waited for her response.

She narrowed her eyes. "I'm not sure what you want me to do, but if you have legitimate work, then I accept. I won't be paid to do nothing."

My heart returned to its steady rhythm, and I leaned back in the booth. This night had been full of surprises. I'd expected to spend my time harassing Cyn as she tried to ruin her cousin's date.

In the end, Cyn had gotten what she wanted, but none of us could have imagined the ripple effect. Cyn had stolen Nic and left me stuck with her awkward cousin.

But I had discovered a new friend. One I couldn't wait to learn more about.

The added benefit was she might help me uncover Audra's secret. Because this girl was too honest to be part of whatever was happening with Audra's profile. But she might hold the answers I was searching for.

Chapter Fourteen

Fiona
  I felt sick.

Last night with Nathan had been amazing. If he had been my first date, I would have been floating around my room, not caring that I was stuck with my family who hated me, that I was grounded, that Cyn was now openly hostile. Nathan was the first person in Wildwood that I had really connected to. I really liked Ash and felt like I could be friends with Ceara. But Nathan?

I could fall for Nathan.

Except I was a liar and a phony and a chicken.

He had offered me a job which I still wasn't sure what he wanted me to do. But this business was important to him, I could see it written all over his face. And he was letting me be a part of it. I didn't know how many others knew about how he made his money, but I was honored to be one of them.

He'd let me in, opened up the real him. And I was a two-faced backstabber. No, make that a one-faced, two-personality liar.

I stared at my ceiling, not wanting to get up and face the day. Not wanting to see what fresh new drama my cousin had planned. I didn't need her to beat me up; I was doing a great job on myself.

But peace wasn't on the agenda for today.

Cyn swept into my room without knocking. She floated around the space, adding in an occasional twirl. "Isn't this the most beautiful day?" she asked as she hopped on my bed and pulled back my curtains. The sunlight shone through my windows and made me squint into my now bright room.

"What are you so happy about?" I said.

Cyn grinned at me, her expression hinting that I wouldn't like what she had to say. "Everything is coming together beautifully. Nathan is now single, and Audra can go in for the kill."

"Nathan single?" How did that happen? When did that happen?

"He definitely is," Cyn smirked. "He just might not know it yet."

I sat up in my bed and stared at my cousin. "What do you mean?" If Nathan didn't know it, then that meant Genevieve had dumped him. Or maybe... "Did something happen at the party last night?"

Apparently I had asked the one question Cyn wanted me to. Her grin stretched widely across her face. "You could say that." She smirked at me. "Apparently your date was quite happy to escape you last night." She laughed and tilted her chin in a smug expression. "Almost as soon as we walked in the doors, he went to Genevieve and the next thing I knew they were making out in a corner."

"Are you kidding me?" I knew that Nicolaus was a bit shallow, but I didn't think he was capable of stealing his brother's girlfriend. I felt bad for Nathan. Granted, he didn't seem very happy with his girlfriend, but to have her publicly dump him had to be a hit to his ego.

"So all I have to do," my cousin said, "is make sure he knows he's available. Then Audra can swoop in and be his shoulder to cry on."

I had felt sick earlier. Now I was completely nauseous. I knew what she had planned next. There was no way she was going to make her move via text messaging. "I'm not going to do it," I said before she could even suggest it.

"You act like you have a choice. Need I remind you you're already grounded for talking to Nathan. What do you think my parents will do if they find out you didn't go straight home last night?"

My mouth dropped open in shock. How did she know? She was at the party. Had Nathan said something? Had he posted something online? That didn't seem like him. But I couldn't think of another way that she would know where I was. "How?"

"You really are naïve," she said with disdain. "Figure it out. But until then, just know that you can't go sneaking around without me finding out. You're just lucky that I'm in a good mood this morning."

"I don't care." She could do whatever she wanted to to me, but I wasn't going along with this scheme against Nathan. I wanted to be his friend. And that meant my role as Audra had to stop. Today.

Cyn grinned at me. "So what exactly were you doing at that restaurant? And how did you get there? Please," she rolled her eyes, "don't tell me you were there with Ash."

I held myself completely still as I processed what she said. She obviously hadn't seen me there; otherwise, she would have known who I was with. How would she react if I told her that Nathan had taken me? I liked that she didn't know, and I relaxed a bit. "Does it really matter who I was with?"

She smiled and assumed that she had guessed correctly. "I hope you really enjoyed yourself," she said. "Because you won't be doing that again for a long, long time. If you refuse to help me, I'll make sure you never leave this room again."

"Nathan got dumped. In front of all of your friends. Genevieve humiliated him. Isn't that enough?"

"No! Because she did it. Not me. He needs to know that I will not be disrespected. He made a fool of me, and he will pay. And now that Genevieve has publicly embarrassed him, I have to step up my game."

"Is that all you care about? Your ego? No one is even worried about the fact that he isn't dating you anymore. In fact," I had an idea. A last-ditch attempt to change her mind. "I bet people will be saying he should have stayed with you. Because you wouldn't have done that."

"They'll say it even more when Audra dumps him," she said.

My heart sank. She was determined to hurt him. Nothing I said or did was going to change that. But maybe there was a way I could turn it to my advantage. "Does he have to fall in love with her? I mean," I chose my words carefully, "if she publicly rejected him now, wouldn't that be good enough?"

Cyn smiled as she considered my proposal. "Interesting," she said, "pour salt into his wound. I didn't think you had that kind of cruelty in you, Fiona."

It was mean. But in my mind, it was a lot nicer to do this now rather than break his heart later. If I couldn't prevent her from going forward with her plan, maybe I could minimize the damage. "You said that he didn't like the Danvers. What if we used them?"

My cousin nodded with approval. "I like where this is going. What do you have in mind?"

"What if Audra rejected Nathan and then made it official with Oscar? He would go along with it, don't you think?"

She laughed. "That sounds perfect. Then, he'll have had two rejections in a row, and he'll realize he should have appreciated me more. I will graciously welcome him back. And he'll know better than to dump me again."

"You can't still want to date him."

"Of course I do."

I stared at my cousin in complete disgust. "You want to tear him down, hurt his ego, and make him think that you are the only option he has for a girlfriend? That's horrible, Cyn. I can't believe you would do that to anyone."

"Before you get all high and mighty, cousin dear, don't forget what he did to me. He's not innocent in this. He deserves what he gets."

But he didn't. I didn't know Nathan's side of the story. Why he dumped my cousin for her best friend. Maybe I was naïve. But the guy that I'd spent last night with didn't seem like the kind of guy who would do that. He seemed kind and genuine, and he was funny, and he was sweet. And maybe he'd made mistakes. But so had I. My gaze wandered to my laptop.

Cyn noticed the direction of my gaze. "No time like the present, Cousin. It's show time." She grabbed my laptop from my desk and brought it over to us. She flipped it on and logged into Audra's account.

"I can't talk to Nathan like this," I motion to my hair and face.

"You did when you were blubbering like a baby," she wrinkled her nose at me, "Trust me, this is a better look."

She scrolled around the screen for a minute and then said, "It's your lucky day. He's not logged in right now."

She pulled up a message and quickly typed *I just heard the news. I'm so sorry. Do you need anything?*

Then she hit send and logged out of that account. "Let the games begin," she laughed. "Now I need to sweet talk Oscar into our plan. That shouldn't be hard."

She bounded off my bed and practically danced to the door. "Play your cards right," she said, "and maybe I'll convince my parents to lift your grounding. Maybe." She cackled as she left the room.

I knew better than to trust Cyn and her promises.

And I hated how determined she was to hurt Nathan.

But what I hated more was that I had a role in it.

Nathan
 I woke up to a ton of text messages. Most of them were pictures from my so-called friends of my brother making out with Genevieve. If she had been my girlfriend, I would've been mad. If I cared for her and thought she cared for me, it would've hurt. But the great thing about having a deal with your ex girlfriend was no one got

hurt. She had finally made her move on Nic, and I was officially free.

I needed to clear the air with my brother first. But after that, I wanted to talk to someone. Someone who would understand what was going through my head. My first thought was Fiona. Which was stupid. We'd only connected last night. Before then we had barely interacted. So why would she be the first person I wanted to talk to after I was officially broken up with my girlfriend? It didn't make sense.

I could talk to Ceara. But she would only gloat that I never should have dated Genevieve in the first place. Ash and I were friends. But we didn't talk about our personal lives. And Ben, he would listen and understand, but he was currently in his own drama with his stepbrother Bobby.

I logged onto social media and went to Genevieve's account. There, in black and white for all the world to see, was her relationship status. Dating Nic.

I got dressed and went to the kitchen, and sat across the table from my brother, who refused to look me in the eyes.

"So you had quite a day yesterday," I said.

Nic reluctantly met my gaze. "I'm sorry." He grimaced as if waiting for me to lash out at him.

"It's only fair, right? You asked her out first."

I wasn't going to get into the whole defense that she had asked me. The most important thing was they were together, and they had my full support. I wanted out of that drama as quickly and neatly as I possibly could be.

"So you're not mad?" Nic narrowed his eyes at me.

"I should be," I said and shrugged, "but it was obvious that she and I weren't compatible. If she makes you happy, then I'm fine with it."

Nic leaned away from me. He didn't believe me, and that was okay. The only way I'd gain his trust was for him to see I truly didn't care.

We ate our breakfast in silence, with Nic giving me brief looks as if he expected me to attack any minute. I ignored his suspicion and let my mind roam to his disastrous date with Fiona and my attempt to make her feel better. I wondered how she felt this morning. I knew without a doubt that Cyn would rub the latest news in her face. That immediately after her first date with Nic, he connected with someone else. I hoped that didn't hurt Fiona too bad. Though it had to sting. She had to care for my brother, at least a tiny bit. Otherwise, why would she have accepted his date? I rejected the idea that Fiona had a crush on Nic. She was too smart to fall for someone as shallow as him. Still, I wondered if she was okay.

It would be perfectly fine as a new friend for me to check on my friend. There wasn't anything weird or wrong about me wanting to make sure she was okay. It didn't mean anything more than exactly that. We had become friends, and I looked out for my friends.

Anything else was just blowing a simple situation out of proportion.

In fact, I wouldn't be surprised if her number was one of the many who had sent me a message to make sure that I was okay. I rushed through my breakfast and then went upstairs and grabbed my phone. I scrolled through all the numbers. But they were all people already on my contact list. No new numbers, no potential for Fiona to have texted me.

Maybe she didn't have my number and didn't want to ask her cousin for it. That would make complete sense.

I logged onto social media, but the only message that I had was from Audra. I stared at Audra's words and tried not to be a little disappointed. The message was kind and thoughtful. But it hadn't come from the profile I wanted.

I tamped down my disappointment and sent a quick note to Audra. *Thanks, I'm okay.*

I hovered over Fiona's profile. We weren't connected on social media. And as a new friend, it wouldn't be weird or strange to make that connection online. But I hesitated. My brother had just publicly embarrassed her. Even if very few people knew that they had gone out. Was she solely focused on the hurt and embarrassment that she felt? Maybe that's why she hadn't reached out to me. Would it be the right thing to do to connect with her?

I wasn't sure. Even though she could read me, I struggled reading her. But I had promised myself I'd be more direct. And that's what I would do. If this wasn't the right time or she took it the wrong way, then I'd explain myself.

I clicked on the button that requested a connection between the two of us. Now the ball was in her court. What happened to our friendship was up to her. But if she needed me, she'd see I was there.

Chapter Fifteen

Fiona

"Thanks, I'm okay." Cyn mocked. "That's all he has to say to us? We're trying to be a friend to him, and he brushes us off. What a jerk." She took one pillow off my bed and threw it across the room.

I held in my smile. My cousin's plan would never work if Nathan wasn't interested in Audra or her fake sympathy. "Maybe he didn't want to talk about it," I said.

Cyn took another pillow off my bed and threw it in the opposite direction. "What are we supposed to do with that? He didn't leave us any openings."

I shrugged. "I don't know. Maybe give it some time. Maybe he just needs some space."

My cousin scowled at me. I was sure she wanted to throw another pillow, but there were none left on my bed. "Give him some space? If we don't strike now, some other girl is going to snatch him up. A guy like Nathan never stays single for too long. He always has girls throwing themselves at his feet."

"Well, maybe that's where Audra's different. Maybe she gets his attention by being his friend. Not coming on too strong."

Cyn huffed and retrieved my pillows from the floor. "You know nothing."

It was getting harder not to smile. Obviously my cousin wasn't the revenge mastermind she thought she was. Either that or she didn't know Nathan at all. Sure, she'd known him well enough to hook him in the first place. But all the bait she was throwing out to catch him with Audra wasn't working.

"Maybe he doesn't like her," I said. That would be the best thing ever. If he wasn't interested in Audra, then nothing Cyn tried would matter. And the thought of Cyn's plans being thwarted because Nathan didn't care about Audra made me very happy. Although, if I was honest with myself, that meant that he wouldn't be interested in me, either. Not that I ever planned to date the guy. But I couldn't shake the warm, fuzzy feeling I had whenever I thought about our friend date.

Cyn flipped open my laptop and logged into Audra's account. "Nothing," she said, "absolutely nothing."

She slammed the lid closed. "Hey!" I said. "Don't break my laptop."

She ignored me. She got a notification on her phone and pulled it out of her pocket. With a frustrated groan, she threw the phone onto my bed, nearly missing me.

"What was that?"

"Oscar being a jerk."

"I take it he didn't agree to the plan." I struggled to hide my happiness. It seemed Cyn's plan was blowing up from multiple directions.

"No," she plopped down into my desk chair, "he said you were too young for him. He said go for Charlie."

"So Audra is supposed to fall in love with Charlie Danvers?"

My cousin pounded her fist on my desk. "He told *me* to date Charlie."

I shrugged. "What's wrong with that? Didn't you say Nathan was jealous of Charlie?"

Cyn placed her hands over her face. "None of this is working out. I've got to rethink my plan."

I didn't press her on my question, even though I found it completely fascinating that she threw away the idea as soon as Charlie was involved. I had gotten the impression from our outing that maybe Charlie was interested in my cousin. So maybe Cyn had a shred of humanity left and didn't want to string along a friend. I sat there quietly while she swung back and forth in my chair. Her frown etched deeper and deeper as whatever thoughts she processed didn't give her the results she wanted.

Without a word she stood up, grabbed her phone and left my room, slamming the door behind her. I breathed a sigh of relief. More than anything, I hoped this meant that she was giving up her revenge plan on Nathan. Hoped, not expected.

I grabbed my laptop to make sure she hadn't done any damage to it. I was frustrated when I saw a tiny crack in the plastic casing at the corner of the computer. When I got a chance, I'd find some duct tape to tape over the tiny crack. It would be ugly, but hopefully would prevent the case from cracking further. I couldn't afford to buy another laptop just because my cousin threw a temper tantrum.

I logged into my social media account. I still had a feeble number of connections, but I noticed I had two new requests. Ceara Vega. Nathan Hollingsworth. I immediately accepted Ceara's, grateful that she was giving me a chance. My mouse hovered over the accept button for Nathan. Of course I wanted to connect with him. I wanted to be his friend. And the fact that he sent the request hopefully meant he felt the same. That he didn't regret the offer he had made last night.

I sucked in a deep breath of air and quickly clicked the mouse button, accepting the connection. Seconds later, I had a message from him.

So yesterday...

I waited for him to say more, and when he didn't I typed back *yeah, yesterday.*

Apparently it was the right thing to say, because he immediately came back with *how are you?*

I should be asking you. It seems like your brother dumped us both yesterday. It was a little bolder than I had intended to state it, but there was no point sugar-coating the truth.

That's one way of putting it.

So, are you okay?. The issue with messaging was not knowing how the other person sounded. I didn't know how he felt about Genevieve, but I really hoped he wasn't heartbroken over her betrayal.

Instead of texting back, I got a video request. My hands shook as I accepted the call.

"Are you okay?" he said. Before I had a chance to ask him.

I shrugged. "Except for worrying about my friend, I'm okay."

He smiled at me. "Then we are in the same boat. Geni and Nic are perfect for each other. So, I'm glad they worked it out."

I sat back in my seat and stared at the face coming from the screen. It was a lot harder to read body language via technology. But from what I could tell, he seemed completely open and honest. "If they were perfect for each other, why did you date her?"

I wasn't sure if it was a glitch of the video or if Nathan was actually blushing. "If I tell you, it's going to make me look really bad. I don't think I'm ready to put our friendship to that kind of test yet." He grinned at me.

"You've dumped my cousin to date her best friend. There's not much else you could say that would make you look worse," I smiled at him to soften how harsh my words sounded.

He let out a surprised bark of laughter, and too late I realized that I'd responded like Audra. Not Fiona.

"But," I scrunched up my face, "we all do stupid things."

He rubbed his hands together. "Oh, that sounds juicy. Care to share?"

I raised my eyebrows at him. "I don't think I'm ready to put our friendship to that kind of test yet."

J. LEIGH JAMES

Nathan's lips twisted into a tight grin. "Well played, Houghton. Well played."

"So let's agree that will save that conversation for another day. Okay?" I shocked myself by almost winking at him, amazed at how easy it was to flirt with him. It shouldn't have felt so natural, so easy.

"Works for me," he said. "Are you sure you're okay?"

"Absolutely."

"Good," he said, "so how about a little outing tomorrow?"

"I wish I could. But I'm grounded, remember?" My uncle hadn't given me an end date to the punishment, and I was sure if Nathan was involved, he'd turn down any request I made.

"Even if it means a part-time job?"

That, I wasn't sure. I knew they expected us to have a carefree summer, but maybe having a job would ease their restrictions on me. "What do you have in mind?"

"Well, partly it involves an idea I have for the Vega Farms goat milk products. And partly it means supporting Ceara's soap-making class at the library."

"I'll ask my aunt and uncle," I said, "that's all I can do."

He nodded. "The class starts at 2 PM tomorrow. If they agree you can go, I'll pick you up at 1:30."

I laughed. "There is no way they are going to allow you in this house. Did you forget you're enemy number one here?"

Nathan leaned forward in his seat, his blue eyes piercing me even through our screens. "Really? Even after what Nic did to you, I'm the villain?"

I shrugged. "All they know is you hurt Cyn. In their eyes, that's unforgivable. If they let me go to the class tomorrow, then I'll walk there. It's not that far away. And I'll have a better chance of getting their approval if I go by myself."

Nathan's lips twisted with amusement. "We're sneaking around?"

I ignored the connotation of those words and the small thrill that ran up my spine. "No," I raised my chin and looked down my nose at him, "I'm going to support Ceara."

He laughed. "What a coincidence. I am, too."

"Then I'll ask. Wish me luck," I said.

He crossed his fingers and held them in front of the camera. "Good luck, Fi. I hope I see you tomorrow." Then he signed off.

I quickly signed off and shut my laptop. Placing my hand over my chest, I willed my heart to slow down its beating. He wasn't asking me on a date. He was thinking about his business. We were becoming friends. That's all. And the fact that he was handsome and charming was not important.

I gave myself a few minutes to calm down while I thought about how I would approach Aunt Lisa and Uncle George about the soap-making class tomorrow. I took several deep breaths, with my plan in my head, and slowly made my way to the living room where they were watching TV. I hoped my approach worked.

Because I really wanted to see Ceara tomorrow. And Nathan.

Nathan

I paced around the small meeting room the library had set aside for Ceara's class. When the old Victorian house had been someone's home, I imagined this was someone's bedroom. Now it was an open space lined with chairs and one long table set across the front. Ceara had set up all of her materials and was anxiously waiting for people to show up. There was 15 minutes before her demonstration, and she fidgeted with various items in the room as we waited for other people to show.

"Why are you so nervous? I'm the one giving the demonstration." She placed her hands on her hips, and I walked away from the doorway where I'd been examining passersby.

I couldn't tell her the real reason that I was on edge. I hadn't heard from Fiona since yesterday. I didn't know if she was going to make it, or if she had gotten into worse trouble simply by trying to attend. If she did get permission to come, did that mean that she had to bring Cyn with her? Was she always going to have a chaperone whenever she wanted to do something? I just wanted her to show up. One, because I wanted her to see Ceara's process and hear my idea for creating new and unusual combinations of scented soaps and two, I wanted to know she was okay.

"Do you think Ash will come?" Ceara said. "I invited him for moral support. But I don't want to make a fool of myself in front of him."

I walked over to her and placed my hand on her shoulder. "You're going to be amazing. How many soaps have you made in your lifetime?"

"Too many to count," she laughed.

"Then you're going to do great. So don't worry." I pushed aside my own concerns for Fiona and concentrated on supporting my friend.

"But what if no one shows?" She frowned at the thirty empty chairs staring back at her.

"People will show. Even if I have to drag them into the room." I turned from her like I was going to make good on the threat.

Ceara laughed. "Please don't. How embarrassing would that be?"

I heard a noise behind me and turned to see Mabel walk into the room. Right behind her was Margaret. Ceara greeted the older ladies and gave them hugs. "What are you doing here?"

"Supporting our favorite girly," Mabel said and gave her a kiss on the cheek.

"Thank you so much," Ceara visibly relaxed.

In the next few minutes, half of the seats in the room were filled. But Fiona wasn't there. I brushed away my disappointment. She had wanted to be here. I knew if she could, she would. But obviously she was still grounded. A couple minutes before Ceara was scheduled to start, Ash walked through the door. As soon as my friend saw him, she grinned and all her nervous energy fled.

It was nice to see that. Even though they hadn't admitted to each other how they felt, it was obvious to anyone watching. They had a bond. They supported each other, and they were there for each other. When one was around, the other felt invincible.

One day I'd have that. I didn't know when. But one day.

Since I really didn't care how to make soap, I took a seat in the last row in the back of the room. Ceara took her place by the table and grinned at Mabel and Margaret, who were sitting in the front row. As she started to introduce herself, someone sat in the seat next to me. They leaned over and whispered to me, "I'm so sorry I'm late. Have I missed much?"

Without turning my head away from Ceara's demonstration, I leaned over and whispered to Fiona, "You're just in time."

My whole body relaxed. I hadn't realized how tense I was waiting for her, worrying about her. We sat there in silence as Ceara taught her class, me simply watching the show, Fiona furiously taking notes in a notebook she brought along.

When Ceara was done, she opened it up for questions and almost immediately Fiona raised her hand. She asked something about the temperature of the ingredients, and Ceara answered her question confidently. Then others asked questions and before we knew it, the librarian was at the door signaling our time was up.

Fiona rushed to the front of the room and began helping Ceara pack up her stuff while she shared her congratulations on a successful class. Ash and I joined in, and Mabel and Margaret stood there and chatted while we all worked.

"This is cause for celebration," Mabel said. "You did such a superb job, girly. I'm so proud of you."

Margaret's voice was softer, more demure than her sister's. "I baked a fresh pie today," she said.

"I'm so bummed," Fiona said. "I have to go back home."

"How can Natey celebrate without his girl?" Mabel winked at me.

I avoided Ash's and Ceara's gazes. I knew they'd have tons of questions about why Mabel thought Fiona was my girl.

"Did you drive here?" I asked her.

Fiona shook her head. "I walked."

"How about I give you a ride home?" I offered. "It's on the way." It wasn't exactly on the way to Sally's. But it wasn't completely out of the way, either.

"That's not the best idea," she said. "Public enemy number one, remember?"

"Then I'll give you a ride to the end of your street. And you can walk the rest of the way. Sneaking around, remember?" I teased her and held back my grin when a slight flush covered her face.

She shook her head. But I got the impression it was more about my tenacity than it was her refusal to ride with me. I wanted to hear how things went down with her family, and I knew she wouldn't want an audience. When she didn't say anything, I said, "Well, that's settled. Let's get you home. Because I have pie waiting on me."

The others laughed, and Fiona and I walked to my car. Without thinking, I grabbed her hand and led her to where I had parked. It just seemed natural, and I hadn't noticed I'd done it until I let her hand go to open the passenger door for her. She refused to meet my eyes, and that's when I realized I might've crossed a line. But she didn't say anything, so I didn't bring it up.

LOVE YOU LIKE A CATFISH

Going forward, I just needed to be aware of my impulses. I didn't want to ruin this friendship before it even began.

Chapter Sixteen

Fiona

"You know this isn't necessary," I said, "This ride will only take two minutes." I laughed.

"That means we can sit in the car for 10 minutes and chat and then I can drop you home."

My heart hammered in my chest. Even though I knew he wanted to talk business, it felt way too intimate sitting in his car all alone. To dispel this false sense of intimacy, I dove into the topic. "So what was your business idea?"

He turned on his car to get the air conditioning going and cool us down from the heat of the afternoon. He turned on his radio, so that music played softly in the background. It didn't help my nerves at all.

"I want to experiment with essential oils and the Vegas' soaps. Maybe create an aromatherapy line that would be unique and not something that anyone could get anywhere. If we get the right combination of products, then the Vegas could open an online store, and we could reach a wider market."

The idea wasn't bad. "Do the Vegas want an online store?" I didn't know a lot about their business, but from what I had seen, all the products were made by Ceara. If they adopted Nathan's idea, then they would need help.

"Not exactly," he said. "But I want to get a plan together and convince them to at least try. I think they're doing something special, and I want to help them make it big."

"They're not the only all-organic, goat milk beauty line out there," I said. "You can try adding new scents, but I don't know if that's going to make them unique enough. Especially if they're not interested."

He drummed his fingers on the steering wheel.

"I'm sorry if that messed up your plan," I said, "but I have to be honest with you."

"That's what I appreciate about you, Fiona." He turned sideways in his seat and faced me. His eyes searched my face, making me feel as if the space between us had shrunk. "You tell me the truth."

I wanted to sink into my seat. I told him the truth. About most things. But there was one big lie between us. And I wasn't confident enough in our friendship to reveal it.

I glanced out the passenger window. "I'm not saying you can't do this. I just want you to be aware of the competition."

"Hey," I felt his hand on my forearm, "I'm not mad. I appreciate the advice."

"Maybe instead of the product being unique," I said. "Maybe your marketing should be unique." I didn't want to have a conversation about our friendship. I didn't want him reminding me that I wasn't what he thought. That I wasn't completely truthful with him. I hoped that keeping his mind to the business aspect would prevent us from having a conversation I wasn't ready to have. I'd have it one day. Just not today. Or any time soon.

"Like what?"

I don't know," I said. I thought about his other venture with Ash. How they had renovated the house and had sold it. "What if you combined the two businesses?"

He was silent for a minute. "Like air fresheners or something?"

"Or," I bit my bottom lip as I thought. "A Welcome Home gift basket with products from local companies," I said slowly.

"That's not bad," he said. "Not bad at all."

I gave him a small smile, happy that I had given him an idea and happy that we had avoided other topics. He pulled on his seatbelt and drove the car from the parking lot. As we drove the short distance to my street, he began brainstorming the different products, different companies that could be included in the welcome-home package. He even mentioned contacting realtors to see if they'd like to go in the venture. The more he talked about it, the more excited he got, and I watched him, barely holding in my smile. His enthusiasm was contagious, and he reminded me of a kid opening presents at their birthday party. I was sure not many people got to see this side of Nathan, and I was honored I was one of them.

When we got to the end of the street, he pulled to the side of the road and reached for my hand. "You have some great ideas, Fiona. Thanks for sharing them with me."

I shrugged and unbuckled my seatbelt. The feeling of our space shrinking returned, and I found it difficult to draw in a full breath of air. "That's what friends are for," my voice held a slightly breathless quality, and I hoped he hadn't noticed.

"Friends," he said and narrowed his eyes as he examined my face.

I nodded and ignored the heat building in my cheeks. "At least I hope so," I said.

He had an unreadable expression, and I wondered what was going through his head. His eyes traced the outline of my eyes, my nose, my lips, and I got the impression there was something he wanted to say. But I was afraid of what it might be.

"This was fun," I rushed to say, "Thanks for inviting me." Then I slipped out of the car as quickly as possible, gave him a quick wave goodbye and hurried down my street. I had the weird sensation that I was running away, although that didn't make sense to me.

I'd planned to lock myself in my room and relive what had just happened. Hopefully, I'd sort out my tangled emotions. However, the minute I walked into the house, I knew something was wrong.

Aunt Lisa met me at the door and wordlessly crooked her finger to follow her. She led me into their dining room where Uncle George and Cyn were waiting. "Do you have anything you want to tell us?" she said as she sat down and motioned for me to take a seat.

I glanced at my cousin, and her smug expression said she'd thrown me under the bus. Over what, though, I had no idea. And I wasn't going to confess to anything until I knew what I'd been accused of.

"Is something wrong?" I asked.

Aunt Lisa's expression darkened. Of course it was the wrong thing to say. I never said what she wanted to hear.

"So you're going to deny everything?" Aunt Lisa said.

"I'll tell you the truth," I vowed to her. "I just don't know what you want me to say."

"You said you were going to the library," my aunt said, "You failed to mention going with Nathan Hollingsworth."

"I didn't go with him," I said and rushed to continue, "I met him there. Along with Ash Ellis. Because Ceara Vega was teaching soap making, and we wanted to show her support. So when I asked to go to the soap-making class, that's exactly what I was doing."

"Then why did he give you a ride home?" Cyn leaned forward and grinned at me.

I had told them I would say the truth, and I meant it. "He offered me a ride home, and I took it." Even though I knew it would get me in trouble, I had to know. "How did you find out?"

Cyn opened her phone and clicked open an app. A tracking app. "You really should learn technology, Cousin," she said. She clicked one of the menu items, and I saw that she had a tracking for Nathan, as well.

"How are you doing that?"

She laughed. "It's easy. You get the phone and install the app. I installed it on yours when you got here, and I installed it on Nathan's when we were dating. I got suspicious after I found you chatting with him online. That you had a secret relationship with my ex-boyfriend. That my best friend wasn't the reason he broke my heart. You were." She ended that statement with an award-winning sob.

"That's not true," I pleaded to my aunt and uncle to believe me even though I knew it was useless. "He broke up with her the second day that I was here. I'd never even met him before."

"I don't know how you did it," she actually had tears rolling down her face. The girl was an excellent actress. "We opened our home to you. And you played all innocent while Mommy and I were talking about setting you up. But the real set up was you stealing my boyfriend. All because you wanted to be popular." Cyn buried her face in her hands, and her crying sounded completely real.

"I'm so disappointed," Uncle George said. "I know your situation was hard. But I just don't understand why you would do this to us."

His heartbroken expression made me want to cry. "I didn't do it."

But they weren't listening to me.

Aunt Lisa smirked as she held out her hand toward me. "I will take your phone now. I've already removed your laptop from your room. You will have no more contact with Nathan. Or any of Cyn's friends. We are calling your parents tonight and demanding that they get you. Now go to your room, and we'll bring your supper to you. Right now, I don't think any of us want to see your face."

I did as my aunt told me and went to my room. Just as she said, my laptop was missing. I closed my door and threw myself on my bed. I didn't care about being grounded. But Uncle George's hard expression was going to bother me for a while. I didn't know how I felt about my parents coming to get me. A part of me was glad. After all, it had been what I wanted all along. They never should've left me here.

On the other hand, I was disappointed. I had wanted to make friends with Ceara and Ash. And Nathan. I'd wanted to get to know

Nathan better. I didn't hold out any hope that he was interested in me. But it was nice hanging with him, getting to know him, finding out things he didn't share with other people. I felt close to him, even though it made no sense. As Fiona, I'd barely spent any time with him. I'd had some time with him as Audra. But in those times I'd insulted him because I thought that he had hurt my cousin. Now I wondered if my cousin even had feelings to be hurt. She saw everything as a game, and I was just a casualty of it.

I buried my head under my pillow and tried to quiet all the thoughts in my head. I was just starting to feel comfortable. Just starting to make friends. Just starting to develop a crush. And with the snap of her fingers, Cyn took it all away.

I didn't know what my parents would do. But they weren't going to be happy. And I didn't know if it was worth even arguing my side of it to them. What was done was done. They were coming to get me, and they'd have to take me with them because there was no place else for me to go.

My time in Wildwood was over.

The end.

Nathan

"Okay, spill it," Ceara said.

We had finished our mini celebration at Sally's, and Ash had gone to mow someone's yard. That left the two of us alone, and she immediately lit into me.

"What am I supposed to spill?"

"Where your brain has been the last hour. Because it hasn't been here with us." She tapped the table between us.

"I don't know what you mean." Though I did. My mind kept straying to Fiona. How much I wished she was with us. How incredibly smart she was. How I always seemed to smile when I was with her. But most of all, how I had held her hand without a conscious thought. Like it was the most natural thing in the world.

Ceara rolled her eyes. "You can't fool me. We've known each other for too long." Then a teasing smile graced her lips. "Is it a certain blond?"

I didn't play dumb with Ceara. I could either spill my thoughts now or spill them later. Either way, she'd get it out of me.

"It doesn't make sense." I laid my hands palms up on the table as if I was showing her I had nothing to hide. "I've only known her for a few days, but I feel like I've known her forever. And the way she talks to me feels like she's known me forever."

"Oh," Ceara laughed. "So she makes fun of you and insults you?"

"Ha ha, funny," I said sarcastically. "It's like she sees through me. Where other people are fake or want something from me, I don't think she does."

"Is that a good thing or a bad thing?" Ceara said.

I thought about her question before I answered. "It's good that she's not fake. That she doesn't care about my money. I guess I just don't know what to do with that. How do you get to know a girl who doesn't want anything from you?"

"Wow." My friend sat back in her seat. "You sure are jaded in your old age."

I gave her a smile. "Present company excluded, I haven't met a girl who didn't have some ulterior motive."

Ceara frowned. "That's the saddest thing I've ever heard you say," she reached out and grabbed my hand.

I brushed away her concern. "Not sad," I said, "just the truth. I don't know anything else."

"The question is, do you *want* to know anything else? Or do you want to keep doing what you've been doing?"

I thought about her words. Did I want a relationship that was deeper than what I had in the past? Did I want one like Ceara and Ash where there was complete trust, mutual respect and genuine affection? Sure. Who didn't want that? But I guess I'd never looked for it, because I'd never had it. But even admitting that I wanted it didn't mean that Fiona was the one I wanted it with. I didn't know this girl. Not really. And for me to be so hung up on her after such a short period of time completely confused me.

"I don't even know why we're having this conversation," I said to her. "I don't know this girl."

"Chemistry doesn't make sense," she said. "It just happens. Sometimes it's fast. Sometimes it's slow. There are no rules. No rhyme or reason. It just is."

"Well, that's an inspirational message," I said sarcastically.

She laughed. "It wasn't meant to inspire you. It was to remind you to get over yourself. If you have feelings for this girl, you just have to go with it. You can't control it."

Just go with it. That meant taking a backseat and letting things happen. That wasn't typically my nature. But maybe she was right. I could just spend time with Fiona, become her friend and see what happened after that. It sounded like a horrible plan. But it was the only one I had right now. There was no reason to rush into anything else.

When I got home, I pulled up social media. Since I still didn't have Fiona's number, I sent her a message. She wasn't online, but I hoped that she got it soon. As I was typing it up, I saw her indicator come online, and I breathed a sigh of relief.

Hey Fi. Tomorrow I'm going to Wildwood Bakery and tell them our plan. I thought it'd be a nice touch to have fresh-baked cookies or muffins in the welcome home package.

She didn't answer for a moment, and I waited impatiently for her response. Finally she sent a message back, and I read it over several times, not believing what was in front of my face.

I bet your sister will love cookies in her welcome home package.

I'd never mentioned Beka to Fiona. We weren't planning a welcome home for Beka. The welcome home package was Fiona's idea. How could she get it so wrong? I stared at the words again, and a pit hardened in my stomach. This wasn't Fiona. It couldn't be. I didn't remember a single time I'd told her about my sister, but even if I had, I knew I'd never mentioned her being away.

Fiona had come up with the welcome home concept while we were sitting in my car. Whoever was on the other side of this text didn't know about the idea.

I was talking to Cyn. Every instinct told me the person on the other side of this message was my ex-girlfriend.

I was being played.

The hardened knot grew heavier in my stomach. Did this mean that Cyn and Fiona were in this together? What about Audra? Were they sitting around looking at my message and conspiring on what to say to me? I wanted to believe Fiona's innocence. If she'd conspired with her cousin, then they wouldn't have made this mistake. But this was Fiona's social media, and Cyn had access to it.

I should have known. Of course, it felt like Fiona knew me forever. Because Cyn had. They had probably sat down and done an entire rundown on me so that Fi could play her part. And I'd fallen into it.

I wondered why they had done this. Why they'd gone to so much trouble to lure me in and play me like this. But the answer was right in front of my face with the words that I was sure Cyn had typed.

I had broken up with Cyn. And she was getting revenge.

And I was a fool for thinking that I had any connection with Fiona.

Chapter Seventeen

Fiona

My parents couldn't get away immediately. It would be a couple more days before they arrived. Aunt Lisa had given my phone back long enough for my mother to chew me out. My parents were furious. And if I had done what I had been accused of, then I wouldn't blame them. But it was all a lie. Cyn had made it all up and had gleefully told me several times how upset her parents had been when she'd told them about my betrayal.

She went out with her friends the next day while I was forced to stay home. I wasn't even allowed to go to the library anymore. So as soon as Aunt Lisa left for work, I grabbed my ereader and went to the hammock and tried to concentrate on a story. But I couldn't focus my mind on an imaginary world when the real world consumed all my thoughts. I felt bad that I was going to disappear without a goodbye to any of the people I tried to make friends with. Of course, once we moved away I could use social media to send Nathan a message. But it would mostly be a message of goodbye because I would be gone.

I hadn't taken Cyn's threat seriously enough. She said she could make me miserable. Mission accomplished.

And we both knew she had won.

I heard a door slam from the front yard, and I walked around the side of the house to see Ash's beaten-up truck in our driveway. He walked towards me, and I said, "George didn't say anything about you mowing today."

Ash smiled at me. "Nope, not mowing," he said. "Just wanting to hear your side of the story."

"My side of the story?"

"Yeah, Cyn is telling everyone you're leaving town. Nate says you're a liar. Ceara doesn't know what to think. And I don't believe any of them. So tell me the truth."

Tension filled my shoulders and chest. Of course, Cyn was talking badly about me. That, I had expected. But Nathan thought I was a liar. I wasn't prepared for the pain those words caused. The people I had hoped would be my friends were questioning who I was. I didn't blame them for not giving me a chance to explain. Not when I was a Houghton, and they knew Cyn. What surprised me was that Ash had bothered to come at all.

"You don't know me. Why would you even ask for the truth when I could completely lie to you?"

He shrugged. "I've always been pretty good at figuring people out. And you're not like Cyn. You help out and don't expect anything in return. You work hard. You're kind. Whatever else is going on, you're my friend. And I want to hear your story from you. Not from anyone else."

I opened the gate, and we walked to the porch swing in the backyard. I was fighting the tears that his words brought. Despite what other people were saying, people that he'd known for a long time, he was putting his trust in me. It was easy for me to open up to him, because he was one of the few people I hadn't lied to in this town.

So I spilled my guts. I told him everything. How my parents had dumped me here. How Audra had been something fun my cousin made up as she helped me build my own social media profile. How I was torn between loyalty to my cousin and giving Nathan a chance. And by the time I got to explaining the night Nathan had taken me out for apple pie, I had tears running down my face. I'd even mentioned how I had been attracted to Ash until I realized what he and Ceara had together.

At that statement he paused for a moment in the story and asked, "You thought we were together?"

I shrugged and wiped the wetness from my face with the heel of my hand. "It's obvious you like each other. I don't know if there's something that's preventing you from being together. But if there's not something serious stopping you, you need to tell her how you feel."

"Do you know how you feel? Are you feeling the same about someone we both know?"

"I didn't understand how I felt until it was over." And that was the truth. The kindness I'd seen from Nathan. His thoughtfulness, his seriousness about his money, and even his reluctant generosity to pay for things when his friends took advantage. They all pulled at my heartstrings. But he thought I was a liar. Ash had even said so. And he was right.

"It doesn't matter." I wrapped my arms around my waist as if to hug myself from the truth. "Not anymore. I can't ask for forgiveness. At least not until I get my phone and laptop back. Which may be months from now. I ruined all my parents' plans. They're going to be livid."

We sat in silence for a few minutes, swinging back and forth, lost in our thoughts.

"Are you willing to tell Nathan everything you told me?" Ash's deep voice held an emotion I didn't dare identify.

"What's the point?" I didn't know when he'd gone from thinking of me as a friend to thinking of me as a liar. I didn't know what stories Cyn was spreading about me. But even if Nathan knew the truth, and even if he forgave me for my role in the deception, I was still leaving. My parents would be here in two days and then I'd be gone. What was the point in clearing my name when I'd never see him again?

Ash raised his eyebrows and waited for me to answer his original question.

I thought about it. Would I tell him the truth if I got the chance? Yes. As embarrassing and humiliating and horrible as it would be to see his disdain and dislike, I would do it. He deserved to know the truth.

"Yes," I said. "I would. And I'd accept if he hated me."

Ash rubbed my shoulder. "That's exactly what I thought you'd say. I'll figure out something."

"I don't have my phone or my laptop," I told him. "They were taken away from me when I got back from Ceara's class."

Ash scratched his chin. "Okay, that's a challenge. But I'll figure out something." He stood up from the swing and waved goodbye, and within minutes he was gone.

I watched him drive away and realized it was probably the last time I would ever see him. The tears started up again, and even though I was alone, I ran to my room and locked the door so that I could cry in private.

Nathan

This had to be the dumbest thing I'd ever done. Somehow I'd let Ash talk me into taking his truck and his mowing equipment over to the Houghton's house. He promised me that no one would be home. He told me he'd accidentally double booked his mowing appointments, and he needed me to do this favor for him.

Ben and Ceara had both been there. Ceara encouraging me to help Ash. And Ben daring me not to.

And as much as I hated it, Fiona's voice echoed in my head about adding my muscle to Ash's work.

So here I was mowing the lawn at the last place in Wildwood I wanted to be.

As I unloaded the mower from the bed of the truck, a voice said, "What are you doing back? George didn't say you were mowing today."

I slowly turned and faced the girl who'd spoken to me. Her long blond hair was in a ponytail. She wore a faded vintage T-shirt and cut-off shorts and no makeup. "Fiona? Or are you Audra?"

The girl winced. "Fiona," she said. "I promised Ash I would tell you the whole truth if he gave me the opportunity. I guess this is it."

She turned around and went back into the house. I left the mower where it was, threw the ballcap I was wearing into the cab of the truck and followed her inside. Obviously this was a setup.

I found Fiona in the kitchen, and she motioned for me to sit at the kitchen bar. Then she handed me a cup of coffee. Black. And I blinked a couple times, realizing she knew exactly how I drank my coffee. The feeling that she knew me returned, but I pushed it back. I didn't want to be blinded by the weird connection I felt with her. I wanted to know the truth. I wanted to know her role and what happened.

"Are we alone?" I asked. "Ash said no one would be home."

"My family went back to the water park. I'm on house arrest. So I'm not allowed to go anywhere."

"What did you do?" Although my guard was up, a part of me hoped she was OK. I wondered if she'd been grounded because she'd lied to her family, too.

She shook her head. "That's not why you're here. Let's just get this over."

I took a sip of my coffee and waited for her to talk.

She stood on the other side of the bar; her hands folded tightly on the countertop. She reminded me of the Fiona I met at Genevieve's party. The girl uncomfortable in a social setting, who took a while to warm up to anyone who spoke to her. At least, I knew that wasn't an act.

But after the last two days of Cyn texting me from her account, I didn't know what else to believe.

She took in a big breath of air and slowly blew it out before she forced herself to look me in the eyes. She was obviously nervous, but I respected that she was going to face this head on. Whatever it was, she had to say.

"My parents dumped me here. I didn't have a choice. All I wanted was to fly under the radar. But Cyn said that was impossible."

I didn't say a word, but I agreed with her cousin. If this girl standing in front of me just as she was this moment had shown up, people would have noticed. The girls in my group would have noticed. The guys would have noticed. And if I was honest with myself, I would have noticed.

"My aunt didn't want me here," she continued, "Cyn didn't want me here, and I didn't want to be here. I was just trying to get along until I could figure out how to get my parents to change their mind."

She paused, and I didn't know if she was simply gathering her thoughts or she expected me to react. But I refused to say a thing until her whole story came out. So I took another sip of my coffee and waited for her to speak again.

Fiona unclenched her hands and wrapped them around a glass of soda. She didn't drink any, just moved her fingers up and down, tracing the condensation lines.

"Cyn disapproved of everything about me. My clothes, my shoes, the fact that I had no social media. It was easier to go along with her, because it was harmless. A couple of new outfits. My own profile online. No big deal, right?"

She paused in her story, but I didn't think she expected me to answer her question. Instead, it seemed she was asking herself. She let out a small, angry laugh and then spoke again.

"She kept telling me how naïve I was. And I really was. I didn't even know it was possible to create a fake online account until she showed me."

My throat closed up, and my chest felt tight. I didn't want to contemplate what she was telling me. I didn't want it to be true. But my mouth said what my brain refused to process. "Audra."

Fiona sighed. "Audra."

I wasn't surprised. Something hadn't felt right for a long time. And I had realized that my interactions with Audra were inconsistent at best. "Does she even exist?"

Fiona lifted her face and stared me squarely in the eye. Her cheeks flushed, and her eyes glistened. But the fact that she looked near tears didn't sway me. I had seen her cousin cry on demand more than once, and this girl was admitting to lying to me. I didn't trust the emotion I saw her exhibiting.

"Cyn used the Audra account to teach me how to make my own. She said that she would delete it, and I believed her. We didn't make it with the intention of lying to anyone. Not at first."

Her story rang true. Though I wasn't sure if I believed her. But if she was telling the truth, then I could see events playing out as she described.

"Then you dumped her for Genevieve."

"And you decided to get revenge," I said.

"No. At least not through Audra. We went out with the Danvers because Cyn thought it would bother you. I didn't know she planned to post those pictures on Audra's account until after I saw them there."

"So you're claiming you're innocent in all this?" I challenged her. I wasn't sure what she had told Ash to convince him that we needed to have this conversation. He had obviously believed her. But I wasn't buying that she was an innocent bystander in all of this. And I prepared myself to call her out.

"No," she said. "I am not innocent. When you sent that first video chat, I opened it. Cyn didn't want to. But I was so mad that you were reaching out. To someone who was obviously Cyn's relative after you had just dumped her. I didn't think twice about pretending to be Audra." She swallowed a couple of times and shook her head. "As much as I want to blame my cousin, she wouldn't have gotten far if I hadn't played along in the first place. I made Audra real, because I let you and Nicolaus and all of Cyn's friends think that they had met her. And after that it just got out of control."

I respected that she told the truth, but I was still angry. "So all those times I video chatted Audra," I clarified, "that was you."

She nodded.

"And when you came to Genevieve's party. What was that? An act?"

Fiona laughed, a bitter, unhappy sound. "No, unfortunately, that was all me. I was scared of meeting Cyn's friends. I was scared that people would realize I'd lied about Audra. And I'm more comfortable in small groups than I am a large party of strangers." She laughed again. "Cyn described it as being extra Fiona. And she was right."

If this girl was acting, she was good. Because I found myself believing her. It didn't change the fact that she had lied to me and broken my trust. But I did believe she was telling me the truth. Or at least mostly the truth.

Everything was becoming crystal clear to me. "You were Audra's face," I said, "You video chatted. And Cyn told you what to say."

She interrupted me. "No, she never told me what to say. Sometimes she was in the room with me. Sometimes she wasn't. But everything I said I take ownership of."

"And Cyn chatted with me when your face wasn't needed." It wasn't a question. Just confirming what I already knew. I had been confused why my interaction with Audra felt electric during our video chats and dull and flat when we texted. It was because I'd had a connection to Fiona all along. And instead of reassuring me, it made me mad. This indescribable connection that I felt with her had started since the very beginning. And I had been too stupid to realize it.

"I like to you, Nathan. I won't deny that. Whenever Audra was involved, I wasn't completely honest with you. But I want you to know that whenever I was Fiona, I was completely me. None of that was a lie. Not that I'm expecting you to forgive me or for us to be friends." Her voice caught at the last word, and she cleared her throat before continuing. "I just wanted you to know the truth."

I narrowed my eyes at her. "Everything with Fiona was true?" I shook my head. She didn't realize I had caught her in the lie. The texts I'd received over the past couple of days via her Fiona profile were obviously Cyn. She referenced things that Fiona had no way of knowing without Cyn being involved somehow. "No. I wanted honesty. And I believed you until now."

Although she still had a hurt expression on her face, Fiona stood taller and squared her shoulders. "I can't make you believe what I'm telling you. And if you're not willing to hear me out, I guess this conversation's over."

I stood up. "Agreed."

Fiona held up one finger. Her face flushed deeper, and this time I realized it was with anger. "Wait here one minute," she said and rushed from the room before I could reply. While I waited for her to return I dumped the remainder of my coffee in the sink, washed out the cup and set it in the sink. I looked around the kitchen that I'd visited many times over the four months I had dated Cyn. I never thought I'd be in this situation. Made a fool of by my ex and her cousin. Sure, my pride was hurt. But what bothered me the most was that I'd really felt something for this girl. Finding out she lied to me hurt more than I had expected. Especially when she couldn't stop lying.

Fiona returned with a small stack of paper. She thrust the pages in my hands and said, "Believe whatever you want, Nathan. Obviously we're not gonna work this out. I was waiting until I got my laptop back to type these up and make it more legible. But I don't see the point now. So take these and use them or not. Your call." Then she stormed to the front door and held it open, waiting for me to leave.

I fisted the papers in my hand and stormed out the front door. I didn't say another word to her. Not even goodbye.

When I got to Ash's truck, I threw the pages on the seat next to me, loaded up his mower and drove off as quickly as I could.

As I saw the Houhgton house disappearing in my rear-view mirror I said out loud, "Goodbye Cyn. Goodbye Andra. Goodbye Fiona." Because I never planned to speak to any of them again.

Chapter Eighteen

Fiona
My family arrived the next day. And although I was happy to see my brother, the whole night of crying had left me emotionally drained. I didn't know what I had expected from my encounter with Nathan. I guessed I was hoping he'd hear the truth. That even if he didn't forgive me, then there was a chance he would in the future. That obviously wasn't happening. I'd had crushes before. But this one had felt different. It felt like we knew each other. The connection that I had with him, whether I was Audra or Fiona, felt very real to me. And I thought he felt it, too.

Apparently I was wrong.

Frank engulfed me in a massive bear hug the minute he saw me. Then my parents sent him outside to play while they led me to the living room. Aunt Lisa and Uncle George sat with us at first, giving their account of everything that had happened. I didn't recognize the girl they described. The one who was ungrateful for everything they'd done for them. The one who willfully targeted her cousin's relationship because she wanted the boy for herself. The one who lied to all her family. The one who had been a nuisance from the moment she walked in the door. Once they had done their butcher job of my character, they left me to face my parents alone.

My mother and father stared at me in horror and disbelief. My mother was the first one to speak. "What happened here? I knew you didn't want to stay. But did you take your anger for us out on your family? Family is everything. They're the ones who will always be there for you. What were you thinking?"

I had expected this. My mother wanted us all to play nice together. She didn't like drama, and she didn't want to believe that family could turn on each other.

"What do you want me to say? None of this is true? The only parts that are true Cyn twisted to make me look like a villain and her innocent? This is punishment from my loving cousin because I wouldn't go along with her plan to hurt her ex-boyfriend? What's the point? You already believe them."

My parents stared at me with open disbelief. I couldn't remember the last time I had lashed out at them. And I bet they were thinking the same thing.

"So that's it then?" my dad said. "You won't tell us what happened?"

"Do we have to do this here? Can't we do this at your new house? I promise I'll tell you everything you want to know. I just don't want to be here anymore."

My parents looked at each other for a second, and then dad sighed and stood up. "Fine. We'll do this later. Go get packed."

"I already am."

My mother and my aunt followed me to my bedroom where my suitcase and backpack were packed and ready to go. I had folded the comforter on the bed and pulled off the sheets and the pillowcases so they could be washed. All the clothes that Aunt Lisa had bought me I had neatly folded on the bed. I motioned to them and said to my aunt, "I've worn them and washed them. So you probably can't get your money back. But I thought I'd leave them here in case you wanted to try."

Lisa frowned at me. "We bought them for you. They're yours. Take them."

"Thank you," I said, "I know you won't believe me, but I do appreciate them." I stuffed them into my suitcase and took one last look around the room to make sure I hadn't forgotten anything.

Lisa followed me as if double checking every step I made. I didn't know if she was ensuring I hadn't taken anything of hers. Or she just wanted to make sure no trace of me was left behind. As I peered into the closet, I saw the small pink dot of paint. It probably wasn't the time or place, but I wasn't sure I'd ever get another chance to ask. I pointed to the one blemish in the room. "I've been dying to ask," I said, "why is this here?"

Lisa peered at the splotch of pink on her pristine white wall. She ran her finger over it and then rubbed her forefinger and thumb together as if expecting the paint to be wet. She shook her head. "I didn't know this was here." She glanced in the direction of my cousin's room, completely confused. "Cyn's room is the only one with this color."

"Did the painters make a mistake?" my mom asked.

Lisa frowned as if she was trying to solve a deep, complex mystery. "Cyn painted her room. We kept a small amount for touch ups. But that was thrown away years ago."

It was obvious what had happened, even though my aunt refused to believe it. At some point, her precious daughter had gotten angry and taken the bright pink color and stabbed it onto the wall. Somehow that made me like the color even more. One, it wasn't supposed to be there. Just like me. Two, it was proof that my cousin wasn't as perfect as her parents thought. That she did things out of spite. And her parents were oblivious, refused to see the truth.

I wasn't surprised when Aunt Lisa's next words said that she'd cover it up immediately. Because that's what they did. They saw the evidence that Cyn wasn't perfect. And they buried the truth.

I had never been more grateful to be away from them than I was right now.

I grabbed my stuff and walked to the front door where Cyn was standing there with a sad expression pasted on her face. She and I both knew it wasn't real. But everyone else was fooled. My aunt and uncle and my parents stepped outside, leaving me and Cyn alone a few final seconds. "I'm sorry it's ending like this," I said.

Cyn smirked. "I told you not to mess with me. All you had to do was play along. And everything would have been fine. I might have even let you have Nathan. Once I was done with him, of course."

I frowned. She didn't get it. Not even a little. And I think that made me more sad than anything else. "Family is forever, Cyn. We'll never escape the fact that we're tied together by blood. But I was hopeful that we might actually like each other one day. Or, heaven forbid, even love each other. But that's obviously not what you wanted. Your revenge on Nathan and your pettiness against me were more important than any relationship we could've formed. You'll always be my cousin. But until you change, we will never have a relationship. That's the sad part. And you don't even realize it."

"You're pathetic," she said.

"Yeah, but at least I have a heart." And with that, I stepped out of her house and into my parents' car.

Nathan

"You have company, Loser," Nic said as he popped his head into my room. "Mom says you have to come downstairs."

That meant my company was a girl. Girls weren't allowed into our bedrooms, so when one came over we had to see them in one of the public rooms in the house. My first thought was Fiona. That somehow she was no longer grounded and was allowed to come see me. I slowly got up from my bed and ran my fingers through my hair. I wondered what she'd say. If she'd repeat what she'd told me yesterday.

If she'd tell the truth.

Though something she'd said had been nagging at my conscience all last night. *When she got her laptop back.*

A part of me wanted to believe that statement meant more than it did. That it could exonerate her from Cyn's deception. I hadn't looked at the papers she had given me. I was so angry and frustrated that I'd left them in Ash's truck without glancing at them. Part of me didn't want to give up hope, believed I might get my answers from those pages. But I couldn't allow myself to go there. I'd been manipulated by Cyn Houghton one too many times.

I stepped into the living room to see that I had not one but three visitors. Ceara, Ash, Ben. No Fiona. The tightness I suddenly felt in my chest had to be relief, I told myself. It couldn't be disappointment. I never wanted to see that girl again.

"What's up?" I said to the group.

"You left trash in my truck," Ash said and pointed to the crumpled papers lying on the coffee table in front of him. My heart picked up its pace, and my fingers itched to grab the notes in front of me and discover what secrets they held.

Instead, I stared down my friends. "You came all the way over here to complain that I was messy?"

"We came over," Ceara said, "to tell you that you're brilliant." The smirk on her face told me she was joking.

I sat down in the empty recliner across from them. "Seriously, what's up?"

Ben held up his phone. "Checking on you," he said. "You didn't respond to any messages last night. Just wanted to make sure you were okay."

"I'm fine."

"Are you mad at Ash?" Ceara said. "Because if you are, you should be mad at all of us. We agreed that you needed to talk to Fiona. You at least needed to hear her side of the story."

I stared at my friends in open shock. "You didn't even like her," I said to Ceara.

She rolled her eyes and groaned. "I never gave her a chance, did I?"

"Maybe she didn't deserve one." She'd lied to all of us. If they were going to defend her, they'd have to explain why they were OK with being deceived.

"You don't believe that," Ash said. "Did you even bother to look at these papers?"

I didn't answer them. What was the point of this visit? It's not like they had been friends with her, either.

"Listen," Ben said, "I've never met her. I didn't make friends with her. I don't know anything about her except that she's Cyn's cousin and your brother dumped her after going on one date with her. Now Cyn is telling anyone who will listen that her cousin is a loser and a liar and is leaving town in disgrace."

I was angry with Fiona. I was hurt that she lied to me. And if I was honest with myself, I was frustrated that she didn't feel the connection I had felt with her. But that didn't mean I wanted Cyn gossiping about her to all of our friends. Especially when she was just as guilty. She didn't get to play the victim and let her cousin take all the heat.

My best friend continued, "If she was nothing to you, you'd tell everyone it wasn't a big deal, that you didn't care and you had more important things to do. You would be out there working on one of your businesses, figuring out another way to make money, or hanging with one of us. The fact that you holed yourself up in your house after talking with her says volumes. Even if you don't want to admit it, you care for her. And she hurt you."

"What do you want?" I said and stood from the chair. I threw my hands in the air in frustration. "Do you want me to say that I like her? Okay, fine. I liked her. I was attracted to her. I liked fighting with her when she was Audra. And I liked hanging out with her when she was Fiona. I loved her ideas for the business. Because she thought of details that I'd never considered. Because she took what we were doing and found a way to make it better. I liked everything about her. Except that she's a two-faced liar. Is that what you wanted to hear," I said realizing that I had raised my voice to my friends. I rubbed my hands over my face and tried to calm myself down. My friends didn't deserve to be yelled out.

"Sorry," I said.

Ceara picked up one of the crumpled sheets of paper and handed it to me. "Just look at these."

I reluctantly took the sheet of paper from her hand and turned it over to see where the page had been divided into four sections. The top left corner was titled Local Welcome Baskets. Underneath was a list of items for the baskets, including Vega Farm soaps. Underneath that was a list of where the baskets could be placed: new-home sales, new to the neighborhood welcome, new teachers and school, new baby arrival. The top right section was labeled Cross Promotion and had a few ideas of how Vega farm soaps could be paired with other local companies to help advertise for each other. The bottom two sections were lists of scents. The left side stating aromatherapy scents and what they could be used for. The right side listing some combinations of scents with the question at the bottom *is it possible to do knockoffs of famous perfumes?*

I stared at this page for several seconds and then looked to the other three crumpled pages still on the coffee table.

Ceara read my thoughts, and said, "Yes. They are all ideas that she had for your business. Some of them are pretty good. Like partnering with the arboretum to develop themed botanical baskets."

I sat down as I processed what was in my hands. She had said when she got her laptop back she planned to type this all up and send it to me. I had assumed it was some letter of apology or some reason why I was supposed to forgive her. Instead, it was a whole list of ways that I could make my business even better.

"That's a lot of brainstorming," Ben said. "I can't imagine anyone doing that just to keep a lie going."

I said more to myself than I did my friends. "She told me the truth about Audra. About the role she played in that profile. She was truthful right up to the point she started talking about our messages. That's when I knew she and Cyn were playing me. Because she sent messages with information she had no way of knowing. Unless she was talking to her cousin."

"When?" Ash said. "Because you know she was grounded, right? Her laptop and phone were taken away as soon as she got home from Ceara's class."

"Her phone?" I said to myself. Was it possible that this was another layer of their elaborate lie? Had she told Ash that her phone was taken away and her laptop was gone just so she could continue the pretense? That didn't seem reasonable. Why do that?

I back in the recliner, tossing the paper back on the coffee table, and leaned over and rested my elbows on my knees. None of this made sense.

"So you were getting these bogus texts the same time Fiona unfriended me on social media?" Ceara said.

I stared at my friend. If Fiona was playing me, was playing us, she wouldn't risk being discovered by insulting one of my friends. There was only one piece of this puzzle that made the whole picture come into focus. "Cyn had her laptop."

"Ding ding ding. We have a winner, folks," Ceara laughed. "That's what we thought, too."

"That doesn't change the fact that Fiona lied to us."

Ben stood from his seat, gathered the papers from the coffee table and set them in my lap. "No. But I think you also have proof that she genuinely cares. It's your choice what to do about it," he said and headed toward the door. My other friends stood up and followed him. After Ceara stepped from my house, Ash hung back.

"I have really big news I want to share," he said. The huge smile on his face said it all, but I played along.

"Yeah?"

"Ceara and I are official," he beamed.

"It's about time," I said.

"You should've said something. I didn't think she liked me like that. I might never have made a move if Fiona hadn't told me."

"Fiona."

"Yeah." He grinned at me. "She told me her side of the story, and I believed her. And then she told me not to waste time and connect with Ceara. Fi made a really big mistake. But I forgive her. Especially since she helped me to see the truth about my feelings for Ceara." Ash patted me on the shoulder and trotted toward his truck.

I watched him jump into the vehicle, lean over and kiss Ceara on the cheek before they took off. Fiona did that. I glanced at the pages in my hand. Fiona had done a lot. And one idea she had outlined in her notes was exactly what I needed.

I raced to my bedroom and pulled out my phone, ignoring all of my missed messages from the last 24 hours. I typed out a text to my three best friends and then sat at my desk to pull together a plan.

Cyn had told everyone Fiona was leaving town, but she didn't say when. Which meant I was on borrowed time. If I wasn't already too late. I stood in my doorway and yelled down the hall for Nic to join me. I was going to need all the help I could get.

Chapter Nineteen

Fiona

    I was grateful my parents believed me. After they'd given my little brother a video game and forced him to wear a headset, we sat down on the beds in our hotel room, and I told them every little detail. They were still upset with me. Because as my mother said, family is forever. And at the next family gathering, which would probably be Thanksgiving, I would have to give a heartfelt apology to Uncle George and Aunt Lisa for the trouble they had been through. But that was the extent of my punishment.

I got my laptop and my phone back, and I logged onto social media to see that I was no longer connected to Ceara or Nathan. Of course I was disappointed. I had hoped they would forgive me, eventually. That seemed unlikely now. I also noticed that I was no longer friends with Audra. Though I was disappointed to see the Audra account still existed. I tried logging into the fake account, but of course, Cyn had changed the password. I made sure that my parents knew I couldn't get into the profile, just in case my sneaky cousin tried something else.

With our adult-only discussion over, my parents interrupted Frank's game. "We have something to tell you," Dad said.

My stomach tied in knots, and I clenched my hands in my lap. The last time Dad had said that, I had been forced to live with my aunt and uncle. I hoped whatever news he had wasn't as disastrous as that had been.

Mom grinned widely and held my father's hand, her body was shaking with excitement. My brother, however, was having the same thoughts I did.

Frank said, "We're not leaving Fiona again, are we?" His little arms crossed over his chest, and he pouted.

I wrapped my little brother into a bear hug and kissed the top of his head.

"No, from now on we're staying together," she said.

The stress fell from my shoulders, and I hugged Frank again. Her next words, though, brought the stress back.

"But this whole episode made your father and I realize something very important. Family needs to stick together. *All* the family."

I sat up straighter and looked at my parents' faces. They seemed rather pleased with themselves; although, they were wary of my reaction.

"I'm very lucky to have George as my brother," Dad said. "And this made me realize how far we've grown apart."

Mom jumped in and said, "We're moving to Wildwood. If we have any chance of bringing this family together, we need to be together."

"Don't expect me to make friends with Cyn." No doubt that's what my mother wanted. But it was impossible. Until she changed, there was no hope I might have a relationship with her. And moving to Wildwood meant I would always be around her. Although...

Moving to Wildwood also meant Ash and Ceara. And Nathan. And even though they weren't my friends, and they were angry that I had lied to them. If I was around, maybe I'd have a chance to repair those relationships. I had no expectations. But having a chance was nice. I wasn't naturally a risk taker, but earning their forgiveness for a chance to become friends was a risk I'd willingly take.

"We found a cute little rental house," Dad said, "We will stay there for the next few months until we can buy a house. Your mother and I signed the lease this afternoon."

I stared at them in disbelief. "Are you kidding?"

My mom gave me a tentative smile. "Is that a happy *are you kidding* or a mad *are you kidding*?"

I honestly didn't know. The fact that we were staying in Wildwood together had totally blown my mind. I shrugged and said to my mother, "Ask me later."

My mother took that as a good sign and laughed and engulfed me and my brother into a big hug. "This is going to be amazing. We're going to be so happy."

Something nagged at the back of my brain. "But Mom, what about your business? You and dad put all your money into this dream. How are we going to live here when all of your money is in Camden Heights?"

My parents grinned at each other before facing me again. "Life has a funny way of turning on you," Dad said. "You see, we thought we had a great business idea — a unique boutique that sourced low-waste home products. And we weren't the only ones who liked the concept. We started getting everything together and getting the word out that our business would be opening soon, and a local businessman heard about it and offered to buy it from us. He had more resources than we did, and he seemed really passionate about the project."

Mom said, "So we sold it to him. The concept, the building, the few supplies we had already pulled together. He bought it all."

I sat there stunned. "What are you going to do now?" I figured they had enough money to cover us for a while, but it wouldn't be forever.

My parents in true risk-taker style shrugged and said in unison, "Who knows?"

I blinked at them. I could never live the way they did. I liked my security. I liked being comfortable. Though I realized I needed to take chances now and then. Although I'd made some dumb decisions, if I hadn't taken the chance I never would've gotten to know Ash or Ceara or Nathan. While taking chances still wasn't my favorite thing to do, sometimes you had to risk it.

The next morning after breakfast, my parents drove us to the house they had rented. My mouth dropped in shock as I immediately recognized the little cottage. "This is a rental house?"

"Yeah," Dad said, "apparently the owner just bought it as an investment and decided to rent it out."

"Wait to you see the inside," Mom said, "It is so adorable."

I was too numb to tell her that I knew this house. The house that was very close to my cousin and her family and not far from the library. The one Ash and I had spent hours landscaping. I dragged my feet as I followed behind them. Frank ran ahead of us and bounced on his heels as he waited for my parents to unlock the front door. As soon as the door was cracked, he took off running.

I stepped into the empty house and listened to our footsteps as they echoed off the wood floors. There was no furniture in the house yet, and my parents told us that our moving truck with all our furniture would arrive in a couple days. Frank rushed through the house asking where his room was, and Dad laughed as he scooped up my brother and took him down the short hallway.

Mom and I stepped into the kitchen, and my mouth dropped in surprise. There on the kitchen counter was a huge welcome basket filled with goodies from local businesses - Vega Farm's soaps, cookies from Tucker's Diner, a potted plant donated from the arboretum. My ideas all come to life before my eyes.

When Nathan had crumpled my notes, I had no hope that he'd ever read them. Now I know he had. The hope that grew in me hinted that maybe he'd forgive me one day. That it might be possible to become friends. Or more.

Frankie yanked my hand, "Come see your room, Fi."

I followed my brother and halted midstride when I stepped into the space that would be my bedroom. Inside was another basket filled with a rainbow bouquet of roses. A note hung from the handle of the basket. I opened it up and quickly read.

Your flower basket idea was great, but I couldn't find a rose that said I'm sorry. So, I got all the colors I could find.

The note wasn't signed.

"Who's it from?" Mom asked.

I sighed. "It doesn't say."

She read the note. "Do you have more than one person who would want to apologize?"

Dad walked in the room holding another note. "I think this is yours." He handed it to me. "It was hanging on the basket in the kitchen."

Mom stood behind me and read the note from over my shoulder.

Fiona, don't forget your promise to bring your mom to our shop.

The handwritten note was written in a flowery, loopy handwriting, a different handwriting than the other note I was holding. It was Ceara. Hope grew even more. She had forgiven me. I hoped she'd welcome the news that I was staying.

"What shop?" Mom asked.

I told her about the store and the products, and we agreed to visit after we'd unloaded the car with the few belongings my parents brought with them, including the huge tent and gear that we'd use to camp out in the backyard tonight.

As soon as it was set up, Mom and I went to the Vega Farm. Another huge surprise met me when we walked into the building. The walls had been painted, a new floor had been installed, and one side of the building had new wooden shelves. "This is amazing," I said as I ran my finger over the shelving.

"I'm glad you like it," Ceara said.

I hadn't realized she was standing behind the counter.

"Looks like they're following your vision," I said and introduced my mother to her.

"We were surprised to hear you were staying," the girl said. "Your cousin has been telling everyone you left town in disgrace."

I shrugged. "The disgrace part might be true."

"Not to the people who know the truth," she said.

"The truth?" I said numbly. The truth that I was a liar.

"That Fiona Houghton didn't run away from her mistakes," a male voice said behind me. "That she's nothing like her cousin."

I turned to see Nathan and Ash. Taking a step to the side, I made sure all three teens were in my line of sight. "I'm so sorry," I said. "I didn't want to hurt any of you."

Ash grinned at me. "We didn't want to hurt you, either."

I gave him a tentative smile and focused on Nathan. "I'll understand if you don't want to be friends."

His expression remained stoic. "Want to take a walk?"

I glanced to my mother, and she gave me a quick nod. "OK," I said and followed Nathan outside.

"Thank you for all the ideas for my business," he said, and a knot of disappointment formed in my stomach. I had no right to hope for more, but if business was how we buried the hatchet, then I'd take it.

"You're welcome. I wanted to give you something to show..." I trailed off. I wasn't sure what the right thing to say was. I couldn't tell him that I cared. I still had some pride left.

He nodded as if he understood. "Message received," he said. "I'm sorry that I didn't give you a chance to explain. I was," he hesitated, "mad."

I had a feeling that wasn't the word he'd originally planned to say.

"I get it," I said. "If I were in your shoes, I'd be mad, too."

"But I realized that I was just as mad at myself as I was at you."

"For falling for the lie," I said and nodded my head.

He blew out a huff of air. "Not exactly. I dumped Cyn, then I dated Geni, and I promised myself that I'd remain single once we were over. I didn't need any more complications this summer. I only wanted to focus on my business. But you," he grabbed my hand, "you were a big complication."

I shook my head.

He continued, "I loved sparring with Audra. When my girlfriend was falling over herself with a fake niceness, she was giving me grief. She didn't care who I was. She only wanted me to do the right thing. To treat my girlfriends with respect. Then along came Fiona, who wasn't impressed with me for a totally different reason. She was reserved and shy and thoughtful. And had a crazy head for business. I loved spending time with her because she challenged me to be better, without any of the confrontation or drama."

He squeezed my hand. "I swore I'd stay single because that was the most practical plan. Then I had these sisters who drew my attention. I was falling for them, and then I realized that Cyn had been sending me messages as Audra and as Fiona. And I thought I'd been played by all three."

"I'm sorry. I never meant it to happen like that."

"I know," he said. "I should have trusted my instincts. They were right."

"About what?"

Nathan tucked a stray strand of hair behind my ear. "That I liked you. That I respected you. That I was starting to fall for you."

I gasped, and my heart hammered in my chest. "You can't mean that."

He leaned against a large apple tree and pulled me next to him. "Why not?"

"Because you don't know me."

"I know Audra and Fiona, and both of them are you. I want to explore the chemistry we have and see where it takes us. On one condition..."

The joy I'd felt at his words subsided. He didn't trust me, and I had no right to expect him to. "And that is?"

"Let's communicate in person or on the phone. I want to see your face and hear your voice."

"To make sure you can trust me?" I said and tried to hide my disappointment.

He grinned. "To make sure your cousin hasn't stolen your phone or laptop again."

"I can live with that," my shoulders relaxed as I realized his distrust was aimed at my cousin. Not at me.

He wrapped his arms around my waist. "You don't believe I feel this way, do you?"

"Not really," I said. As much as I liked what he was saying, feeling his nearness, my heart was at stake. I could get seriously hurt by this guy, and it was a risk that scared me silly. However, it was also a risk I was willing to take.

Nathan sighed. "Then we'll take it slow. I'll prove to you that I really like you."

"And I'll prove to you that you can trust me."

His fingers trailed down my jaw. Slipping his fingertips under my chin, he tilted my head up. "Then let's sign our pact."

He leaned down and made my toes curls with the sweetest kiss.

When he backed away, he grinned at me. "In person communication is so much better."

I grinned back. "I agree. Though, I'm not very experienced in kissing. I might need more practice."

He laughed. "The flush on your face is shy, sweet Fiona, and those words were saucy Audra. I've got two incredible girls in one. Right here in my arms."

I stood on my tiptoes and placed my hands on his shoulders for balance. Even though my face heated furiously, I said, "Kiss now. Talk later."

He wrapped his arms around me and pulled me tighter to him. "That's one thing we'll never fight about," he said and kissed me again.

When we broke apart a moment later, he said, "Thank you for forgiving me."

"I'm supposed to say that."

Nathan leaned his forehead against mine. "You weren't the only one who screwed up. I made stupid mistakes. And I'm not used to a girlfriend who actually cares about me and my business."

"No one is perfect," I said, "not even Audra, and she was fake."

He laughed. "I really like you, Fiona Houghton."

"I really like you, Nathan Hollingsworth."

"From now on it's going to be the real you with the real me."

I readily agreed. It was time to leave the fake profile and the lies behind us. While playing Audra had been wrong, she'd helped me to tap into a stronger side of me. One that could fiercely defend my family and talk freely to a boy without getting tongue-tied and selfconsious.

I only wished I'd been able to learn that about myself without lying to the boy I loved.

I gasped out loud, and Nathan lowered his eyebrows in concern. "Are you OK?" he asked.

Now wasn't the time to confess my feelings. I'd learned to be a risk taker, sort of. But I wasn't ready for this level of riskiness yet. One day, though, I'd tell him I loved him, and hopefully he'd say it back.

In this moment, I only wanted to enjoy the feel of his arms around me, knowing that I had forgiveness I hadn't deserved with a guy who understood me.

This was going to be the best summer of my life.

Epilogue

Nathan

"Congrats, King," Fiona kissed me on the cheek. I dropped my football helmet and wrapped my arms around her. The Homecoming court had been announced during half-time during our Homecoming game. I'd been announced king, and Cyn had been queen.

Fi handed over the crown she'd been holding for me while I finished the game. I grinned at her and placed it on her head. It was a little big and fell lower on her forehead, nearly covering her eyes. "You could have had one of your own," I teased her.

As people started nominating the Homecoming court, Fiona had adamantly told everyone she didn't want it. Our classmates had planned to vote for her anyway until Ceara, Ash and I insisted she meant it. My girlfriend didn't like the limelight, didn't want to be popular, and it was one of the things I loved about her.

She rolled her eyes. "Thanks for making sure I didn't. I don't know how you get out there," she pointed to the football field, "every week with all those people watching you."

I shrugged. "I don't know how you find the perfect houses to flip." Over the summer, she'd found a house her family loved, and Ash and I had fixed it up after her parents had bought it. Soon after that, she'd found another house for Ash and I to fix up and sell. I was on track to pay back my dad around Christmas, thanks to my entrepreneur-minded girlfriend. "We all have our talents," I winked at her. "The team is going to Tucker's. Want to join us?"

"I don't think so. I need to get ready for our big date tomorrow night."

I nodded. It was her first school dance, and she and Ceara were making it a huge event. "Then I guess I'll see you when we pick you ladies up tomorrow."

She gave me a quick kiss on the lips and began to walk away. "Fi," I called after her, and she turned around. "Love you."

She smiled and before she said anything else, I added, "Catfish."

She narrowed her eyes at me even though her smile never left her face. "Love you, too, jerk."

I laughed as I watched her bounce away. The more we knew each other, the more we fell in love. She was the perfect blend of sass and sweet. I didn't think about how we almost missed our chance together, how Cyn and Audra had stood in our way. I liked to believe that we'd have found each other eventually, because she was my heart, and she challenged me to be a better man every day. And tomorrow, at our Homecoming dance, I was going to give her a ring. A simple, silver infinity symbol to show everyone that we were forever.

She'd refuse it at first. Because she genuinely loved me for me and not my wealth. But she'd give in when she realized I meant what the ring said.

We may have had a shaky start with distrust, revenge, and lies. But we'd formed a solid bond, and I'd love her for infinity. Just like she felt about me.

Because there were no more secrets. No more lies. No more fake social media accounts. Only the real me. Real her. And real love.

Don't miss out!

Visit the website below and you can sign up to receive emails whenever J. Leigh James publishes a new book. There's no charge and no obligation.

https://books2read.com/r/B-A-UDTL-DWLIB

BOOKS 2 READ

Connecting independent readers to independent writers.

Also by J. Leigh James

Faux in Love
Love You Like a Catfish
Pretend You Love My Brother

Watch for more at www.jleighjames.com.

About the Author

J. Leigh James lives in Texas with her amazing husband, "bad apple" daughter, and neurotic cat. She began writing in middle school when a beloved story had an unsatisfying ending. After rewriting the ending to the story, she became addicted to creating love stories with happily-ever-after endings.

She loves connecting with her readers, so check out her website and sign up for her newsletter.

Read more at www.jleighjames.com.